THE ANGEL'S
LAST WAR

SEAN T. SMITH

This is a work of fiction. Names, characters, places, and incidents are products of the author's imagination or are used fictitiously and are not to be construed as real. Any resemblance to actual events, locations, organizations, or persons, living or dead, is entirely coincidental.

World Castle Publishing, LLC
Pensacola, Florida
Copyright © 2025 Sean T. Smith
Hardback ISBN: 9798298147026
Paperback ISBN: 9798891264571
eBook ISBN: 9798891264588
First Edition World Castle Publishing, LLC, September 16, 2025
http://www.worldcastlepublishing.com

Cover: Cover Designs by Karen
Editor: Karen Fuller

For Tracey, my happy ending and new beginning.
Your love makes me believe in God.

CHAPTER ONE
THE WORST DEATH

33 A.D.

That first death hurt the most. He was only an hour old when he died, and he did not know his nature yet. His demise was preceded by the worst thing he would ever see, the worst thing anyone could see.

Malak opened his eyes for the first time on a sun-scorched rocky hillside to blinding light and the sounds of hammering and cheering and wailing. He wore tattered robes and a scruffy beard, with sandals on his feet. He possessed no memories, no sense of context, while he trudged up a hill in the general direction of the calamity.

Where am I? Who Am I?

He knew how to walk and form thoughts, though he did not yet understand how he knew these things. It was hot, and somehow, he comprehended this, the knowledge of hot and cold. He puzzled how he knew enough to wonder.

He picked his way in the direction of the commotion. A walled city sprawled behind him. Smoke snaked from chimneys, armored soldiers glittered in the harsh light, and the air tasted wrong and despaired. More cheering rolled down the hill, a certain frenzy in it, the kind that gets in the air and pollutes everything it touches.

With each step, Malak felt purpose and awareness building in his chest. It was a terrible fury and fear, urgency mixed with anguish and dread. He quickened his pace, ignoring smashed shins and toes, reckless with the need to act. He did not know why he felt these things, only that he could not deny the impulse.

He crested the hill. One rise away, three men hung nailed to wooden crosses. He was too far away to make out the details, though over the next two thousand years he would relive every one. The taste of the rock, the scent of his own sweat, and the cries of the crowd would always be with him, no matter how many times he died.

His heart hammered, and his head throbbed, and the crowd roared. He felt something akin to hunger, a kind of pressure pent up in his chest demanding release.

He sprinted up the opposite slope, not knowing precisely what to do, but certain of the need to strike and defend.

And then there were Roman soldiers.

"Where do you think you're going, Jew?"

Malak understood the words, though he did not ponder this because he had no time.

"Make them stop," Malak gasped. His voice felt as wrong as the air and the light.

The soldier smashed him in the stomach with an angry fist, followed by a kick to the face. He dragged Malak up the hill by the hair.

"I hate Jews," the soldier said. "Troublemakers."

"Ugh," Malak coughed at the second blow. He'd never been struck before. He did not know how to strike back, so he took it. He hurt, and pain, like everything else, was new to him. The soldiers beat him with casual vigor, in no particular hurry. They chuckled while Malak crawled forward, blinded by blood, his face caked with tiny pebbles. He clawed in the direction of the next hill, fingernails torn and raw. He felt a sharp blow to the back of his skull, and his vision blurred and narrowed to a dark tunnel.

"So much for your king," one of them said.

A soldier yanked Malak by the hair, pulling him up to his knees, and forcing him to watch a spear pierce one of the men nailed to a cross. The crowd erupted in a cacophony of cries, euphoria and despair at war on the wind.

Malak raged and trembled, and something tore in his soul, and he felt an electric connection to a weeping, convulsing universe. Then there was hot steel on his throat, and that was the first time Malak died.

———

Malak would spend centuries struggling to understand that a hero is not necessarily the hero of his own life. Throughout his many lives, he would battle his own demons of anger and guilt, along with very real demons who walked the earth. His path was long, rocky, and mean.

Time flowed like an implacable river in only direction, even for Malak. He could never go back, only remember what he'd done. When he died, he always resurfaced somewhere down the line, often with many years passing in between.

That first death was the worst one, though, and it stayed with him forever.

CHAPTER TWO
WINGS INCORPORATED

Now

"This interview is being recorded," said the American in a tired suit. Sweat stains peeked from around his armpits as he bent to pick up a manila envelope, which he dropped loudly onto the desk.

"You have no rights. You gave up your rights when you decided to become a terrorist. You may call me John. If you cooperate with me, things will go better for you. So. State your name."

"You may call me Mal."

Clad in an orange jumpsuit and shackled to a steel chair at his wrists and ankles, Malak smiled serenely. His dark hair hung to his shoulders, and his beard was unkempt; his body ached from the repeated beatings delivered by the Saudi Secret Police. John sat across from him at a desk in the center of a sad concrete room illuminated by a single harsh light bulb. Malak shifted his heavily muscled frame in an awkward attempt to both convey his earnestness and also relieve the pressure on his lower back.

"I have nothing to hide," Malak said. *This guy is a low level spook. A CIA operative, most likely.*

"Let's start at the beginning," John said. Malak chuckled at that.

"Does this amuse you?" John asked affably, raising his eyebrows.

"You hate this posting, don't you?" Malak shook his

head slowly. "Tell me. Was it politics that landed you here, or did you do something truly incompetent? It must be one or the other."

Mal was reasonably certain that he was still in Quatif, located in the northern part of the Eastern Saudi Arabian province. Heat hung in the city in a way that got into your pores and then multiplied. It lingered like a stain upon the land, hovering just beyond the next breath, and refused to be banished by nightfall. It was unrelenting. The locals here were as hostile to the westerners as the climate.

"See, you're something of an enigma," John said. "You are not on any watch lists. In fact, you seem to not exist. Your skills and lack of history smack of a state intelligence agency. You work for someone. Who? Are you with the Israelis? Mossad?"

"You wouldn't believe me if I told you," Malak replied.

"Why did you kill the Prince?"

"Because he's been funding terrorists right under your nose. Believe it or not, I'm on your side."

"The Saudis are our allies. Your attack did nothing but destabilize the region."

Mal laughed. "A bit late for that, don't you think?"

"Who do you work for?"

"I work for no man, no government."

The interrogator, who said his name was John, produced a plastic case with several syringes inside and said, "First, we'll try this, give you some time to think. Then we'll get more creative. You know how these things go, Mal. You might as well accept the fact you'll never see the light of day again."

"Why don't you just execute me?" *That would make things easier.*

"Despite the rumors, we don't work that way." John

stuck a needle into Mal's bicep, cocking his head, an almost friendly look on his face. "Sweet dreams," he said.

———

Malak had spent the last year undercover in the guise of a private security contractor. He drove around in bulletproof cars armed with an earpiece and a machine pistol. He traveled with various members of the Saudi royal family as a silent bodyguard. He cleared hotel rooms from Bahrain to Shanghai, waiting, learning. The firm was international, well respected, and, as far as Malak could see, on the up and up. They were a means to an end.

He communicated with his own team of ex-special-forces and intelligence operators via encrypted emails and burner phones. He'd started this firm back in the nineties, which he'd called Wings Incorporated, with a wry sense of humor. He employed about a hundred men and women, from trigger-pullers to some of the best hackers on the planet. He'd lured smart, good-hearted people away from Microsoft, Apple, the FBI, CIA, NSA, and every branch of the military.

This particular Saudi prince was as dirty as they came. He'd cultivated the image of a brash playboy who cared for nothing but a lavish lifestyle, complete with yachts, opulent parties, beautiful women, and a penchant for charity.

This prince had built some of the most lethal terrorist training camps in the world, hidden in war-torn Africa and the jungles of Indonesia. Beneath the public facade was a man who believed in the overthrow of the West, the spread of Islam at the tip of the sword. Malak had counted many Muslims his friends. This man was despicable.

The prince enjoyed driving his four-wheel drive truck out into the desert with his friends, making a day of bouncing over the sand dunes. Mal got tapped to go on one of these excursions.

The prince left for the dunes early in the morning with a posse of twenty other young, affluent men and a few women. Mal waited in his SUV, the air conditioner working overtime because the temperature outside was well over a hundred degrees.

He was not going to act that day, was planning on using poison or a bomb later. He'd only recently gotten the confirmation he needed that the prince was indeed a closet terrorist. Mal had become a careful planner over the years, was reticent to act rashly because there was always a price.

Early in the afternoon, the Prince's truck got mired in the sand, and he called Mal over to help him pull the vehicle free. The prince was alone.

Malak grabbed chains from the back of his vehicle, brought for that very purpose, and walked toward the prince. The pick-up was stuck on top of a dune, the wheels buried in soft sand. The Prince grinned at Malak.

"Perhaps we shall go home after this," said the prince.

"Yes," Mal replied. "Tell me, prince, how do you sleep at night? Do you dream?"

"What?"

"Do you dream? Do you see the faces of the children you have murdered?"

"I'll have you shot! You can't speak—"

"Oh, but I can," Mal said, closing on the prince, who wore flowing white robes and who looked afraid for perhaps the first time in his life.

"So much blood on your hands," Malak said. "I'm truly curious what you see when you close your eyes."

The prince reached for a cell phone inside his truck. Mal swatted it from his hands.

"Allah—"

"God is great, yes," Mal said. "And now you will be

judged by Him."

Mal struck the handsome prince in the chest, and the prince keeled over in the seat, dead. His face rested sideways against the steering wheel, and his eyes were open.

That should have been the end of it. He would have made it out clean, but one of the Prince's girlfriends in a four-wheeler one dune away saw the whole thing. She shouted and screamed. Mal got back into his vehicle and hit the gas.

Waves of nausea rolled through him, and he felt the pressure of an elephant standing on his chest. His head ached. *There is always a price.* He felt heavy, weighted down as though he wore a lead cloak, and his vision blurred. Often, when he took a life, he absorbed something from the dead; he could filter it in time. He was out of time now.

Rounds peppered the hardened exterior of his vehicle and pinged off the glass. A cloud of sand bloomed behind him as he hurtled across the open desert. The main road was more than five miles away. He felt his wheels digging a hole in the sand as the truck labored up a mountainous dune.

He slammed into reverse, losing precious seconds. Several rounds cracked against the back glass.

This vehicle was heavy, not designed for the kind of afternoon the Prince had in mind. Mal knew he was not going to make it.

Four wheelers closed on him, along with a dune-buggy and two pick-up trucks. Not all of the drivers and passengers were armed, but there were enough firearms that Mal figured he wasn't going to be walking away from this one.

He checked his weapon, a compact Uzi capable of cutting a man in half at close range, but ineffective at longer distances. He had a choice to make. Most of these people were innocent.

He left the Uzi on the passenger seat and stepped out of

the truck, expecting to be shot, hands on his head. He swayed in the heat, fought to remain standing. *This guy must have been something truly spectacular. I haven't felt this bad in what? Twenty years.*

The desert was spinning. *Almost through it.* He put his hands on his knees then and vomited. While he was doing that, somebody cracked his skull with a rifle butt, and he woke up in a Saudi cell.

The Saudis tortured him, though he had experienced far worse. They shocked him with electrodes and a car battery, and they beat him with a metal bar. It lasted less than a day, Malak was fairly sure, before the CIA found him and whisked him away to wherever he was now.

———

"I believe you," the American said.

Mal groaned, feeling groggy and drugged.

"Tell me more about Wings Incorporated."

"What?"

"Fascinating," the American said. "You should still be in dream land. And you are healing faster than anyone I have ever seen."

"Who are you?" Mal mumbled.

"A better question," said John, "is who are *you*? More to the point, *what* are you?"

Malak was still restrained at the table in the dingy concrete room. His head swam.

"We've got all the time in the world," the American said, producing another syringe.

Mal decided he had underestimated the American, his last conscious thought as the drug took him.

CHAPTER THREE
FIRST BLOOD

Rome, February 64

Malak waited for his eyes to adjust to the gloom, disoriented amidst the scent of death which lurked heavy and thick in the damp, close air. He heard coughs and groans nearby.

For him, no time had passed since the Romans killed him in Jerusalem. There was steel and anguish, followed by this place. He discovered he was sitting with his legs splayed, with his back propped against a cool rock wall.

"Water," said a broken, disembodied voice in the shadows.

Mal stood and smacked his head on a low-hanging stone ceiling. There was cheering again, and he thought about what he had witnessed earlier, still reeling from the pain of it. This crowd, this thunder of applause, was clearly larger and more enthusiastic than the one he had died listening to the last time.

He crouched, groping in the dark, and moved in the direction of the voice.

"Where are we?"

"Over here. I can't reach the bowl."

Mal felt something soft and yielding against his right foot.

"Watch it!" said another man. Mal stepped over him.

Mal was perplexed. He continued ahead, able to see now that he was in some kind of narrow cave or tunnel. Faint light came from ahead. Torch light.

Lying in a corner, he found the man asking for water. Iron bars covered an opening ten feet away, and beyond this, a single torch burned.

The man had an iron shackle on one leg, and there was a bowl of water just beyond his reach.

"They think it's funny," the man said in a hoarse voice.

Malak handed the man the wooden bowl. In the dim, shifting light, Mal saw that the man was badly wounded. Dried blood caked the man's tunic, and Mal could smell corruption in the wound on his shoulder.

"I haven't seen you before," the man said, sputtering and choking down the water. He dropped the bowl, and it clattered on the stone. "Where did they find you?"

"I don't remember," Malak said. "I don't know anything."

"Ah," said the wounded man. "Head wound. Knocked out your stars. That happens sometimes."

"I see."

"You probably won't have to fight today. It's getting late. Then again, they're thirsty. You can hear it."

"I hope I don't have to," Mal said. That seemed appropriate.

"It's good to hear my language again before I die," the man said. "You're not from the north, though, by the look of you. How is it you know my tongue?"

"I wish I knew, friend," Malak replied. "How were you hurt? Let me see."

"Don't bother," the man replied. "I'm finished. It was cats, by the way. The biggest cats you ever saw. I'd heard the stories, but by the gods, I wasn't ready for that. Bigger than a man, with fangs and claws out of a nightmare." He shuddered.

"Let me look."

Malak pushed back the man's tunic. Deep gashes festered.

"There's spirits in my blood," the man said with a heavy sigh.

And then something unusual happened, although over the years, Mal would come to understand it better. It did not occur often enough, but when it did, it was wonderful. In those early years, it was much more frequent.

Malak placed his hands on the wounded man's shoulder, following instinct, guided by something vast and unseen.

"What in the world?" the man said.

Malak was radiating white light. A feeling of peace infused him, a sensation of being clean and whole.

This was followed immediately by paralyzing pain. Mal slumped against the wall, exhausted and in agony, while sharp needles seemed to tear through his skin. The feeling passed, and in that instant, he saw a cold land of mist and stone, fields of green and fresh spring air.

"How?" the man stammered. "You healed me."

"No," Malak said. "Not me. I don't understand, either."

"Are you a witch? You have power."

"I don't know what I am," Mal said.

Heavy footsteps echoed down the corridor outside, and there was the sound of great doors creaking open. Several soldiers armed with spears walked to the metal door. One of them carried a torch. He produced a key and opened the cell, the flame dancing in the darkness.

"One, two. Maybe three, the soldier said, walking through the gloom, kicking lifeless and maimed bodies on the floor. "Two."

"Get up," the soldier growled.

Malack and the other man rose, heads stooped. The

soldier unlocked the shackle on the man's leg.

"Walk, *meat*."

"What is your name?" said the man.

"Malak." He uttered this for the first time, feeling the rightness of it.

"I am Drust. I will die with my friend this day."

The thunder of the crowd grew louder as Malak and Drust wound up wooden steps.

A bored Roman soldier handed Malak a short blade, a *Gladius*, Malak instantly knew. He had a flash of something akin to memory, though the memories did not belong to him, but to the man he had healed, his newfound friend Drust. He saw the *ludus*, a school for gladiators, sweaty and hot, felt the clash of dull blades beneath the Roman sun, under the baleful eye of his teachers.

The soldier opened a door, and light flooded the tunnel. Malak felt the butt of a spear at his back. He stepped into the arena.

"Well," Drust said, "at least there aren't those cats."

Three helmeted men fanned out on the dirt of the arena. The crowd erupted while the door slammed shut.

The spectators sat and stood in rows, a riot of color and motion.

The three attackers were armed differently. One with a long trident and a net. Another with an oblong shield and sword. The third held a small shield and light blade. The enemies wore light leather armor over tunics.

A horn blew.

"Take the trident first," Drust said. "That one is dangerous. He'll hang back while the other two come for us."

The attacking trio fanned out, moving with knees bent, closing the gap, shields raised. The enemies were bronzed by the sun, large men who moved with predatory grace and lethal intent.

Malak raised his blade in front of him, fear in his chest, and the taste of sweat on his lips. He felt like he was vibrating, a thrum in him. He crouched, readying himself.

Two men lashed out, springing toward Malak and Durst from the flanks.

Malak dropped, ducking beneath a slashing sword, rolling and then exploding to his feet and cutting backhand as he rose, a lightning strike to the back of the attacker's knee. He felt the blade grate through sinew and launched himself directly at the man with a trident.

The net, weighted down at the edges, came at Malak, who did not slow or turn, but instead leaped ahead. The edge of the net caught his head, and he tossed it aside, his own blade held in his right hand, poised.

The trident blurred to the left and shifted, too fast for the eye to follow, and Malak grunted when a sideways blow caught him on the temple. He went down, instinct propelling him, rolling and then coming up, light on the balls of his feet.

Behind him, he thought he heard a scream over the crowd, but Malak kept his focus on the burly warrior with a long trident who meant to skewer him. The man circled Malak and lashed out, jumping forward with his right leg extended, the wicked trident seeking Mal's throat in a quick jab.

Malak danced backwards.

Durst was beside Mal then, swinging the net over his head with practiced efficiency. The man with the trident retreated, his plumed helmet swinging from side to side, watching, waiting.

"Rush him," Drust instructed.

Mal came at the man, anticipating the counterattack. This time, there was no feint. The big man was quick as a snake, and one of the prongs gashed Malak's left forearm.

Malak brought his blade down, knocking the trident to the ground with a clang.

The net was on the gladiator then, and he struggled to free himself. Malak hit him on the temple with the pommel of his sword, and the man slumped down in the dirt. The crowd went wild, then grew quiet.

"Face him," Drust shouted at Malak, who stood sweating and bleeding.

Drust towered over the unconscious, entangled man with his sword raised.

Malak followed his gaze and beheld Nero Claudius Caesar Augustus Germanicus standing in a box, clad in a flowing white toga with a purple stripe. Nero raised his thumb in the air, along with most of the people in the crowd.

Mal dropped his sword, and a group of heavily armed soldiers emerged into the arena to escort him back into the darkness while the crowd cheered, and Malak wondered what dream he was in.

CHAPTER FOUR
MIRACLE

Now

Mal strained to lift his head and found he could not. This room was not the cell he'd been in before. He heard subdued beeping sounds and low voices under harsh fluorescent lights. The room had the sterile feel of a hospital. He wiggled his fingers and toes. *I'm not paralyzed, at least.*

His head seemed to be immobilized by some sort of unyielding foam. A restraint across his chest kept him from inhaling deeply. More bonds kept his legs and arms fixed in place.

He took a slow breath and relaxed, finding a quiet place deep down. He concentrated on the voices, though he caught only fragments.

"...a phenomenal discovery," a woman was saying, "that could change everything."

A man's voice interjected, and Malak heard something about DNA. They were speaking English.

Mal shifted his eyes around the ceiling, looking for anything that might tell him where he was. The ceiling was white. That was about all he could discern.

"He's coming out of it now," the woman said, this time closer.

Malak heard footsteps on the floor, the swish of clothing, and the whisper of perfume.

"Hello," said a man beyond Mal's point of view.

"I'd shake your hand," Mal said, "but I'm a bit tied up

at the moment."

"Yes, I do regret that," the man said. "I apologize. Someone wants to talk to you. After that, I think we can reach some other accommodation for you."

"That's kind of you," Malak said.

"Where are you from?" the woman said. She sounded breathless, bursting with curiosity.

"Forgive my colleague, Dr. Rose. She is of the opinion you are of extra-terrestrial origin."

"I've never been anywhere but this rock," Malak said. He chuckled. "Sorry to disappoint. Mind if I ask where we are?"

"Again, I hope you will forgive me, but I am not at liberty to divulge that information."

"I understand," Mal replied. "And what might your name be, good doctor?"

"Adam," the man replied. "Dr. Adam Bass."

"It's nice to meet you, Doctors Bass and Rose. Might I trouble you for a drink of water?"

"I'm terribly sorry, but I'm not authorized to do that. You have a saline drip; you are not dehydrated."

"I see. And when will I have the pleasure of meeting my mysterious visitor?"

"Very shortly," Dr. Bass replied. "You awoke on schedule."

"And whom might I be meeting?"

"His name is Doctor Louis. That's all I know, and all I am at liberty to say. Speak of the devil; here he is."

Malak heard more footsteps. A normal human being would doubtless have been terrified, being confined, tortured, drugged, and interrogated with no end in sight. Malak was more bored than anything and annoyed at the fact that these people were wasting his time. He was racking his brains for a way to force them to kill him.

"Greetings, Malak," Louis said.

"Louis, where have you taken me?" Mal said.

"In time," Louis said. "Let's just say you're a rather long way from where I found you. You are safe. We will not harm you in any way, you have my word." A delicate, suntanned face framed by ash blond hair appeared a foot from Mal's own. He smiled down at Mal.

"Dr. Bass, please remove the restraints around the patient's head and chest." The doctor complied.

Malak raised his head and looked around the room. It resembled an operating room, the walls lined with machinery and luminescent display screens with bewildering data sets streaming. Electrodes on his chest, arms, legs, and head apparently fed information to computers. The room was cramped. He lay on a narrow bed with metal rails. The two doctors retreated to a glass door, wearing white lab coats and hesitant smiles.

"So I'm a patient, then? Funny, because I feel healthy."

"You are indeed healthy. Impossibly so, in fact."

"Well then…"

"You came to my attention thanks to a colleague," Louis said. "We're going to get to know one another very well. I believe we'll be friends."

"Is that a fact?"

"It is indeed. Of course, you will need to make certain compromises and concessions."

"Hmm. So you know, then, I'm just a guy who does some security contracting."

"That is an excellent, if euphemistic way of putting it, Malak." Louis laughed then, a musical sound. "You have lost your way. I can help you find it again."

Malak shivered. He had not felt true fear since Berlin

in the spring of 1945.

"Ahh," Louis said, a faint smile on full lips. "You don't need to fear me, *brother*."

Malak strained at his bonds, staring at the man who called himself Louis. His muscles ached, and he tried to break free with sheer force of will.

Louis pursed his lips and shook his head. "Well, friend, I wanted to stop by and introduce myself, get a good look at you. We have much to discuss, but I see you are not quite ready for that talk just yet."

The vise around his head tightened, and Mal found himself immobile again. *Okay. Now would be a good time for some help.*

He felt hot breath on his forehead, but he could see nothing but the lights. "Do you think," Louis whispered, "He cares about you? He doesn't. Not even a little bit. See you soon." Louis kissed him on the head, a tender gesture in the way of a father kissing his son, only it was creepy and terrifying.

The doctors must have put something in the drip, because Malak went to sleep, remembering the war before he could reply.

CHAPTER FIVE
REMEMBERING

Normandy, 1944

Perhaps death is not darkness but dawn, when hope sings over the horizon and burns bright, promising a world reborn in the sigh of waves and dance of light, a place of refuge and inspiration and beginnings rather than endings, a doorway to the unknown and beautiful.

That's not how it was for Malak.

He was erased by a German artillery shell in Poland early in the war, only to reappear in a Soviet uniform. He bound wounds and rushed into enemy fire, was toasted for his heroism, as he watched Russians die by the trainload. He was cut down by a Kraut machine-gun nest outside Leningrad, and then found himself at Omaha Beach wearing American fatigues.

He picked himself up from the blood-stained sand and went to work, crawling ahead while rounds hummed and cracked over his head and smacked the sand around him, the cries of the dying mixing with the thunder of artillery and explosions of shells launched from ships offshore as they hammered entrenched German positions.

The beach, which was not a friendly sun-kissed expanse of sand and relaxation in the way of the word, exploded and tilted. A German artillery round detonated ahead and to the right, and sand and bits of men rained down on his helmet.

He crawled ahead, toward a man screaming for his Momma, the soldier trying to put his intestines back inside a bloody cavity that had been his abdomen.

Malak did not know his purpose here; he touched the man, though, and felt the searing pain that came with healing. He emanated a blue-white aura as he worked, though he ignored this. He felt weak, but he kept moving. He wished and prayed he could do more. He took the carbine from a dead man's hands, along with two Mark II fragmentation grenades.

A German pillbox ahead unleashed terrible machine-gun fire, the rounds seeking men behind Malak who were still struggling to make the beach, and those hunkered down behind the metal obstacles the Germans had laid up and down the beach. Mal pulled his helmet close to his head, belly in the sand, the scent of blood on the air and gunpowder and screams and terror.

Planes churned overhead, bombers and fighters attacking the German positions on the Norman coast. He looked over his shoulder, saw the landing craft, ungainly steel boxes that pretended to be boats, crashing into the surf and disgorging platoons of men who fell beneath a hail of gunfire or vanished under the implacable ocean.

And then he felt that thing.

In his mind, he called it "the glory." It was a sense of certainty of action, a security of violence, he rarely experienced. For a moment, his power did not belong to him.

Malak ran ahead through German rounds and artillery shells. The American troops crouched down and advanced behind him, and Malak *knew*. He charged, an M1 Garand in his hands and a scream in his heart. Enemy shells exploded in the dirt, sending geysers of sand and mud high into the air.

His steps were light, and he sped into the hail of lead. A sand berm loomed ahead, lined with barbed wire, and beyond that was the German bunker. Malak saw the muzzle flashes and felt a wind of angry projectiles cracking and hissing around him, breaking left and right without touching his flesh.

He cut to his left, staying out of the direct field of fire from the heavy guns. He knew from experience he did not have long.

A German trench, perhaps five feet deep, ran parallel to the beach, connected to the bunker. The trench was lined with soldiers firing down the beach. Malak jumped into the trench.

A startled soldier fired a burst from an MP-40 submachine gun at Malak from only a few feet away. Malak closed the gap, wrenched the weapon from the man's hands, and broke his neck.

Other soldiers ran and shot, backing away from Malak, who fired controlled bursts from the MP-40. Some ran away from the bunker, and he let them run. His goal was to take that bunker.

He pulled the pins on the frags and tossed them into the bunker, not bothering to wait for the explosions. He stalked into the grey, dusty building, the smell of propellant and smoke heavy in the air. He could hear the heavy machine guns upstairs chugging away. He took the steps two at a time, stepping over bodies of men torn by the grenades.

An officer waited atop the steps, covering the machine gun crews. He was a middle-aged man with blue eyes and an aquiline nose, sharp featured. Perhaps he was a father to young children back in Hamburg or Berlin. Maybe he was a good man in some way.

Malak did not care at the moment. The officer was protecting the gunners who were killing men every second.

"*Ich Uebergebe!*" the officer shouted, raising his hands.

"No," Malak said.

Malak shot him in the chest. The crews were turning, reaching for side arms. Malak picked one of them up with his left hand and tossed him through the opening in the bunker. With his right hand, he hit the other soldier in the chest, and the man flew ten feet and smashed against the concrete wall, lifeless.

The power left him. He was depleted and sick, an image seared into his mind imparted from the dead officer. Furnaces and mass graves. Something called the Final Solution. He was turning for the door when a round went through the base of his skull.

————

When he opened his eyes again, he was alarmed to discover he'd missed much of the war. He found himself wearing a medic uniform again. There had been a big German offensive, which, the men said, was bloody and cold. But now, the war would be over soon.

He walked through the mud into camp and sat down at a fire without introduction. One of the soldiers offered him a smoke, which he accepted.

"Howdy," the man said. "You look like you've been through hell, too."

"Yeah," Malak said. The disorientation he felt at being dead then reborn was passing. He inhaled on the cigarette.

"Names Calhoun. From Macon, Georgia."

"Mal. From here and there."

"Ha. You with the 101st?"

Mal had neglected to look carefully at his uniform. "I'm attached now," he said, hedging his bet.

"What a war," the guy said. "They say it's all but over now. It's a race to Berlin, us and the Reds."

"I'll be glad when it's done," Malak said. "Thanks for the smoke, buddy. I gotta run."

"Sure, Mac. See you around."

Malak had a mission, one he had decided to undertake all on his own, and he was looking forward to it.

CHAPTER SIX
ESCAPE

Now

He was in a different room this time, one with padded walls and a mattress on the floor. He was no longer restrained. Malak pushed himself to his feet and paced the room. Ten by ten. He'd been in smaller cells. He was dressed in a white, open backed hospital gown which reached to his knees.

He peered through the reinforced glass window in the door. The empty hallway held no answers for him.

Malak sat cross-legged on the mattress, closed his eyes, and prayed to a God he was certain of, but did not understand and could no longer feel.

He was sure God existed because he'd felt unfathomable love shine upon his face, been immersed in grace for moments which could sustain his faith for centuries. He'd also felt the wrath and fury which came from the same place. His resurrections, encounters with demons, and the time he'd spent with Ariel erased any doubts which might have crept in. God was real. *But where is He? Why does he allow such terrible things to happen to people?*

It seemed to Malak in his darkest moments that the question of belief was easier for mortals, and part of him envied the simplicity of choice that humans enjoyed. Take a leap of faith, or don't. Be certain of what you have not seen, and seek God. Most of the time, Mal recognized that his own dilemma was no different at its heart than what humans faced, other than the fact that he'd been dealing with these questions for longer. He'd been a witness to more, both good and evil, than any mortal man.

After two thousand years, Malak was still trying to figure out his own place in God's plan. He'd felt unworthy of love, been crushed by failure, and seen his own actions unleash catastrophic ripples through time. Free will, his own and that of humanity, seemed to be at odds with any kind of grand plan.

He tried to wrap his mind around that concept, envisioning God on the scale of the universe itself, billions of galaxies, trillions of stars, and still this encompassing, powerful force behind all of it. He believed in God, but doubted His benevolence at times.

God had a sense of humor, of that Malak was certain.

———

The door opened, and the American doctor Bass entered the room, carrying a computer tablet, smiling warmly at Malak.

"Good morning," said the doctor.

"Is it?" Mal said.

"It is morning, and a good one at that."

"Hmm."

"We're moving you to a larger facility, one I hope will be more to your liking. You will have your own quarters, much more freedom than you have enjoyed over the last few days. Again, I regret all of this. If it were up to me, I'd let you walk out of here."

"Your hands are tied. Following orders, right?"

"Precisely."

"From Louis."

"Dr. Louis is my boss's boss," the doctor said. He looked like he wanted to wring his hands, but he couldn't because he was holding an iPad.

"Who do you work for? Where am I being held captive? Why?"

"My superiors are very intrigued. Your blood work is completely normal. MRI scans of your brain show nothing unusual, but for an enlarged hippocampus and highly active cerebral cortex. Yet you are able to repair wounds at a cellular level more quickly than should be possible. You could be the key to curing all sorts of diseases that have plagued mankind. You might hold the key to longevity beyond our wildest dreams. The word 'miracle' is being bandied about."

"So rather than asking for my help, you're going to hold me indefinitely while you poke and prod. That sound about right?"

"Indeed, you are too valuable to science. Again, this is what my superiors say. You can't just leave. We need to understand you."

"What if I told you there is a war going on, one you will never understand? That there is a storm coming which will make all wars in human history seem tame? And that I seem to have a role to play."

"I'd tell you that you suffered from a form of schizophrenia," said the doctor, "although we have not found markers for that. Tell me, do you truly believe what you just said?" He cocked his head to the side and peered at Malak.

"I am certain of it."

"Interesting."

"So you're not going to let me go, then Doctor? I'm doomed to a life of needles?"

"Not indefinitely, but for the time being, yes."

"I'm sorry, then."

"Why?"

Malak took two steps and struck the doctor in the solar plexus. The doctor fell to the ground, his mouth open, fighting for air that refused to come, eyes shocked and wide.

Malak crossed into the hallway, the hospital gown he wore flapping behind him, bare feet slapping on the tile floors. He passed under more than one security camera.

He noticed other cells lining the hall, and he sprinted toward the end of the hallway, where double doors opened, disgorging a knot of armed men in military uniforms. They knelt, weapons aimed at Malak, from twenty paces away.

"Halt!" one of them shouted.

Malak did not slow. He sprang for the right wall, placed one leg on it mid-way up to the ceiling, and kicked in the opposite direction, descending onto the men from above.

Two soldiers fired Tasers, the darts zipping beneath him. The men were shouting. One of them fired a sidearm, and the shot was deafening in the confined hallway.

He hit the ground, rolled, and leapt into their midst. His legs were weapons, his elbows bludgeons, and his fists blurred with merciless ferocity. It was over in less than six seconds.

A klaxon blared, raw and jarring.

Malak took a submachine gun from an unconscious soldier and went through the double doors.

Straight ahead, another long hallway stretched for fifty yards. To his right was another set of doors. He hit a metal button on the wall, and the doors slid open.

The room beyond looked like a nurse's station at an ER. There were banks of monitors at a central, circular desk. The remaining doctors, nurses, and security personnel ran amuck, scurrying for exits on either side. Someone screamed, no doubt alarmed by the wild-haired man garbed in a loose white gown, wielding a submachine gun.

He charged toward what he hoped was the exit and emerged in a metal stairway. He pounded the steps, taking

them two at a time. He overtook the staff and thrust them out
of his way.

This seems a bit too easy.

He paused at a landing, listening. Behind him, he could
hear people climbing the stairs, muttering and cursing, their
steps ringing in the confined space. He looked up and saw he
was nearly to the top. Two flights to go. No one was coming
down.

He reversed direction and came barreling back down
the stairs. An Asian man in a lab coat tried to turn around
when he saw Malak coming back. Mal grabbed the man by
the shoulder.

"I won't hurt you," Malak said. "Hold on."

"Turn around," the man hollered down the stairway.
Shouts reverberated, and the timbre of the steps changed,
receding.

"What's up top?"

"The hangar. And a parking lot. Many soldiers."

"There's got to be another way out."

"No."

"Help me out here. What's your name?"

"Dr. Lee."

"Okay Lee, we don't have much time, I'm guessing. I
need some quick answers. Can you do that?"

The man looked petrified, as though at any moment he
thought Malak was going to eat his heart or infect him with
some terrible, incurable disease.

"What do you want to know?"

"Where are we?"

"New Mexico."

"Are we at a military installation?"

"Yes."

"Good. You're being very helpful. I appreciate that.

Why don't we start walking down while we chat."

Dr. Lee nodded his head, and Mal took his elbow. They walked back down the stairs.

"Where is the security station? The one down here?"

"Just off the central corridor. Where you just were."

"Let's go have a look, shall we?"

"Did you kill those men?"

"The soldiers? No. They won't be bothering us, though. Are there more of them down here?"

"Not in this wing. There are two more wings, each with a security station. But the only way out is through this stairway. There was an elevator, but a few years ago, there was a breach. They decided to make everyone pass this way."

"Good to know. What about security protocols? What happens when there is a breach?"

"Containment."

They reached the bottom of the stairs and walked back into the room with the monitors. Lee pointed at a metal door off to the right. "Security," he said.

"Open the door. And what does containment entail? What happens next?"

"We're all going to die," Lee said.

CHAPTER SEVEN
KILLING HITLER

Berlin, April 1945

There was an essential greyness about that city under siege, a grainy black and white feel to it, even though Malak saw it in living color. When he thought about Berlin in 1945, it was always like that. Allied bombs smashing the city, grey uniforms, grey tanks, and piles of rubble and black smoke. Civilians terrified and starving. Their skin seemed stretched and papery and had an ashen palor to it, as if they absorbed the rampant evil, recoiled from it, and were trapped inside it, consumed and condemned to a kind of twilight existence where color is washed out in the murk and coming dark.

Malak acted of his own accord. He was not under orders, either from God or man. He went, as the Army would say, AWOL. Absent Without Leave. That was not something new for him, though. Sometimes it was the right thing; often it wasn't, in retrospect.

He'd spent lifetimes attempting to grasp how fate, faith, and freewill interact, slashing and rippling and devouring history with consequence and purpose beyond his understanding. Mortals only had to live with their mistakes for a handful of years.

He'd felt the ache of making a wrong decision for the right reasons enough times that he was reluctant to act. Hitler had to be put down, though. Malak wished he'd done it sooner, and he questioned the unwritten rules that seemed to govern his existence, even as he took off the medic uniform.

Malak changed his clothing twice before he arrived at the *Furhernbunker*. He left American lines, took off the medic uniform, and put on the bloodied grey of a German officer whose stiff body lay face down beside a burned out armored vehicle.

He cut across ragged German lines and commandeered a car to the capitol. German anti-aircraft raked the low hanging clouds, and sirens blared. At the second checkpoint, a blue-eyed blond Aryan poster in a crisp black uniform demanded identification papers.

The SS commander regarded Mal with arrogant suspicion, perhaps because Malak's appearance was a far cry from the master race ideal.

"Why have you left your men at the front?" he said.

"As I explained, I have intelligence of a classified nature. There is no time."

"Wait here," said the Nazi, turning for the sandbagged command post, probably to find a phone or a radio.

Malak shot him in the back of the head from four feet away with the Luger he'd liberated from the dead captain. Malak's driver sputtered and tried to back up, cursing, and Malak put a single round through the man's right eye.

With nausea and pain racking his body and mind, Malak waded into the group of three soldiers standing behind the machine gun emplacement. They were mere boys, baggy uniforms and helmets too big for their heads. Malak slashed with elbows, knees, and fists, and the boys slumped unconscious to the ground. He dragged the SS officer into the shack and stripped the dead man of his uniform and shiny black boots. He put the body into the back of the jeep and followed his instinct as he drove toward the source of evil.

It was like an electricity, a tingle in his brain, or a repugnant scent which he could follow like a bloodhound.

Here.

A concrete building surrounded by machine guns and SS troopers, though not nearly as many as he'd expected, squatted ahead. There were craters in the walls, and parts of the roof were missing in places. While he sat in the jeep, Russian artillery shells pounded buildings less than a mile away.

Mal jumped from the jeep and strode forward with purpose, attempting to radiate urgency and self-importance. He ignored the Tiger tank crew and the soldiers and went straight for the door. Two SS guards armed with submachine guns clicked their heels at his approach.

"Heil Hitler," they said, stabbing the air in the way of good Nazis.

"Heil," he replied, mimicking the ridiculous gesture.

They let him pass. He paused beyond the door. *It knows I'm here.*

He sensed it was beneath him. Soldiers milled about, looking frantic and hopeless, and Malak attempted to act like he knew where he was going. He found a doorway leading down and followed the steps, down a cement stairway lit by flickering naked light bulbs. His breath was loud in his ears, and he took two steps at a time. The close ceiling shuddered, and small pieces of cement fell as he loped downward. The light went out for a few seconds. He continued on his path, hands on the wall for balance and sense of place. *It's close. On the move.*

The invisible chord he followed pulsated with increased ferocity.

He emerged from the stairway into a group of offices. Tense officers stood over maps. They looked up at him and seemed to accept him, no doubt contemplating their own imminent capture and demise at the hands of the Red Army.

He crossed a hallway and came to a sitting area behind a door.

A patterned couch sat against the wall; a makeshift desk covered with papers squatted in a corner with a bottle of champagne on it.

The bodies of six small children lay on the floor; they had not been shot. Five girls and one boy of maybe ten. Malak shook with rage.

He went out a rear door and found stairs going up. He sprinted up toward the surface.

He stepped into the daylight in the middle of what once had been a beautiful garden. Now, it was cratered and muddy. He was in the Chancellery Garden; Adolf Hitler was standing next to a fire with Joseph Goebbels and Eva Braun. They were clearly planning a getaway. The fire, in a crater made by a Soviet artillery shell, consumed charred bodies. The scent of gasoline mingled with that of burning meat and smoke.

Goebbels stared at Malak, who brought up the Luger as he walked ahead. Hitler looked defeated and small. He'd seemed much bigger in the news reels.

Malak shot him in the temple, and the Führer toppled into the fire. His wife screamed. Malak was assailed by crashing waves of evil. His eyes rolled back in his head with the force of it. If Hitler hadn't been such an evil son-of-a bitch, Malak might have had a chance against the demon.

Goebbels raised a hand, and Malack flew off his feet and smashed against the wall. Malak had not expected that.

"You are too late," said Goebbels. Of course, it wasn't really the propaganda minister, not any more, if indeed it had ever been human.

Malak pushed himself to his feet and began to speak the words.

He glowed as he chanted. Most of the words were Hebrew, some Latin, some Aramaic. He understood all of them.

Goebbels attacked again, and Malak could not speak, his throat clenched as though it was in a vise.

Okay, God. This would be a great time to let me do some smiting on your behalf.

"Events are now in motion, Malak Elohim." Goebbels spat, thin lips, soulless eyes, and an awkward, cruel face fitting his reputation.

The world was going black. Mal fought for breath. He'd never encountered a demon this powerful, and he didn't know what would happen if he died this time. Malak was afraid, staring into those black eyes, the sneering face of darkness. He heard the buzzing sound of thousands of flies bottled up and contained, felt the weight of evil pressing on his soul. He was afraid for himself, but more so for mankind.

"The Prince is coming soon, on *his* terms. There is nothing you can do to stop it."

At least I killed Hitler, Malak thought. Then he died.

CHAPTER EIGHT
MAH-VET

Now

"How are we all going to die?" Malak asked Dr. Lee. The room was empty, the monitors beeped and blinked with mindless efficiency, and Malak wondered where the other staff people had gone.

"Gas," Lee said. He pointed at the ceiling. "Those aren't just sprinklers."

"So let's find us some bio-suits. You've got those down here, right?"

"This is a class V containment facility," Lee said, defeated. "I don't know what the protocol is. They're not letting you out. Or me."

If they think I'm the key to curing cancer, they just might break protocol. I've got to give these people a chance.

Malak stood beneath one of the security cameras and waved at it.

"I'm coming topside. Alone and unarmed. Don't kill these people." He put the weapon on the desk. "Goodbye, Dr. Lee."

Mal climbed the stairs with less eagerness in him than he'd possessed minutes before. At the top, he opened a simple metal door and entered a cramped, sterile room. An impressive blast door barred his way. He waited, hands at his side. Minutes passed.

The door opened with a hiss and a release of pressure. There were no guards, no soldiers waiting for him beyond the threshold. Malak stepped into the gloomy hangar. A hundred yards to his right, bright sunlight illuminated the entrance to the building.

Malak heard vehicles outside, but all he could see beyond the glare was desert. Somewhere, an alarm wailed.

A silhouette cloaked in shadow strode toward Malak.

They met in the center of the empty hangar.

The enemy wore black fatigues and bloused combat boots, every blond hair perfectly in place, and a smile on his face.

"Resourceful as always, Malak. I should have taken a more personal interest in keeping you secure. You've become something of a nuisance. I was engaged elsewhere."

"Who are you?" Malak said.

"You still don't know? Hmm. You once did. It's been a long time."

"What are you talking about?"

"I have had many names."

Malak could not feel the buzz that accompanied a demon. There was no throb of evil emanating from this man. There was an absence of vitality, a kind of void surrounding him. Mal was certain this was no ordinary human being. He began the incantation, chanting under his breath.

"I had great plans for you, Malak, and you served my purposes well. I think I shall reward you. Tell me, would you like to go home?"

Malak did not answer. He kept chanting, fear and urgency building in his chest.

Dr. Louis continued to smile, even as his visage changed and became terrible. His eyes turned yellow, like neon urine flashing with electric energy. Malak could no longer speak; his mouth was sealed shut. He launched himself toward the man. Mid-flight, he stopped, hovering in the air, paralyzed and dangling like a fish on a hook.

"Your time on earth has come to an end. *My* time is just beginning."

As if a gateway had been opened, Malak felt a torrent of evil assail him, cutting him, crawling and swirling and swarming.

Malak had perished by drowning more than once, and what he felt now was worse. He was drowning in evil. It invaded every part of him, and he choked on it. Malak was dying, and he felt sure this death would be final. He prayed while the world got ragged and dark, unable to close his eyes, and staring into the face of iniquity.

Without warning, the attack ceased. Malak dropped to the hard concrete floor, gasping face down.

He pushed himself up to his feet, shaking.

The bunker was no longer gloomy.

Ariel stood next to Malak, radiant, effervescent, and beautiful, white light banishing the darkness, and she touched Malak on the shoulder. He felt better at once.

"Lucifer," Ariel said. There was a trace of sadness in her voice. "You cannot be here."

"You chose the wrong side," Lucifer said. His eyes flashed, and Malak felt heat emanating from him.

"There are no sides," Ariel replied. "You are as arrogant and foolish as ever."

"You are wrong. It is you who are deceived." The room hummed with power, the solid floor vibrating beneath Malak's bare feet.

Ariel raised her hand, and a sword appeared in her grasp, flaming white, more energy than steel.

"*Mah-Vet,*" Lucifer said, pointing a finger at Ariel.

The concussion shredded the hangar, sending twisted metal high into the air, a shockwave on the scale of a nuclear blast disintegrating the walls, overturning vehicles, and tearing apart the soldiers outside.

Malak stood beside Ariel, feeling not even a gentle breeze, as the surrounding area vanished in dust and violence.

Lucifer took a quick step backwards, something serpentine in the way he moved, a coiled, lethal aspect in his body.

Ariel lunged, fluid and graceful. Her sword pierced Lucifer's chest. He slumped to his knees, naked hatred on his face and a trickle of blood on the side of his lips.

"Wait," Lucifer said. "Tell him—"

Ariel pulled the blade from his chest and executed a perfect spin attack. Lucifer's head rolled onto the ground, and his body toppled backwards.

Ariel turned to Malak, smiling.

"Hello old friend," she said. "It's been too long."

She touched him on the shoulder, and they weren't in New Mexico anymore.

CHAPTER NINE
INTO THE FIRE

Rome, July 64

Malak and Drust walked through the crowded slums, following five paces behind the man who owned them.

Caius strutted through the alleyways and narrow corridors, wearing a toga, pausing to speak to prostitutes.

"We should kill him," Drust said under his breath.

"Maybe," Malak said. "They would hunt us down like vermin. Everyone knows we belong to him."

"It might be worth it," Drust said with disgust. "I'm getting too old for the ring. You've been carrying me."

"Bah," Malak said. "You've got fight in you yet."

"I grow weary of this heat. I yearn for home. Sometimes I envy you for not remembering home. It is a powerful thing, that longing."

"I cannot miss what I do not remember, that is true," Malak said. "Caius isn't so bad. He's better than the last one. He treats us well. Good food doesn't make us kill. We don't fight often. It is not such a bad life, my friend. We could be living on the street with these poor people."

"But we are slaves, Malak. I wish I could make you understand. Sometimes I think you are simple."

Malak laughed. The wind was dry and warm, and the sun was sinking low in the sky. Malak enjoyed getting out into the city and considered it a rare privilege. That their purpose was to allow Caius to show them off did not matter to Malak. He was, in fact, simple then.

He did not mind the life of a gladiator. He embraced the simplicity of combat, the adrenaline rush that came with facing death, and the sense of honor in victory. These were the only things he knew.

Caius motioned for them to come closer.

"Men," Caius said. "Take this woman and cut her tongue out." He pointed at a cowering girl of perhaps twelve.

"We have no blade, master," Malak said. *And I just might take my friend's advice, after all.*

"What has she done?" Drust said.

"That does not concern you. Take my blade and cut out her tongue. I don't want to soil my robes."

They stood in the shadowy doorway of a brothel. Malak could hear women wailing in the background over the general noise on the street.

Caius removed a long dagger encrusted with gems from a sheath at his waist and handed the blade to Drust.

The dark haired girl, knees clenched to her chest, whimpered.

And that was the first time Malak got marching orders from upstairs. He stood frozen for a moment, not understanding what was happening to him. The image of flame seared his mind and soul.

He realized both Drust and Caius were staring at him, Drust holding the blade in his hand.

"By Jupiter's balls," Caius exclaimed.

Malak struck Caius in the throat with such speed and force that the Roman flew through the open doorway, feet horizontal, as though he'd been hurled from a catapult. When Malak's fist made contact with Caius, the man burst into flames. His lifeless, burning body hit something highly flammable against the interior wall. Malak thought later that it might have been alcohol, maybe pitch. Whatever it was,

Caius's body ignited an inferno in the brothel.

The people inside ran, screaming. Malak picked up the girl, the power still upon him, and carried her through the streets. Behind them, smoke billowed, and the fire licked the next building, and then the next, hungry. Citizens and slaves stampeded in the streets as the fire spread from rooftop to rooftop.

Drust ran beside Malak, struggling to keep up, weaving through the crowd. The sound of alarm receded some, only to be renewed from up ahead.

A group of armored Centurions came in Malak's direction, shoving people aside.

"We must leave," Drust said.

"Yes. Where?"

"I don't know. We're slaves. Maybe we should find a Ludus in another city. I don't know how we will get there."

"We'll become Romans," Malak said.

"I don't understand."

"Like this."

Malak put the girl down on the street, and she ran away. The Centurions were twenty paces away, and they were noticing Malak, who was enveloped in a brilliant blue-white aura. He was unarmed, but he felt certain that would not matter. He faced six soldiers who were barreling down upon him at a run.

Malak dropped low to the ground, slashing with his right leg, supporting himself with one hand and his left leg. The blow shattered the knees of the first two Romans.

A blade flashed at Malak's head from the side, a killing blow which should have ended it. The blade deflected as though it bit stone, and the soldier swore. Malak hit the man in the groin, and he went down. Drust was at his side then, swinging a gladius, spinning, slashing. Malak felt the power leave him, extinguished like a fire doused in water, and he fought, weakened now, vulnerable.

The last soldier stabbed Malak through the stomach, and the blade wrenched in him, tearing vital things. Mal sank to his knees with his strength gone and blinding pain radiating from his midsection.

Drust picked Malak up and put him over his shoulder. The next hours were full of smoke and screams and darkness.

Drust, at some point, put Malak into a cart with two dead Centurions. Later on that night, Drust helped Malak put on the Roman uniform.

They left the city under the cover of night, and in the distance, Malak could see that the fire he started would engulf the city. The orange glow blotted out the stars from many miles away, and the smoke drifted on the wind. Malak wondered how many people were dying in the fire he started.

They were given shelter the following day by an enclave of Jews many miles from the city, and there, Malak began his real education.

———

He would always wonder about that night. *What if…*

What if I had not attacked those soldiers? They may well have put out the fire that consumed two-thirds of the city.

What if there had been no fire? Nero needed a scapegoat for the flames, and he found that in the sect of Jews worshiping the Christ. In the years that followed, Christians were persecuted with great vigor. Nero executed them by the thousands, placed them in the ring to die under the sword, and in more creative ways, too.

Peter and Paul were put to death. Men I wish I'd known.

What have I done?

CHAPTER TEN
ARIEL

Now

Malak felt the lurching disorientation he usually experienced after being killed. He was sitting beside Ariel, who now appeared human. They wore casual hiking clothes, complete with backpacks, canteens, and sunglasses. Her fine, blond hair danced in the cool wind.

They sat on a rock overlooking a placid blue lake, mountains and forest all around them. He knew this place.

"You're a comedian," he said to Ariel.

"It seems fitting," she said, laughing. "Inspiration Point does have a certain poetic ring to it."

He'd been here more than once, though it had been a wild place then, and now that the Teton Range was a tourist attraction, he'd decided not to return.

"How have you been, Malak? I've thought about you often."

"Is that all you have to say? It's been hard."

"I know. How is your heart?" She placed her palm against his chest, and he felt the healing in her touch.

"I'm working on it. I could have used some help before, you know. I prayed. A lot."

"You have doubts still?"

"I do."

"Yet I am here with you now. And He will never abandon you."

"I take issue with the last part. And you did. Abandon

me."

"Malak, I died."

"I know."

"Then you know it's not the same."

"You never came back for me, Ariel. *I* looked for *you*. I felt you nearby, and sometimes I swear I saw you."

"I am sorry. I had no choice."

"It seemed to me that you did… was it all an act?"

"Of course not. I can't explain it properly, because I don't fully understand myself. For a while, I was like you, I think, but then after I died, I recalled *everything*. And then my choices were no longer truly my own. I obey."

"Well," Malak sighed, "it was long ago. It's good to see you now. I mean it."

She cupped an elegant hand against his cheek, leaned close, and placed her forehead against his, gazing into his eyes for a long moment. Malak took a deep, aching breath, savoring her touch.

"It was not a lie, Malak. I am sorry that you hurt. That your life was not easier. But no one said it would be easy," she said. She gave Malak a sad smile, pushed her hair back from her eyes, a human gesture which brought back memories both good and bad. "I would do something different if I could. I hope you know that."

"I've spent my life being confused," Malak said. He laughed without humor. "My life. Lives. Everything must be cryptic. Why is that?"

"I only know what I know. The truth is within you, all around you."

"See, that's exactly what I'm talking about. Riddles."

"It's part of your journey. The most important part."

"What am I, Ariel?"

"You are who you are, though not who you will be,

nor who you have been."

Malak groaned.

"Ariel, tell me the truth. I've encountered you and Gabriel. I'm nothing like you or him. I'm something else. I'm weak, flawed. I'm... broken, perhaps. Never enough."

"You are not weak, nor are you insignificant. We each have different roles to play. You are unique, Malak. It is a gift."

"It is a curse. I would rather be a normal human and be allowed to die a proper and final death."

"You will be called home when the time is right."

"And where exactly is home?"

She smiled serenely at him and caressed his hand with her fingertips, light as a feather.

"Tell me what to do, then. Help me understand. Please," Malak said.

"That is not my role, my friend. Your freedom, your choices, belong to you. The war draws near once again, and it will spill out onto the earth."

"You were there at the beginning, Ariel. Why would He allow any of it?"

"I do not know. Lucifer was not always evil. Pride twisted him, destroyed him. There are consequences, and mankind suffers. For men make choices, too."

"What did Lucifer mean when he said 'tell him' right before you lopped off his head?"

"Lucifer believes he will be victorious, as do those that follow him. He is mistaken. He is the deceiver, trying to make you doubt what you know to be true. I weakened him, but he will return."

"How do you know he's *wrong*?"

"Goodbye, Malak," Ariel said. She vanished without a sound.

A family sweated up the rocky trail in his direction, the children squealing with joy at the vista. The father hunkered down beside Malak.

"Well, that was worth the hike," the man said, drinking from a plastic bottle of water, out of breath.

"Yep," Malak replied.

"Inspiration Point, kids," the man said. "It almost makes me believe in God."

———

Malak lingered on that rock until night fell. He chatted with hikers who paused to admire the view, and when the sun slipped below the mountains, he relished the feeling of peace that came with solitude.

For a time, the mountains were his temple, mosque, synagogue, and cathedral. He meditated, he prayed, and there were moments when he felt restored, too fleeting, as doubt assailed that irrational, essential part of him, the bedrock of faith that he'd tried to stand upon even as it was eroded.

For him, this was not something new. He'd long attempted to reconcile his experiences with his faith. There were many things that did not add up in his mind. He'd long held the suspicion that he'd been misled, abandoned, even betrayed at times. He felt this not just for himself, but for all of mankind. He longed for the zeal and reckless abandon stolen by years of bloodshed and unanswered prayers.

He pulled himself back to the present and considered facts. He was hunted now, by the American government, and by something else, too. He needed to get in touch with his team. They had probably already been compromised, he reasoned, but they were a smart, loyal bunch. There were protocols he'd put in place in the event that he was captured or killed. He had not checked in for several days, maybe more, for he did not know how much time had passed. His people would know that something was amiss. If the NSA, or anyone else, tried to hack the Wings system, his people would probably be ready for it. He had purchased safe houses and offices all over the world, preparing for such an inevitability.

If war was coming, the kind of war that was more than a war, then he intended to be in the fray. More than anything, he hoped he could stop it before it started. Despite his doubts, he believed there were good guys and bad guys, and he aimed to be on the right side, even though he'd gotten that part wrong sometimes.

There was a great deal of money flowing into extremist groups in Russia at the moment. The prince he'd killed was one of the sources, but there were others. Israel was under threat from its neighbors, but that was nothing new.

When Israel became a nation again in 1948, Malak had rejoiced. He almost forgave God for what had already happened, almost believed again without reservation. It was a fulfillment of ancient prophecy. Then Israel got attacked over and over again, and Malak saw that the rebirth of the nation did not mean peace. Quite the opposite. Israel's existence paved the way for Armageddon.

Now, Lucifer walked the earth again, and the world was poised to burn. Nuclear arsenals were armed and ready. China expanded its navy and took an aggressive stance toward disputed islands in the Pacific. Russia rebuilt Soviet-era bases in the Arctic and spent billions of Rubles updating its nuclear triad of submarines, bombers, and missiles. The United States stood beside Israel, even as the Israeli government bombed the Gaza Strip with merciless precision. Terrorist groups and radical Islam continued to spread throughout the Middle East. ISIS inflicted misery upon the West with orchestrated terror attacks, fighting to reestablish the Caliphate.

Religion, Malak reasoned, would be at the heart of it.

Money and power led to war between men. Religion could destroy mankind. Sometimes money and power *were* the religion, the worship of those things, by men who held armies on a leash. The worst of it was when money, power, and religion all combined. At the end of the day, it was always some kind of religion.

CHAPTER ELEVEN
SWORDS AND SCROLLS

64-70

The rabbi took an immediate liking to Malak. He was initially intrigued by Malak's affinity for language, and a friendship was born. Under his protection, Malak and Drust traveled from the outskirts of Rome to the city of Corinth across the Mediterranean Sea. The teacher's name was Erastus.

Erastus was a wealthy public official in charge of the construction of buildings and roads and was well respected in the community.

Erastus gave Malak and Drust food and shelter in his home and treated them like family. In the evenings, they shared wine and bread together at a long wooden table, often joined by members of the synagogue. Malak listened to the stories and lively debates, and he felt a truth resonate in him.

When Erastus learned that Malak was literate, he allowed him to read the Tanakh. Malak devoured every scroll he could get his hands on. The stories fascinated him, spoke to him.

On the Sabbath, Erastus would preach in the synagogue of a new hope, a light in the world.

This was the happiest time in Malak's life, a season of possibility. He learned history, the nature of right and wrong, and humility. Drust denounced his Pict Gods, and he and Malak were baptized in the Aegean Sea.

Visitors traveled from Ephesus, Rome, Antioch, Jerusalem, and beyond. Malak talked to merchants, sailors, fishermen, and former slaves who flocked to the city with news. There was tension brewing between Erastus's synagogue and some of the other centers of worship. Judaism and Christianity were becoming separate religions. As time passed, Malak felt darkness pressing upon him.

In 66, Jewish zealots started a widespread revolt against Rome. Malak heard first-hand accounts of the slaughter of tens of thousands in Galilee. In the city of Corinth, violent clashes between sects became a daily occurrence. The powerful priests, attempting to maintain power, collaborated with the Romans, trying to stamp out the spread of a new religion, yet Jews of any kind became objects of wrath in the eyes of the Romans.

Malak fled Corinth with Drust and Erastus, hoping to find safe haven in Jerusalem. They could not have arrived at the gates at a worse time, but they did not know where else to go.

———

They waited in a long line of refugees beyond the East Gate. Erastus had risked much coming here, vacating his wealth and position in Corinth.

"Malak," Erastus said, "fetch some coin. We need to offer a bribe. It'll speed things up."

"All right," Malak said, reaching into his robes for the dwindling pouch of Denari. He was hungry and thirsty. Their cart was almost empty now, thanks to all the bribes they'd already doled out to Roman soldiers along the way. They were lucky to have made it this far.

"What's taking so long?" Drust said in Latin. He'd learned Hebrew, Latin, and Greek over the last few years.

"The city is bursting with barely contained violence," Erastus said. "The High Priests know the Roman army is on the way. The more people they let in, the less food and water there will be to go around if there is a siege. They are turning people away."

"Perhaps we should go elsewhere?" Malak said.

"There is nowhere safe anymore. Not for Jews. Not for us. Our only hope is to reach a peace with Rome."

"Not bloody likely," Drust said. "I know Romans, and Romans don't know peace."

"Wait here," Erastus said. "Let me see if I can find a sympathetic ear. Or a greedy palm."

He walked, stooped with age, toward the city gate.

"Might as well sit," Drust said.

Malak walked to the donkey and gave it a piece of dried fruit, patted the beast on the nose, then joined his friend on the cart, legs dangling over the back.

"These Romans," Drust said. "I despise them."

"We're not really supposed to do that."

"Well, I do. There is no love in me for them."

"I understand." Malak thought about the last time he had seen this city. The day Christ was crucified.

"They are arrogant," Drust went on, "and cruel. So drunk with power and conquest, they are unable to smell the stench of decay in their hot air."

"I see."

"I doubt you see what I see, though I believe you would if you had the chance. Romans do not understand the freedom of a sunset on the vale, when the wind is right and the air itself is a promise. A woman warm and close with love on her lips to share the sky with and little ones waiting by the fire. These Romans, they will never know it."

"We are not the same men we were when we left Rome, my friend," Malak said.

"You changed me," Drust said.

"No."

"Yes. I understand things better since that day when you healed me. I know not whether that is for better or worse. You have made me more clever, I think."

"Maybe you were smarter than you knew to start with," Malak said.

"My woman would disagree with that," Drust said with a laugh. He gave Malak a direct, appraising stare and hesitated. "My friend, we have never spoken of things. But they happened. I saw with my own eyes. Do you think that perhaps you are..." he pointed toward the sky.

"What do you mean?"

"You know. Don't make me say it. The prophecies, the healing. It makes sense. He said he was coming back soon. Maybe when you lost your stars, you forgot who you were."

Malak sighed, feeling heavy. "No, Drust. Don't speak of that again. Trust me, I am certain of this."

"But how can you know when you don't remember. It could be that--"

"Because I was *there*," Malak said. "I saw." Tears came to his eyes with the memory. "I did not know what I was seeing then. It was only later, hearing the stories."

"But, how?"

"I wish I knew. That is my first memory. I was outside this city. I saw the cross from a distance. Romans killed me, and the next thing I knew, I met you. From one moment to the next, nothing in between, though decades passed."

"Why didn't you tell me?"

"Because I.... I don't really know. I did not want you to fear me. I did not understand what I had witnessed. And later, maybe I wanted to keep that memory safe, sacred."

"I will not question you again, my friend. Your heart is your own. I believe, though, great things are in store for you. You have work to do."

"I fear you are right."

———

Erastus procured lodging with friends within the city slums. They slept on a bare floor, and food was scarce. Over the next month, Malak and Drust seldom ventured out into the city, where fear and suspicion were rampant.

When Titus crested the hills with a vast army of three legions at his back, swords and spears glittering in the afternoon light, banners cracking in the wind, the citizens were terrified. The zealots were not well organized, but they were defiant and determined, believing God would spare them.

Erastus met with religious and civic leaders, urging capitulation. "We cannot win this fight," he told Malak. "There are too many of them. They will breach the walls, and the streets will run red."

During the siege, the Romans would allow pilgrims to enter the city on the Sabbath, then refuse to allow anyone to leave. Those who did were either killed on the spot or enslaved.

"Our water and food are almost gone," Erastus said. "They're letting people in because they know we are already starving."

"Let us fight," Malak said.

"You want to join the zealots?" Erastus said.

"There is a battle coming. I'm better at fighting than I am at praying. So is Drust."

"So be it," Erastus said. "I'll speak to a commander I know. He'll be glad to have you."

———

Malak and Drust trained with the soldiers, and Malak learned to follow and loathe orders. He developed skill with a bow, though he still preferred a sword and small shield. He earned the respect of Samuel, his immediate commander. The zealot forces were composed of some professional fighters, but most were farmers, merchants, fathers, and old men who had never held a blade. What they lacked in training, they made up for in ferocity and courage.

On the night of his first raid, Malak walked through the ranks of men gathered on the wall, slapping them on the back, offering words of reassurance. He and Drust would be the first men over the wall.

He dropped to the ground, gripping the rope in his hands and springing off the rock wall to slow his descent. He moved down the wall, staying in the shadows, while other men followed him. They found the cache of weapons beneath a pile of rubble that spies had snuck out of the city over the previous week.

He crept toward the nearest group of tents and fires on a hill. Most of the buildings that had been there before the Legions arrived were leveled. The rocky ground enabled him to move with almost no sound. He smelled the campfires ahead, heard the Legionaries laughing and joking as he got closer.

Malak lay on his chest while the men fanned out around the Roman position, which spies reported guarded a supply of grain and dried meat.

He looked to the flanks and saw that the fighters were all poised to strike. Malak sprinted for the light of the torches and fires, and he heard the urgent sound of feet on stone behind him. No one shouted. There was no battle cry.

The first two sentries saw Malak coming, but they were slow to react, surprised, no doubt by the audacity of the attack. He was almost upon them before they cried out in alarm.

One of them wielded a spear, the other a sword. The

soldier with a spear danced to Malak's right, while the man with the sword came to greet violence with violence. Malak parried the thrust with the shield in his left hand, and the clang of steel on steel rang out in the night. With his right, he lunged forward, stabbing beneath his shield into the soldier, piercing his abdomen. The man screamed.

The spear came at his chest, and Malak stepped back, bringing his shield up and absorbing the blow, conscious of keeping on his feet, maintaining balance.

There were shouts and oaths in several languages. Malak led with his shield, closing on the Roman, readying his arm and shoulder for the counterattack. The soldier reached to his waist and pulled out a dagger, held close to his body.

The spear came for Malak's head. Malak swung his shield up, deflecting the blade with the edge of the shield rather than take the blow on the center, and stabbed the soldier in the groin.

The Roman grunted, slashing with his dagger even as he fell. The dagger caught Malak in the shoulder, and hot pain rippled through his torso. He swung his sword again, slashing this time, and the edge of the blade cut through the soldier's throat. Blood fountained from the wound, splashing Malak, hot against his face.

He saw that the fight was over. The zealots had overwhelmed the sleeping soldiers and were already running back toward Malak. The unarmed men they'd brought along carried sacks of grain and flasks of wine and water.

The Roman army, though, was awake.

Horns blew, and the rustle of men and weapons grew louder. Malak ran for the wall, a feeling of euphoria in him mixing with the fear. He reached the stone and continued running until he reached the concealed entrance. Sentries on the wall hailed him, and the stone door opened.

The men celebrated the victory, which came at great cost. Of the thirty fighters that went out that night, only twelve returned. The food they brought back was good for the morale of the city, but gave a false hope that victory could be had.

Malak went on more raids like that. Titus was displeased and angry. The siege engines came for the walls, and the full might of the Roman Empire came crashing at the gates.

When they breached the second wall, Malak prepared himself for a fight to the death.

"They're in the city," Samuel said. "All is lost."

CHAPTER TWELVE
THE FALL

Jerusalem, 70

He fought in the streets. The Romans were an incoming tide of death. There were too many, and there was no mercy in them. They flowed through the breached gates, slaughtering every human they encountered. Babies fell under implacable blades. Malak witnessed a woman cover her two children, perhaps three and five, under her robes, while an armored Roman soldier towered above her.

She cried out for mercy, and she called out to God.

The centurion cut her throat and did the same to the children.

Malak sprinted at him, screaming, aware that Drust was calling him back. He ran heedless into the throng of soldiers, incensed, violated, enraged.

He laid waste to those around him. His blade and shield flashed in the sun, and he slashed and stabbed and pummeled and bit. He head-butted a Roman soldier, though the Roman wore a helmet, and Malak took the pain and sparks in his eyes, coming close, and slipped his sword into the man's guts, twisting and savage.

He stood for a moment in the cobblestone street, some of the attacking soldiers retreating in the face of his onslaught, his blade dripping and hungry. The city was on fire.

"Malak! Pull back," Drust screamed, sounding far away.

He stood in the road, wanting, needing, someone else

to kill. The Romans did not make him wait.

The soldiers counter-attacked, shields raised, snaking down the street, stepping over bodies as they came. Malak wanted to kill them all.

"Fall back to the temple," Drust shouted.

Malak retreated, sword in his right hand, shield in his left, as the Roman soldiers advanced. He knew from his time in the ring that he could not prevail. He had faith, though. He believed. He'd heard the stories, read the scrolls. The time was now.

He attacked, hurtling into the massed Roman soldiers. At his back, the temple was burning. Zealots retreated, fighting as they back-pedaled. He waited for that "glory" while his blade sought flesh.

It never came.

He killed several more Legionnaires. He was bleeding from many wounds, yet he continued to spin, whirl, parry, and duck. A spear lanced his shoulder, and he dropped his shield. The Romans swarmed him.

They hacked off his right arm, and he continued to battle, fountaining blood and losing consciousness. On his knees and still fighting with a dagger in his left hand. The pain was blinding and terrible.

He saw Drust impaled on a Roman spear, the big man skewered through his stomach, cursing and sputtering and slashing, until the sword dropped from his friend's hand.

Malak fell sideways onto the cobblestone street, forgotten, dying, and inconsequential, while the Roman army dismantled the temple and killed everyone they could. He did not watch it for long because, despite his ability to regenerate, he was finished. It was longer than it should have been, though.

While he languished, he healed enough to prolong his

death, and the bodies of the innocent continued to mount. Malak was mostly dead, unable to move, paralyzed, burning with the need to act without being able to do so. *This is hell. This is what it must be like. There can be nothing worse.*

The temple burned, razed to the ground. Malak caught glimpses, gasping for air and bleeding to death with inhuman slowness, but one of many in heaps of corpses.

When they dragged him onto a pyre, he screamed.

"Look at this one," said the guy dragging Malak by an arm. "He thinks he's still alive."

"No!" Malak tried to say. Then he was out again, and when he woke, it was with pain and the smell of roasting meat, and then darkness, death, and rebirth.

CHAPTER THIRTEEN
THE MONK

Northumbria, 715

The air was rich and salty and filled with the sound of singing birds. Malak rose to his feet, unsteady for a few seconds, out of place and time.

He stood upon a rocky shore, and tidal flats stretched out for more than a mile between the island and the coast of a much larger island. He took a lungful of air and looked out at the ocean. He was on a peninsula, with the flats and the coast in one direction, and the vastness of the ocean in the other. He watched the waves, fascinated by the foaming dark sea, which was different from anything he had ever seen.

This place was foreign, raw, and cold. He thought about his friend Drust and decided the warrior would have liked it here.

He was in no hurry. He stood, embracing the wind in the pale of the day. The sky was painted with strokes of pink, orange, and purple, and the water shimmered and danced. Past and present became one thing, for a time. The wind lashed his face, and he remembered, listened, and let the coming night hold him.

He noticed he wore simple brown garb, similar to a tunic, with a rope at the waist.

He heard voices behind him, and he turned in that direction. Several figures picked their way toward him down a steep slope. He saw goats with them.

"Who are you?" said a man with a grey beard and eyes

bright with mischief, and something else, deeper, wise. "Who sent you?"

"My name is Malak. I've traveled far, from a land of sun and sand."

"Ah, yes. From the south, then. You are of the order?"

"Yes."

"I heard no news," the old man said. "But that's not surprising. We are at the end of the earth here." He cackled and squinted at Malak. "Where are you from, son?"

"I do not know. I am weary."

"You are home now, my son. My name is Eadfrith. I'm the Abbot and Bishop. And you are most welcome to join us. Come. It is almost time to eat."

"I am grateful for your hospitality."

"Are you a pilgrim, or have you come to join us? Do you bring news from Rome?"

Malak considered this. He had no idea when or where he was. He did not like Romans much.

"I seek shelter," he said.

"So be it," Eadfrith said. "I look forward to hearing your tale. You have the look of a man who has seen much, despite your youth."

"Thank you, Rabbi," Malak said.

The old man stopped and looked into Malak's eyes, searching.

"What did you say?"

Malak realized he had used the Hebrew word, rather than whatever language they were speaking now. He'd done it from reflex.

"I said thank you, teacher."

"Yes, yes. I know what it meant. But you spoke an ancient language few understand, let alone speak."

"I meant no offense. I studied much, and sometimes I

forget."

"You can read and write? Hebrew? Greek? Latin?"

"Yes..." searching for the right word... "father."

Eadfrith laughed. "What a find you are, then. You will appreciate something I have been working on for the last twenty years. Indeed, you will. Glory be to God."

They walked the rest of the way in silence, although Malak sensed his new friend was bursting with questions. Eadfrith's companion, garbed in brown as well, said nothing and averted his eyes when Malak tried to make eye contact. He was a young man and seemed lost in his own thoughts, afraid of Malak.

"Welcome to our Priory," Eadfrith said. "We bring good news to the pagans. We study and we pray for the world."

The Priory was a rather sad set of buildings of log and thatched reeds. Torches burned in an open courtyard, and goats, pigs, and chickens wandered about. This was a far cry from Rome or Jerusalem.

"Theo," Eadfrith said, "introduce our new brother to the others. I will join you shortly."

"Yes, father," the young man said, eyes downcast. "Follow me," he said to Malak.

The dining area was lit with candles. Malak was used to raucous talk and lively conversation when it came to eating with other men. These men were somber, silent. They waited at long wooden tables, hands folded and heads bowed with eyes closed. Malak could smell the meat cooking, and he realized he was hungry. These men kept sitting at the table, saying nothing. They did not acknowledge his presence, did not stand to greet and welcome him. They sat in denial of his existence.

This went on for a long time. Malak heard stifled burps,

smelled farts, and saw, squinting through his eyes and folded hands, some of the younger men poke and prod each other, trying to make the other laugh. No one did, though, and the older monks were dead serious about whatever it was they were doing.

Eadfrith bustled into the room, and he began to speak in Latin. He prayed for the world, for the return of Christ, for the Church. Teenagers came into the room with steaming plates of meat, bread, wine, and cheese. Eadfrith went on about peace and love and obedience. That lasted for a long while, and the food smelled wonderful.

"Amen," Eadfrith intoned.

Malak grabbed a piece of meat from a silver platter and tore into it, letting his teeth rake against the bone. It was heavenly.

There was a collective gasp.

Malak had grease dripping down his arm, and a mouthful of tender, slow roasted meat in his mouth. Everyone in the room was staring at him. Some of them made odd gestures with their hands against their chests, and Malak froze, realizing his error, but chuckling inside as he swallowed. The meat was succulent.

"Sorry," he said, through a mouthful of food.

Their eyes were wide and shocked.

He heard one man laugh. It was a wheezing, kind laugh, full of joy and the breaking of rules.

"This one," Eardrith said, "endured a long journey to be with us. He is not familiar with our…ways."

Malak put down the piece of meat. He wanted to drink from the cup, but he was afraid that might make these men swoon.

"My apologies," he said, swallowing hard.

"We sing before we eat, son," Eadfrith said. "But this

night it will be a short song, yes? We are all hungry. Our appetite is for the Creator, but we need sustenance. We sing, and then we eat while we give thanks."

Malak bowed his head, following the lead of the other monks.

The monks took up a song. The words were Latin, and he knew them. He had never heard such a beautiful sound as that singing, and he wished he'd waited to eat, because he could have listened to them for hours, despite his physical hunger. The words were more than words, and the melody was ethereal and exultant, reverent, and perfect.

They sang in harmony, with the high notes weaving around the low ones, and the song was love, plaintive and true and soaring. It was transcendent.

The song was brief, as promised, and when it was over, the mood changed. The men became men that he understood, and they laughed and drank wine and tore into the meat with the abandon he was accustomed to. He wanted to pause and ponder what he had heard, but he was also hungry, and he ate and drank with gusto.

Malak became a monk that night, washed in forgiveness and melody, drinking hope and acceptance. It was more than a night; it was the beginning of a life.

———

Those years were good ones for Malak, memories he held on to through the ages and wished for again. His existence was filled with routine, simplicity, and constant wonder at the small things. The way the water came in and then left the flats, and how the beasts seemed to understand this in a better way than he did. The waters receded, the birds descended, the crabs and small things retreated, and then the waters came again, every day, twice, and there was a rhythm to it.

Sometimes, walking along the beach when the sun was not up yet and the sky was metal and grim and the sea was out, he would toss creatures back into the sea. It mattered to them, and it mattered to him, for they lived. He thought about the men he had killed, and he grieved, even as he tossed a floundering fish to safety.

He followed the rituals and he learned the prayers. When it was time to get up in the dark of the night to pray, he followed a procession of brothers and candles, and he prayed. When singing was in order, he sang, though truth be told, he listened more than he contributed because they could *sing*, while he could not find the right note. His voice was awkward and unruly, and the brothers preferred it when he kept his voice mostly to himself.

The Bishop was a friend and mentor to Malak. Eadfrith was a fascinating, wonderful man in a way that inspired without effort. He was an artist at heart, and his joy was to God.

"This is what I'm supposed to do," Eadfrith said the morning after Malak arrived at the island of Lindisfarne. They stood in an open room over a wooden desk covered with scrolls. In the center of the desk was a work of art. "I would like to complete this before I die."

Malak gazed in awe at the pages. He turned the pages, Latin upon vellum, bound in leather and illustrated with the kind of care and patience only a monk can bestow.

The pages were on vellum, the pictures in loving color. Eadfrith invested his life on earth in these pages of color and truth. Malak never read the gospels, the books of Matthew, Mark, Luke, and John.

"Would you like to help me finish this, Malak?"

"Of course, Rabbi, though I am not worthy."

"Let us get to work then." He gave Malak a tour of the

Scriptorium. The room was small, lined with shelves which contained scrolls, bound books, and manuscripts written on vellum. The pigments used for the colors, Eadfrith explained, came from as far away as Asia, but most were local.

He used sharpened reeds to ink the text. Malak learned to form the letters over time, but he never tried his hand at the artwork. Eadfrith was a master at it. A single page could take as long as a month or more, such was the detail and artistry.

While they worked, they talked. Malak was evasive about his own past, and Eadfrith accepted this without question. When Malak asked him why this was so, the old man shrugged.

"Our ways are not His ways. All that matters to me is where your heart is. I am certain it is in the right place. You are where you are meant to be."

Reading the text, Malak felt a sense of wonder. He had heard the parables before, but there was much he had not heard contained in these writings. Every time he read about the crucifixion, he felt his soul clench, convulse, for it brought back memories of that day. When he read about the resurrection and ascension, he wished he had been there. The art was beautiful, and the words were art.

Malak led a quiet, fulfilling life. When he woke before dawn, he was eager to greet the day. He prayed for forgiveness and understanding. He fasted sometimes, feeling cleansed and whole.

When he learned the year, he was aghast. He had been absent for more than six hundred years, and he found it hard to wrap his head around this. He considered, more than once, revealing the truth to his mentor, but he never did.

When Eadfrith died in 721, Malak carried on his work, completing the last page of the Lindisfarne Gospels.

Over the following decades, Malak continued to be a

simple monk, sheltered and happy in the monastery. He used gray pigment to dye his hair and beard to give the illusion he was aging. When some of the monks who were younger than he when he arrived on the island began to look ancient, they questioned his vitality.

"It must be my heritage," he explained. "My people are notoriously long lived."

His fellow monks liked him, though, and were able to suspend their disbelief because they wanted to. He never jockeyed for power, never yearned to leave the island to make a journey to the mainland or to Rome. He worked in the cold and in the sun with his brothers and lit candles in the darkness.

CHAPTER FOURTEEN
REUNIONS

Now

He hiked down the mountain in the dark, following the rocky path. The air was cool and clean, green with the scent of pine and wildflowers.

At the bottom, he followed a trail around a lake and emerged in an empty parking lot. He couldn't remember how far it was to Jackson, but he figured if he couldn't catch a ride, he'd make it in a few hours on foot. He started jogging. He heard coyotes howling and passed a startled moose on the side of the road.

He made it to the edge of town well before dawn.

He walked the quiet streets, waiting for the town to wake up. There were upscale art galleries, ski shops, restaurants, and posh hotels catering to affluent vacationers.

After eight in the morning, he walked to the grocery store and purchased a burner phone, pleasantly surprised the store sold them.

Kelli picked up on the second ring.

"Hey," he said.

"Mal?"

"Yep."

"Thank God. What do you need?"

"Protocol *Pandora*. Get our team together. Just the inner circle. I'm in Jackson Hole, Wyoming. You can brief me on the jet."

"Damn. We'll be there this afternoon."

"Good."

He hung up. The line *should* have been secure. Voice recognition had come a long way in the last few years, though, and he had to keep the call short. He wasn't sure where he stood with the American government at the moment. Someone would be looking for him, of that he had little doubt. Whether the NSA or CIA connected the incident in New Mexico to him, he could not know. From here on out, he would be extra careful.

The company jet, a sleek Gulfstream IV, taxied down the runway at the Jackson airport. He walked out to the plane and boarded while maintenance crews from the airport came out to refuel the aircraft.

The jet was titled to a shell company owned by a business not connected in any way to Wings. He held more than fifty of these corporations strewn throughout the world. One of the benefits of being immortal was the ability to amass a tremendous amount of wealth. He had caught onto this over time and eventually became adept at the skill. In the late nineteenth century, he'd invested heavily in gold and railroads. He had stockpiles of gold bars in safe deposit boxes and holes in the ground. In the Twentieth Century, he discovered the staggering power of compound interest. He owned legitimate businesses he never saw, and sponsored charities all over the globe.

He climbed into the plane and sat on a leather seat while his team looked at him with raised eyebrows.

"Sorry about that," Malak said.

"What happened? You went dark for three weeks."

"I got myself captured," he said. "I think it was the CIA. Then it was something else, something worse, but I won't go into that. Suffice it to say, we've got to tread carefully."

He smiled at his team, trying to project more confidence

than he felt.

"We followed protocol," Kelli, his operations chief, said. "Locked down the computers, then after a week, we destroyed everything. I've got crucial data backed up on flash drives and tablets, but Wings no longer exists. Your public assets were frozen by the IRS the day you went missing. We dismissed the employees and went to ground."

She was one of the smartest people Malak had ever met. In her late forties, she had been with him since she graduated from MIT. She was sitting in a wheelchair, which was mounted to the flight deck of the plane. She'd suffered a spinal injury when she was ten, jumping into a pool and landing wrong. Though she could not walk, her mind soared to places few could ever know. She was one of two people here who knew Malak was more than what he appeared to be.

Tim McDonald, the strike team leader, spoke next. "So now what?"

Tim, nicknamed Tiny, was Malak's right-hand man in the field. He and Tim worked together in Afghanistan shortly after 9-11. At the time, Malak was posing as an Afghani interpreter, attached to a Delta team inserted into Tora Bora to hunt Bin Laden. Tim was boisterous, loyal, cocky, and ice under fire. He was a big man with a big personality.

He was the only other person who knew about Malak, and this was because Malak healed him in a remote valley of the Hindu Kush mountains after an Al-Qaida round severed his femoral artery. They had been friends ever since that day.

"We'll head to Florida. I've got a place in Lake City that's got an airstrip. We can fly into Jacksonville, then split up. We'll need a couple of vehicles and a Cessna. From there, we'll figure out the next move. Now it's your turn. What's happening in the world?"

"Your activities have not gone unnoticed by the rest of the world," Syed said. "The Saudis are blaming the U.S. There are burning flags and effigies of the president from the West Bank to Kabul as we speak."

"Why?" Malak said.

"Nobody believes that the U.S. government was not behind the assassination."

"I understand that. But why does anyone care about some asshole prince?"

"That asshole," Syed said, "had many powerful friends, and they are calling him a martyr. It's all over social media."

Syed Kamani was a former ISI intelligence officer, the Pakistani intelligence agency. He met the man on the same op he'd met Tiny Tim.

"What are the ramifications?"

"It is too early to tell," Syed replied. "But the Muslim world is up in arms." Syed was a devout Muslim himself.

"Israel attacked the Gaza Strip again yesterday. They sent in armor this time. They are leveling buildings," said Ben Cohen. Ben was a former Shin Bet agent Malak had crossed paths with in Jerusalem ten years ago. Ben never talked much about his time within Israeli counterintelligence, but his knowledge of the region was encyclopedic.

"I'm guessing Hamas is responding?" Malak said.

"Rocket and mortar attacks," Ben said. "A suicide bombing in Tel Aviv this morning at a school bus stop."

"Dear God," Malak said.

"It gets worse, my friend," said Zhang Wei. Zang was a Buddhist in his early sixties, a former MSS agent with China. Mal met him in Taiwan back in the eighties.

"The chatter within Russia is getting worse. Something is about to happen."

"What?"

"A potential coup in Russia. The Russians know about it, the Chinese too. The Americans must know."

The plane was powering up.

"Speaking of Russians, where is Vladimir?"

Kelli chuckled. "He's got a tractor trailer full of gear, awaiting orders. He emptied out the armory when we lost you. He's paranoid, and sometimes that's a good thing."

"Well, let him know where to find us. I'll read your briefings en route," Malak said.

He let the speed of the plane push him back into his seat. He loved takeoffs and landings.

The world was going to hell, and there was nothing within his power to stop it, but he would die over and over again trying.

In Jacksonville, they split up. His team would purchase used cars with cash, then meet him in Lake City that night, while he and Kelli flew a single engine aircraft that he leased under the name of one of his shell corporations.

She slept on the flight, no doubt badly sleep deprived, and he thought about the day he'd met her at the summit of Brasstown Bald in the north Georgia mountains.

———

The autumn leaves were bright with color, and low clouds swirled just beneath the forested mountain peak, and the air was wet and cold, invigorating. He tried to get to the mountains, at least for a weekend, every year in the fall.

Malak had climbed up the long way, hiking along ridges of maple and oak, climbing over rocks and streams. He emerged from the rustic trail onto a paved path, which covered the last half mile to the peak. There were a few tourists here and there who had driven up to the parking lot. It was largely deserted, thanks to the weather.

When he reached the peak, below a building with a

lookout and a fire tower, he saw a woman in a wheelchair, her eyes closed and hands outstretched, head tilted back to catch every shivering drop of mist, a look of peace on her face.

She opened her eyes and looked at him as he walked past her.

"Beautiful, isn't it?" she said, smiling.

Malak paused. "Indeed."

"I was hoping for a day like this. It's been too warm this fall."

"Are you from around here?"

"Ha. Hardly. No, I'm from the West Coast, but I've been hanging around here all summer. I just graduated from MIT."

"Congratulations."

"I'm supposed to either be back in school working on my PhD, or gainfully employed. I'm neither. I'm a bum."

"It looks like you are enjoying it," Malak said. He sat down on a wooden bench a few feet away from her.

"At some point, I guess I'll have to become a grown-up," she said. "I've been trying to figure out what I'm supposed to do with my life. I was hoping the mountains would tell me, I guess. No luck so far."

"What do you want to do?"

She laughed. "I wish it was that easy. I want to help people, I guess. I don't know how. Maybe as a software developer, educational programs. That's the best I've come up with. Maybe find a job with the U.N. or the Red Cross. Or NASA, I've thought about that, too. I'm not as scatterbrained as I sound, I promise."

"You're a computer person?"

"Oh, yes."

Malak studied her, intrigued. Her dark hair was cut short, and she wore no makeup. She had a light all-weather poncho around her waist and a backpack strapped to the back of her chair, which looked like it was designed to handle rough terrain. Her eyes were bright, playful, and alive.

"You didn't take the tram up here, did you?" Malak said.

"Nope. That's a steep half mile, too. My arms are still burning. It was worth it, though."

"Are you up here with friends or family?"

"At first. My friends went back to the world in August. Two of them are going back to school, but the other one is working for I.B.M., making a ton of money, that one."

"Why did you stay?"

"Like I said, I'm trying to figure things out. It's like I'm waiting for something, a weird feeling."

"Well," Malak said, "perhaps things *do* happen for a reason. How would you like a job?"

"Doing what?"

"What you are meant to do."

She was skeptical, and it took months before she finally committed, phone calls and letters back and forth. She'd left the mountains and headed for warmer weather down in the islands. By the spring, though, she'd made up her mind, and she showed up at Malak's office unannounced, wearing a deep tan and a grin.

That was almost thirty years ago.

———

The plane landed on a long grassy strip, a runway shared by about twenty other homeowners in the area who liked to fly, and who respected privacy.

There was something about Lake City that Malak liked. Live oak trees laden with Spanish moss lined his yard, and folks in town were friendly in an old Southern fashion. The sweet tea was perfection, the smiles sincere, and the pace as slow as the drawls.

He had not been here in more than a year.

Kelli, as usual, refused his help in getting out of the plane, allowing him only to get her chair onto the ground.

He grabbed laptops, tablets, and boxes and carted them into the house, and she was inside before he was. He went through the house, removing the plastic sheeting from furniture, turning on the air conditioner, and dodging the occasional wolf spider the size of his palm.

"Man, it's hot," Kelli said. "I don't know why you like it here."

"It's got a certain charm," Malak said.

"Of all the places in the world, you decide to bug out here. Hawaii would have been nice. Southern France. That place you've got in Maine. Anywhere but here."

"Sorry," he said. "Believe it or not, I've got reasons."

"I'm sure you do, Mal, but they're not good reasons."

"Trust me."

"Oh, sure," she huffed. "Famous last words."

She got to work, spreading out her laptops and firing up the computers at the workstation he had built to her specs.

"I need coffee," she said. "Gallons."

"I'm on it," Malak replied.

He brewed ten cups while she typed away at multiple keyboards.

"You lost almost a billion dollars today," she said. "In your hedge fund. But you've probably got some other fund that made it back, betting against you. But the markets are not doing well, from what I can see. Investors are worried that the Middle East conflict is going to widen. Gold prices are on the rise."

The coffee, a robust Jamaican blend, was rich and hot, and he brought her a steaming cup, black the way she liked it.

She touched his hand when he placed the oversized mug on her desk.

"Mal, I'm glad you are safe, even if you brought me to this shithole. I was really worried. Tell me, are we looking at the end? Is this how it starts?"

"Maybe," Malak said. "The world is teetering on the brink again. I'm worried it's going to get a shove."

"You saw *her*, didn't you?"

"Yes."

"Then we should be afraid."

CHAPTER FIFTEEN
STORM

Lisdinfarne, 793

Spring brought fierce storms to the island; wind, lightning, and rain assailed the monastery. Malak would look out at the churning sea, dark and powerful, and smile. Sometimes he left his pallet and walked the shores in the middle of the night while the heavens roared and thunder crashed in great spine jarring power.

He would run along the rocky shores, free of the illusion of old age, leaping from rock to rock while the rain pelted his face.

There were whispers among his fellow monks that something unnatural was afoot. He had outlived most of his contemporaries, and no matter how much grey he put into his beard, how much hesitation he placed into his steps, there was no way he could keep up the act much longer. The only way he managed to continue was by becoming a recluse, enigmatic, and someone to be feared and revered, a cackle in his voice and a bit of madness in his eyes. He was fairly certain some of the other monks had convinced the Bishop to send him away to Rome.

On one of those jaunts in the midst of a glorious storm, he found her washed up on the shore.

She wore white robes, and her blond hair was as drowned as she was, face down on the flats where the tide would take her back to the sea.

He picked her up and carried her beneath a rock

outcropping, laid her down on the ground, trying to decide if she was dead, when she sputtered and coughed and met his eyes in a flash of lightning.

Her robes clung to her body, revealing perfect breasts and the outline of nipples. Never before had Malak understood why men spoke of these things with admiration or relish. He'd heard ribald tales in the monastery, witnessed men copulating with women in the Roman *ludus,* and been perplexed by the fascination with sex. It was something he never understood, for he had never felt the faintest inclination of lust.

Under the rocks with that storm raging, though, lust found him. He touched the woman's cheek and felt lightning in his loins, in his arms and legs, and his whole body seemed to vibrate. He was afraid of this physical reaction, for not only was it alien to him, it was also a violation of his vows.

She did not speak with words, and she did not need to. She kissed him on the lips, and the physical world slipped away, and there was nothing but storm and fury and rhythm and the crashing of waves and the destruction and rebirth of his heart.

Wrapped around each other against the cold, which was no longer lonely and frigid because she was next to him, at some point in the early dawn, they must have fallen to sleep.

Malak woke to sharp shouts and the sound of metal and the grating crunch of ships running up onto the shallows.

He bolted up and looked at the beautiful woman, inflamed with lust again, yet knowing something was wrong.

"Who are you?"

"I do not know," she said. "Who are you?"

"I am a monk. Malak. I do not know what to say, woman. I am sorry. It is not in me to behave the way I behaved.

I do not understand myself, and I will burn for it."

"Malak," she said. "That is beautiful. You were not alone in your transgression last night. I think we're both at fault, if we were.

"I have done you great harm," he said, wanting to do nothing more than lie with her again, but hating himself.

"No, you have not." She laughed. "Quite the opposite."

"Follow me," Malak said. "We can discuss this further later, but I fear we are in danger."

He was at war with himself, despising his weakness without understanding it, shaking with need. At the same time, the sounds he heard from the sea were rife with things he remembered; memories repressed and senses long dormant came to life.

He stood for just a moment at the shore, peering into the swirling fog. He was sure he saw a dragon, a serpent fanged and colorful, attacking.

There were oaths and the rasp of drawn steel from within the mists. Footfalls slapped the shallows, and the clatter of sword and shield was in the wind.

"Run!" Malak said.

He took her hand, and she followed him up the slope toward the monastery. The brothers would be wondering where he was.

They ran across the meadows and pastures, fog swirling around them, and Malak felt a pressure in his chest, a pounding in his temples.

He was aware of her touch, the warmth of her palm in his as she matched him step for step. They darted past a startled shepherd and headed for the chapel, where most of the monks would be at this hour.

He opened the heavy wooden doors, and heads turned in his direction. Some of them covered their faces at the sight of the woman, and others crossed themselves.

"We are in danger!" Malak shouted. "Hide the relics. Arm yourselves!" The idea of arming themselves was, at that point, ludicrous. There were no real weapons in the monastery.

The monks bustled about, but defense was alien to them. This island was a place of peace and worship, a sanctuary.

He found a broom in a corner and snapped it. It was not long enough to be a proper spear, but it was all he had.

He cast his eyes about the room and saw that his gentle brothers were noticing not only the woman, but the sudden spring in his step.

"There are soldiers coming," Malak said.

"From where?" said a young monk. "We are at peace."

"From the sea. Go!" Malak thundered. "Save the relics. Bring the young men. We will try to hold the gate."

His brothers gazed upon him with awe and fear, and did not act.

"Move!" Malak shouted. "Fetch the Bishop." He did not wait for an answer. These men knew Malak as a decrepit scholar, one who spent his days steeped in scrolls and ancient manuscripts. They seemed to be more fearful of his transformation than the attackers storming the beach.

He ran out the door, aware of the beautiful woman behind him. He thought he should tell her to go back inside, but not only did he not want to be away from her, he also sensed she would only laugh at him for telling her to do anything.

The monks were awake and alert, and swarming about the priory, but they had no idea of what to do to defend themselves. Some of the young men gathered at the main gate.

"When they come," Malak said, "do not be afraid." He

thought about how foolish this advice was.

"We are attacked. They must come through this gate. Take up their weapons and fight back. There will be weapons on the ground, I promise."

"God will protect us!" someone said, one of the older monks.

"Pick up swords, and protect yourselves," Malak said. "Pray for mercy but show none. For when the Romans come to burn, the burning they shall have. Fight for your lives."

He knelt and crossed himself. Outside, someone screamed, a dying, animal thing, like that of a pig being butchered by a sadistic knife. It was squealing and prolonged.

Malak stepped outside the gate and told his brothers to bar it behind him. She stood with him in the fog, and she took his left hand.

"You could run for one of the boats," he said. "There are some on the other side of the island. You might make it to safety. Get help."

"I cannot leave," she said. "I don't know why. I will die by your side, if that is what God wills."

Malak grunted. "If you do not flee, you will die."

"Then we will die together," she said. She squeezed his hand, and he felt a euphoria akin to one he had felt from wine, but stronger, a drunken longing and loneliness that threatened to bring him to his knees with the force of it. "But I do not believe we will die this day."

"You are wrong about that," he said.

A horn blew from the depths of the mist, and the Vikings stormed the gate.

"Grab the first blade that falls," Malak said. "And stay behind me." He was sure this woman would not listen to him, and he was right. She stepped to his side.

The attackers screamed as they came on, with painted

faces, angry beards, and axes and swords. Some wore helmets, and some did not. They howled as they attacked the monastery, Malak and this woman he had met the night before standing outside the gate.

There were about a hundred of them, and Malak knew there was no way to win. He held his broomstick, broken at one end and sharp, while the crazy, glorious woman in wet white robes stood at his side. The attackers came straight on, blood curdling screams rising up from their midst, and running full out in a ragged line.

Malak waited until the first attackers were within a few strides. He exploded to his right, coming from a crouch, and slashed with the broomstick, using the narrow piece of wood to smash faces and skulls with violent, practiced precision. He had not forgotten how to kill.

He impaled a man through the groin and snatched his sword before it hit the ground, striking at ankles, knees, rolling, slashing, being cut.

A big man with an axe cut at Malak, a killing blow for the neck. Malak ducked below the blow and struck with his fist, and hit the warrior in the testicles. The man fell to his knees, screaming, and then Malak ripped the axe from his hands, punching the man in the throat with his left hand. He hefted the wooden axe, feet apart. He wielded a short sword in his right hand, the Viking battle axe in his left. Malak cut off the man's head, the slap of steel biting into flesh, and then the crack of the spine like the snapping of twigs.

The woman was at his back, a shield and sword in her hands. The knot of barbarians retreated a few paces, circling and hungry.

Some of them, further down the walls, were breaking into windows. Some held torches.

The smell of wood burning mingled with the stench of

the attacking force, a musty, rank smell of salt and sweat, a wild, animal odor.

"Don't let them take me alive," the woman said.

"I won't."

The Vikings paused for only a few seconds before charging again, a collective rush of strong men with teeth bared and blades readied.

Malak and the woman met the onslaught with fury and death. He marveled at her skill with a blade, and she was quick and lethal. Four men lay at her feet, bleeding and moaning, while more came.

Malak lost his left hand and the axe, as a heavy sword severed his wrist. Blood fountained onto the cold ground. He kicked and hacked with his right hand, and felt the heat of a blade in his lower back. He cried out on his knees.

The woman was bleeding, her white robes more crimson than white, and she fought, pushed against the door of the monastery now, cornered. Malak pushed himself to his knees, slick with his own blood.

She was screaming, dragged to the ground. He lifted a jeweled dagger from one of the slain Vikings. Her eyes met his, her arms pinned above her, two more men struggling to hold down her legs, while others broke down the door to the monastery.

He hurled the blade from ten feet away, and the steel buried into her neck. He closed his eyes, swaying on his knees, and the Vikings turned upon him like a pack of angry dogs. He died on his knees.

———

Centuries later, he learned that the Lisdinfrane Gospels survived the Viking attack. He saw them once more, after World War II, in the British Library of London. His old friend Eadfrith was not forgotten, and the pages he crafted

with love and patience over the years symbolized light in
ages of darkness. Through the coming years, the Viking raids
continued, and the monks abandoned the island for a time,
only to return and rebuild.

He would remember his years on the Holy Island with
great fondness, for it was a time of peace and growth for him.
He was glad that even though history had forgotten him,
Eadfrith's work lived on.

CHAPTER SIXTEEN
PREPARATIONS

Now

His team arrived after dark. Malak was relieved, for this meant they had eluded prying eyes and were able to start over again under the radar.

He culled through the internet, searching for patterns. He read the briefings from his team, listened to opinions on where they could do the most good. It was overwhelming.

They were too few, their resources and assets too limited. He was looking for a linchpin, a single thing which might stop the impending wars.

"There are the peace talks in Geneva," Kelli said. "Syed's people are saying there is going to be an attack there to disrupt them."

"Do we know who and when? If so, let's let somebody know."

"Mossad is already on top of it," Ben said.

"I believe," Vladimir Kushkin said, "the greatest threat comes from within Russia."

"All right," Malak said. "What can we do about it?"

"I'm working on that," Vladimir said. "I'm waiting to hear from some of my former colleagues. I will give you a detailed proposal when I have more information. It might be best to send myself and perhaps you to Moscow."

"You should know China is planning on exercises in December," Zhang said. "They have begun to shift armor and infantry toward the northern border with Russia. They have announced a joint naval exercise with North Korea in the Sea of Japan."

"Should we be worried?"

Zhang shrugged. "Who knows? They're not making it a secret. They will have two carrier groups in the Sea of Japan. Neither the Japanese nor the Americans are going to like that much."

"Keep looking," Malak said. "There is a way we can help."

"Why are you so concerned now, if I may ask?" Tim said. He held Malak's gaze. "Do you know something we don't?"

"I have good reason to believe that a wider conflict is brewing," Malak said. "My sources are beyond reproach, but they tend to speak in riddles."

Tim raised his eyebrows at this. "Maybe we should be heading for one of your underground bunkers, then."

"No. If we can do something to avert this crisis, whatever form it takes, then we've got to do that. That's why we are here. Every one of us wants to do his or her part."

———

The next few months were stressful and boring. Malak read reports until his eyes were bleary. He sent his Russian friend to Moscow to keep an eye on things. Ben traveled to Geneva and then back home after the peace accords fell apart. There was no terror attack, at least.

They used encrypted satellite phones to communicate, and Kelli bounced their internet coms through an ever-changing web of firewalls and roving servers.

The weather changed, and the sweltering heat and humidity gave way to glorious, clear days, though Malak seldom left the confines of the house.

In December, there was a cold snap. Malak took a

hike near the Sewanee River, admiring the live oak trees, the swirling dark waters, and the way the sunlight filtered through the leaves on the winding path. He needed a break from staring at the computer screen, yearned for a connection to God he sometimes felt when he was in nature.

He hummed and prayed as he walked.

Why did you send me here, God, if all I ever do is fail? How is that your plan? Where are you while the world eats itself? If I am your servant, please let me serve.

There was no answer.

Not until the Twentieth Century had mankind possessed the ability to cause its own extinction. Malak knew that the combined nuclear arsenals of the world were capable of wiping humans from the earth. There were almost twenty thousand nuclear weapons in the world, most of them in the United States and Russia. The studies he'd read indicated that if only a hundred were used on cities, then the world would likely be plunged into a nuclear winter. The upper atmosphere would be choked with ash, temperatures would sink, plants would die. If thousands were unleashed, the radioactive rain, fallout, and burned sky would kill the planet. Maybe microbial life would survive, but humans would become a memory.

There were other threats almost as frightening. He knew the United States and the Soviet Union invested heavily in biological weapons. While there were treaties in place banning the development and use of these weapons, these documents were essentially worthless. At this moment, while he walked on this serene trail in north Florida, there were men and women around the world in sterile underground compounds, wearing bio-hazard suits and experimenting with viruses and bacteria that were just as deadly as the nukes.

The average human slept and woke every day with a sword hanging over their throats by a fine string, blissful and oblivious to a threat they could do nothing about. They Twittered and Facebooked and watched reality television and lived their lives while sharp steel swung back and forth, closer with each new dawn.

His phone beeped, an incongruous sound in the woods. He answered it.

"Boss, we've got a problem," Kelli said. "Somebody managed to upload a virus into our network. That can't happen, but it did. It's just a matter of time before they track us."

"All right. Start getting squared away. I'm an hour out." He put the phone away and sprinted down the path.

Malak was certain the string was about to break.

CHAPTER SEVENTEEN
SCHOLAR

Baghdad, 821

He opened his eyes to a blazing sun. He was on his back, wearing an embroidered robe, sandals, and a turban. Several feet away, a camel snorted at him. He gazed across a stretch of desert, through the heat and the haze, at a large city of graceful minarets and towers. The rising heat made the sand shift and shimmer.

He mourned the woman whose name he never knew, and his brothers who fell in a much colder place. He wondered how long ago that was.

He felt weighted, leaden, as he led the camel toward the city. The desert ended abruptly, as though a line had been drawn in the sand, and there were green fields and palm trees with canals running through them.

He walked for miles, much farther than he had thought at first, nodding at people working in the fields.

He passed other travelers on the road, men with skin a deeper chestnut than his own, and they smiled and nodded to him. Some of these men rode horses and camels, while others walked behind trains of wagons heavy with fruits, spices, and other trade goods.

He wandered the city, lost and aimless. The city was vibrant, humming with wealth and activity, and he allowed himself to follow a natural flow of humans through the streets, bobbing along from place to place while the sun set. He walked through a marketplace, where men selling food and trinkets approached him, trying to get him to trade.

"That is a sorry camel," one of them said. "He is old and weak, and will probably die tomorrow, but I will still buy him from you."

Malak paused and regarded the man, who was smiling. There were several other camels at a stable behind him, along with a few goats and sheep.

"What do you offer?" Malak said, in Arabic.

"One Dirham, and that is taking food from my daughter's belly."

"Three."

"Ha! You have been wandering the desert too long, traveler. Two and be gone. My wives will curse me."

"Done."

"Good," the man said. He clasped Malak's hand. "My wives might forgive me if I brought a stranger to our home who was willing to pay for a good meal and a clean bed."

"And what might that cost me?"

"I think a price of one Dirham would be fair for a week. You look lost and have nowhere to stay. Accept my hospitality, for you will find none better in Baghdad."

"Three weeks, then," Malak said, smiling, finding the rhythm.

"I don't trust you any longer," the man said. "If I invite you into my home, you will no doubt rob me in my sleep."

"Well, then," Malak said. "I'm sure I can find someone willing to trust me. I plan on staying for a while."

"Why didn't you say so? If you require lodging on a more permanent basis, I am able to accommodate you. Two Dirham, and you may stay under my roof for four weeks. And you will taste some of the best food in your life."

"Agreed," Malak said.

They stood in the marketplace and laughed. The city

seemed to sing, the air redolent with spice and the music of laughter and the chorus of street merchants calling out for customers.

"Peace be upon you," the man said.

"May peace, mercy, and blessings of Allah be upon you," Malak replied. He wondered how he knew to respond thus; he was not entirely sure what he had said.

"We will go soon," the man said. "I am Nasir Al-Qifti."

"My name is Malak."

"What brings you to Baghdad?"

Well, that's a question for another day.

"I come seeking employment. I am a scholar."

"Then you have come to the perfect place. This is the greatest city in the world. The House of Wisdom is unparalleled, though of course you know this."

"I have traveled far to see it."

"I have a cousin who is a librarian there, yes? I will introduce you to him tonight. He will take you there tomorrow morning. Men of learning are always welcome."

"Many thanks, my friend," Malak said.

Malak helped him tend to the animals, securing them for the night along with Nasir's shy young son, Ibrahim. Nasir explained the layout of the city and extolled the virtues of the reigning caliph, al-Ma'mun.

"These are times of wonder. This city is full of poets, scholars, and musicians. You will love it here."

Malak had no way of asking what year he was in at the moment, though he was dying to know how much time had passed.

Nasir's home was clean and airy, and the food was as delicious as promised. He downed goat cheese and milk, and devoured slow roasted meat, sitting on pillows on the ground. Nasir invited his extended family for the meal and treated Malak like a guest of honor, an odd thing for Malak.

He mimicked the gestures of speech, the nuances of physical behavior the best he could, feigning knowledge he did not have, staying silent as much as he could without being rude.

The meal lasted for more than two hours. There was much laughter, and Malak marveled at the way the family seemed relaxed and happy. He was unaccustomed to children and tried to take cues from the other men on how to behave around them. One of the younger children, a boy of perhaps five or six, plopped down in Malak's lap.

"Where is the story?" he said.

The men all nodded their heads in agreement.

"The story, yes, of course," Malak said.

"Tell it," the boy said.

"Do you know what a Gladiator is?" The boy did not, though some of the men nodded their heads. "This is a story about a simple man who became a fighter. He fought because he had no choice. He came from a land far away. Bad men put him in a ring with other men who had to fight each other. Sometimes, they even killed. This kind man, his name was Drust, did not like to kill. It went against Allah. But if he did not fight, he would be killed himself, so he did what he had to do to survive. The Romans were cruel and smart, and they knew how to hurt him. One day, Drust had the chance to get back at those Romans."

"What happened?" said the boy.

"One time, when he was not watched, he slipped away in the night. He found a young boy, about your age, and he told that boy about Jesus, and how there was a light in the darkness."

The boy's eyes were wide, and the candles in the room cast a warm glow. Malak barreled along with his tale.

"There was a fire, but that boy told his mother, and she told her sister. The word spread, and even though Rome burned, the truth itself spread like wildfire. The Romans tried to stamp it out, but the harder they tried, the more it spread until Rome became Christian. That was this man's gift to the world."

"But what happened to the Gladiator?" the boy asked.

Malak wished later he had been paying attention to the rest of the people in the room, but the boy's question was a good one, and Malak was relaxed.

"He died when the city burned. But when he spoke to that boy, he changed the world."

The room grew quiet. The men were looking at him as though he had bloomed leprous sores on his face.

Nasir broke the silence, clapping his hands.

"What a wonderful story," he said. "The best story I have heard in years."

Some of the other men relaxed, but others continued to glare at him. He did not know what he had said wrong.

"You understand the point of the story," Nasir said, "right? If the gladiator had not snuck away that night to tell of the prophet Jesus, then the word of Mohammad would never have been spread. We would not be here in this great city. God is God. God is great."

The tension fled the room, and the men laughed and nodded their heads in agreement, and Malak decided not to tell any stories until he had a better grasp on…everything.

CHAPTER EIGHTEEN
THE GIFT

Now

He careened down winding, dark roads, past mobile homes adorned with Christmas lights and nativity scenes, old homesteads, and mini-mansions with long driveways and wrought iron gates.

He left the beat-up car on the side of the road and jogged through the shadowed, canopied streets toward his neighborhood. The entrance looked welcoming, and he did not see any cars around. He cut through the woods to be safe.

His senses were on high alert, and the slightest movement sent him further into the woods. He listened for the telltale sound of a drone on station.

He ducked into the house from the rear entrance, the one facing the airfield. The computers were crated, supplies stacked. Kelli wheeled into the room.

"We need to go," she said. She looked grave.

"What is happening?"

"It's started."

"What?"

"The war," Tim said. "Russian revolutionaries with access to ICBMs."

"Where are the rest of us?" Malak said.

"Ben is loading the plane. Syed is loading the truck, the newer one."

The last Malak knew, Vladimir was still in Moscow.

"Where is Zhang?"

"Missing," Kelli said. "Along with one laptop and a flash drive. Maybe more."

"He does that sometimes, though," Malak said.

"He left a note," Kelli said. She handed Malak a piece of a yellow legal pad, with Zhang's distinct handwriting, neat and square, on the page.

My dear friends,

There is nothing more any of us can do. War is upon us. I am glad for our time together, a time we spent trying to make the world a better place. This was my fervent belief from the time I joined with you, Malak, my old friend. Now I do you more harm than good by remaining at your side. I will try to find you if I survive what is coming. I am betrayed. I will try to throw them off your trail, but I fear the worst. MSS has been funding the separatists in Russia. There is going to be a war. When it starts, China is going to invade Russia. This war will be global. None will be safe.

Zhang

Malak read the note again, befuddled. He trusted Zhang.

"How much longer till we're loaded?" he said.

"Almost done," Kelli said.

"What is happening?"

"Simultaneous, coordinated bombings throughout Russia and the Middle East. Terrorists have captured hardened missile silos in Siberia. They are threatening an attack."

"Have you been in contact with Vladimir?"

"He's somewhere over the Atlantic on a commercial jet. He's flying into Miami."

"Can you reach him?"

"No."

"We cannot wait. He knows how to find us."

Malak considered their situation. He'd developed a bug out plan long ago. They would fly to Alberta. He owned a bunker on a sprawling ranch tucked away in a remote valley. He'd built the place back in the sixties and spent a good deal of money on updates and renovations over the last fifty years. It was stocked with food and water, and the air purification system could sustain his entire team indefinitely. Vladimir knew where it was.

What Malak was not sure of was whether he should leave with his team. While he'd known war was coming, he believed he would have more time, find some way to stop it. He had accomplished nothing over the last few months, it seemed.

The intelligence his team had gathered and disseminated did not stop the coup in Russia. They had done nothing to alleviate the tension in the Middle East. The Chinese navy was off the coast of Japan at the moment.

His efforts were futile and puny. He was fighting the outgoing tide, swimming against an unstoppable, implacable force. The collective weight of mankind pulled with inexorable strength, a sea of human misery and history and hate dragging the world into darkness.

He did not know how he could be of most use. He made a quick decision, one his team was sure to disagree with.

"Kelli, you're in charge. Go now. I'm going to stay here as long as I can."

"What can you possibly hope to accomplish?" she said, her face pale and washed out from lack of sleep and the stress she'd been living with every day. "If you die, what will we do?"

"You will keep fighting," Malak said. "As to what I can do, I'm not sure. I'm going to contact everyone I can within our network. I'm going to send warnings to media outlets, governments, anyone who will listen. Perhaps the people will rise up for peace. The hour is late, but maybe there is still a way if enough people are willing to stand up."

"You are ever the optimist," Kelli said. "You can do all of that from Canada, though. Are you trying to get yourself killed?"

"I'm not sure what needs to be done," Malak said. "I'm waiting for something. I don't think it's time for me to evacuate yet."

Syed entered the living room, then looked at Malak and Kelli, his eyebrows raised. "The plane is loaded," he said. "Don't tell me. He's not going."

"He won't listen to reason," Kelli said.

"I'm not going to bother arguing," Syed said. "Malak, I hope to see you again."

"As do I," Malak replied.

"Ben's already powered up the plane," Syed said.

"I'm going to kick the hornet's nest from here," Malak said. "Don't try to contact me. Stay off the grid. I'm guessing I'll be having visitors shortly."

"Goodbye, Malak," Syed said. He clasped Malak's hand. "I know you two have more to say, but you'd better make it quick."

Tiny Tim looked down at his feet, and the big man seemed small, diminished. "I don't know what you're thinking, Mal. But Godspeed. It's been an honor." He met Malak's eyes, winked, and turned his back.

Malak watched Syed and Tim saunter out into the night, rucksacks slung over their shoulders. He heard the chug of the small aircraft on the strip.

Kelli reached for Malak's hand, took it with a tenderness born through years of friendship and understanding.

"Let me give you a gift," Malak said. "In case I never see you again."

"No. This is who I am."

"Please. When the war comes, you will have a better chance if you can walk."

"My mind is my greatest weapon."

"You will still have that, Kelli. You refused to allow me to heal you years ago, and I respected that choice. This is different. The world is about to become infinitely more dangerous."

"Thank you, Malak. But no. I don't know what you are. I'm not sure my mind could handle it. You don't make sense. Do you know I've been in love with you for years?"

"You are like a sister. You are family to me. I love you too."

"That's not what I meant, and you know it. I just wanted to tell you, to say it out loud. I know you were aware of it, and I'm also smart enough to know you never felt that way about me. But I love you. You are a wonderful person. You make everyone around you better. You made *me* better, gave me hope and purpose."

He felt a tingle at the base of his neck, the sensation of flies crawling on his skin. *We are out of time.*

He held her hand and squeezed. Memories washed over him, her memories. He felt pain and longing, hope and fear, and he took it into himself, filtered it. His legs grew weak, and he staggered backwards a step. The room was bathed in soft blue-white light that emanated from Malak.

She was staring at him, mouth agape. "What have you done?" she said.

"Run," Malak said. "It is time for you to go."

He bent down and kissed her on the cheek.

"Oh my God," she said. "You really did it."

"Go. I will find you." There was the sound of vehicles kicking up gravel down the driveway.

She rose from the wheelchair and took two faltering

steps toward him. Malak caught her in his arms. Anger and betrayal flashed across her face, and then something else, softer, more forgiving and loving. A sadness and vulnerability she kept mashed down deep within her.

"I'm sorry," Malak said.

She gave him a quick kiss on the lips, and then she turned away. Her steps grew more confident, and she jogged toward the plane without looking back. Malak hoped she understood.

He wanted her to live because she was kind and good, and death was on the way.

CHAPTER NINETEEN
FAMILY

Baghdad 844

Malak did not know how lonely he had been until he became a part of a family. He had been a member of groups before as a warrior and a monk. Family was different. Family was chaos, love unconditional and forgiving, as the children ran amuck and laughed with unfettered, unregimented joy, shattering armor with laughter. There was peace and truth in the bedlam.

He lived as a brother with Nasir and his family, ultimately purchasing a home next to theirs. They knocked down the exterior walls, and the place was open and airy and full of light. Malak slept on a mat on the floor, and he prayed when it was time to pray, joining the other men. In his mind, they all prayed to the One God.

The House of Wisdom, or *Bayt al-Hikma*, was a wonder. Malak never dreamed the world was so huge. He became a student there, and then a teacher, and often both things at the same time. He learned algebra, geography, philosophy, and medicine. His thirst for knowledge was insatiable, and he drank deeply. He sometimes worked for several days without sleep, lost in his work. He was a translator at first, and he read ancient scrolls from Egypt, Persia, and Greece. In time, he consulted with some of the elder scholars on religious matters and came to be regarded as an expert on the early Christian church.

Men traveled to the city from around the world, as word

of the *Bayt al-Hikma* spread to other centers of learning. He encountered priests and monks who made the journey from Rome, others who traveled from as far away as Northumbria.

Malak was well respected within the city, and he earned a good living. His days were full of wonder and knowledge, and his nights sang with laughter and warm breezes.

Nasir grew older and fatter, and toward the end, he became prone to bouts of depression. One night after the family meal, he came into Malak's home and sat down across from him.

"I know your secret," Nasir said. He stroked his long gray beard. He seemed agitated.

"Is that so, my friend?"

"I will reveal it to no one, but I know."

"What is it you know?"

"I have been watching you. You eat like a ravenous goat, yet you do not grow thick in the waist. Your face bears no more lines than it did the day I met you. I have never seen you ill, even when pestilence scourges the city. You came from the desert, from nowhere."

"What is it you are trying to say, my old friend? Get on with it."

"You have never taken a woman, and you do not look at men or boys. I have tried to get you to marry more times than either of us can count, yet you refuse."

"I am not interested in that," Malak said. "All I have to do is listen to your women harry you like a flock of angry Crows."

"You make jokes," Nasir said. "You always make me laugh. But still I know."

"I am your loyal friend. That is all you really need to know, I think."

"That is what matters to me, yes. But you are a djinn,

Malak."

Malak studied his friend, the man's face steeped in shadows cast by the candles mounted onto the walls. Malak smiled.

"I hope you will do me the kindness of saying, at least, that I am a benevolent djinn."

"Ah! I knew it."

"I did not admit any guilt."

"You did not deny it either. But even if you had, I would not have believed you. I have long suspected. I come to you now to ask a favor."

"Anything."

"You know that my son Ibrahim's wife was with child. The baby has come tonight."

"Praise God."

"There is something wrong. The child is not right."

"What is wrong? I am not a doctor."

"No. You are not a doctor. This child does not need a doctor. My only grandson needs *you*."

"Take me to him."

Nasir pushed himself to his feet, grunting with effort. They exited Malak's home and walked onto the cobblestone streets. The air was warm and sweet. Ibrahim lived only two houses down.

Malak heard women wailing, a terrible agonized thing, the sound of pain which never ceases, tears of loss which no amount of time can ever heal.

Ibrahim's wife, Sarah, lay on a pallet of rugs and cushions, the floor around her littered with bloody rags. She looked spent, sweaty, and beaten. A tiny infant, swaddled and silent, nestled against her breast. Her head lolled in her father-in-law's direction. Some of the other women in the room rushed to the door to shoo the men away, hissing. One of them struck Malak on the cheek. He accepted the blow without comment.

"Leave the room," Nasir said. "All of you." Some of the women protested, shouting at Nasir and waving their hands.

"Now!" He thundered.

"Do not take him from me," Sarah begged.

"Let me see him," Malak replied. Sarah looked terrified when Malak bent down and picked up the child. The baby's hair was wet and matted, and his eyes were closed. Malak removed some of the linens which held the child.

He was breathing quickly, too fast even for a newborn, the little chest rising and falling with quiet desperation, fingers clenched into fists. His skin color was not quite right; the baby seemed gray, as though the light had been stolen from his body before he ever had the chance to shine.

Malak leaned close, listening to the child's chest.

"He came too early," Malak said. "He cannot breathe properly."

"Can you heal him?" Nasir said. "Will you do it for me?"

Malak cradled the baby with his left hand, the baby's head on his palm. Infant mortality was commonplace, with as many as one in five children dying before they reached the age of three. Many women died in childbirth; it was a brutal fact of life. Malak owed this kind man and his family a debt, though, and even if it risked his own position by saving this child, there was no question. He would do what good he could, because even if the world around him was consumed by pain, he could make a difference to this one child, to this one family.

"Let me pray," Malak said.

He closed his eyes and sought a connection to the Creator. He felt a peace like an easy river come to him, clear and true, and with it came power. When it happened like this, when Malak felt guided and certain, healing was pure joy.

He touched the child on the cheek, aware now that he was giving off light, the room bathed in blue and white.

The child wailed, his cry strong and hungry. Malak laid the boy down at his mother's breast. She and Nasir were both crying, and Nasir put his arms around Malak in a great hug, lifting him from the floor.

"Thank you, my friend. There are no words."

———

The child learned to walk and then run. Over the next years, word of the child's miraculous recovery spread from house to house. Others in need came to see Malak, and he found he could not refuse.

Word reached the Caliph, and soldiers burst into Malak's home one morning to escort him to the palace.

The new Caliph was less tolerant of other beliefs than his predecessors and had been threatening to shut down the House of Wisdom because, according to him, science was evil. Knowledge was heresy.

Malak knew he would depart Baghdad soon, and he wondered where he would wind up next and whether he would leave of his own accord or through another death.

He stood in the throne room of the palace, an opulent building of stone and gold, and faced the Caliph, who sat upon an elevated dais. Colorful tapestries adorned the walls, works of art which displayed victories in battle. The ceilings were vaulted, and light entered the room from narrow windows, the sunlight glittering from the diamonds and rubies encrusting the solid gold throne. The soldiers who escorted him into the throne room retreated to the walls after forcing Malak to his knees. One soldier remained behind him.

The Caliph was a middle-aged man, bearded and

robed in fine linens, a jeweled turban on his head, and eyes hard as steel.

"People are talking about you," said the Caliph. "There are whispers that you are a devil. I have a proposition for you."

CHAPTER TWENTY
LIES

Now

Malak possessed the kind of patience only an immortal can, one born through years of uncertainty and many deaths, and there was a certain resignation in it, an acceptance which was not the same as surrender. He had learned to *be still within* until battle began. Sometimes this meant biding time before choosing the exact moment to strike, while often it was a fortification of the soul and mind, a posture of defense rather than aggression, but always the stillness.

He waited for whatever was coming, there in that cinder block house in sleepy Lake City, Florida. Evil stalked the earth, and it was hungry for the blood of men, of this he was certain. Whatever came through his own front door, it would be tame in comparison to the greater darkness which clawed at the gates of civilization, eager, mean, and cold.

Humanity existed in a bubble of denial, a limited sphere of lies and smiles and self-congratulatory social media and vaguely functional governments that established order most of the time. The planet Earth was but a speck in the Milky Way, and the Milky Way a small galaxy in a universe more vast than men could grasp. At any moment, an energy blast from a supernova could evaporate the Earth, a burst from the sun could scorch life from the planet, an asteroid could shift its orbit and decide to plunge on a collision course toward the tiny blue oasis men called home.

There were many ways for humans to become extinct,

but worrying about those things didn't change the reality, and men and women went about the business of living and creating art and culture and civilization, loving, living, dying and passing on the knowledge to the next generation, convincing themselves that what they could see was the only reality, mostly oblivious, thankfully ignorant, of how tenuous their existence was.

More deadly than the threat from another star was betrayal from within. Mankind seemed intent upon its own destruction, and Lucifer was more than willing to accommodate that wish. The devil didn't need to be active in an obvious way, for humans did his work for him. A nudge here, a temptation there, and some demons thrown into the mix, and the world was a tinderbox waiting for a spark.

Malak had read many prophecies. Some came true, and many did not. The Old Testament was rife with things which had already come to pass, though. He'd translated passages of Daniel and Isiah from Aramaic into Latin, and he remembered every verse, the fire and destruction seared into his mind. He'd memorized the Book of Revelation, and while that particular book was cryptic and open to interpretation, it was the most chilling book in the Bible.

He'd encountered Gabriel, Lucifer, and Ariel face to face. There was not the faintest doubt in Malak's mind that fire was coming.

Men chose to disbelieve in the war waging around them because it is comfortable to do so. Malak understood why they did it, and a part of him wished he could succumb to that sort of complacency. He knew he'd already been granted that luxury, though, when he was new and almost mortal in his own mind and soul. He had context now, lifetimes that cursed him with a perspective that humans could not possess.

He'd seen the flash of incandescent hate in the eyes of

men, smelled the burning flesh of innocents, screamed as cold steel pierced his guts, and rocked back on his heels when the buck of his musket smacked his shoulder, death all around him and through him while he raged against it. Once you know the truth, there is no forgetting it, no matter how hard you try. The truth changes you. Malak was calm now.

If the CIA or NSA wanted him dead, they would have sent a drone. Somebody wanted to talk. There were other possibilities, though. He felt the buzzing in his head, and he welcomed the chance to hit back. His role was tiny, irrelevant even, he reasoned, but he relished the chance to engage the enemy. The gladiator in him never died.

Malak switched the firing selector to full auto on the customized H&K submachine gun he held in his hands.

He stood at the head of the dining room table, facing the entrance at an angle, the wooden double doors about ten feet away. The table, an eighties glass and brass atrocity he'd bought along with the rest of the contents of the house, was covered by a neatly arranged and somewhat incongruous array of weapons. There was the katana, a Japanese sword Malak was fond of both for sentimental reasons and its ability to hold an edge, along with fragmentation grenades, flash-bangs, a quarterstaff, and a simple steel long sword he'd managed to buy back from the Museum of London.

The headlights from the incoming vehicles slashed through the dark house, and Malak smiled.

Malak tried to hate nothing, for he believed in the Golden Rule. Hate begets hate.

He hated evil, though, and evil was knocking. Sometimes you have to punch evil in the throat to get your point across.

Five sharp raps at the front doors, a "cop knock," not a friendly, neighborly kind of rap, but a demanding, invasive bang on the door.

"Come," Malak said."

The door opened, and the enemy strode inside, wearing a tailored charcoal suit, every blond hair in place, and a thin, sneering smile. The man glanced around the room with the exaggerated sardonic affectation of a king visiting a pauper, pretending to be kind while intending condescension and insult.

"Love what you've done with the place," Lucifer said.

"Said the greatest loser in the history of, well, history."

"Touche, brother. Although you will find I am playing the long game. I've been waiting for this day for millennia. My time is at hand. You know this to be true."

"You may cavort like a peacock and revel for a moment in your evil. But your time? No. Eternity is a long time, and you will be spending it someplace hot."

"You know nothing, Malak. You *believe* you know, which is not the same thing. We have a long history, you and me. The veil will be torn, and you will remember, and perhaps then you will see the truth. You are weak, God is absent, and mankind is undeserving. Let me clarify that. Mankind deserves better than a God who proclaims himself God, yet does not care when millions, billions of his children die."

"You are still the same snake, just wearing a new skin."

"Your head is crammed with *religion*. I care about humans. The bad things that happen are not my doing. I never caused an earthquake or a flood or an inquisition. War among men is inherent to their nature. They need no help from me. It's been such fun. The real fun, that's about to begin. I'm giving you a chance. A one-time offer to take your place at my side."

"What is it about my character that makes you think that's even a remote possibility? And why do you care?"

"Because," Lucifer replied, his voice soft and musical and almost sad, "I know you better than you know yourself."

"What's that supposed to mean?"

"You are not what you always were, nor are you who you were meant to be."

"More lies. Straight from the source of lies."

"It saddens me you cannot remember. That you do not recall the past does not render it less true."

"Enlighten me."

"You were once my brother, Malak. You joined me in the rebellion. You were *there*."

Malak calculated the time it would take him to shoot, keeping his face neutral. Even if he somehow managed to kill Lucifer's human form, which seemed unlikely, he had no idea of what would happen next. That he would pop up someplace else was a certainty. The backlash alone might kill Malak.

"Look within, Malak, and allow the truth to resonate. How is it you came to be? Why are you so...limited? You might as well be human, stripped of your power, alone and abandoned, cursed to walk the centuries in solitude and pain, shunned. Surely you have wondered and crave answers. Do you not yearn for the truth?"

"Truth is," Malak said, "I—" Malak brought the muzzle of the HK up slightly and squeezed the trigger. He shot the devil in the face, and things got interesting.

He heard windows break at the rear of the house.

He thought they'd at least hit him with gas first. There was that buzzing, crawling, revulsion still in the air. He was curious, and he was at peace.

He knew it couldn't be that easy, because it never was. Evil was easy by design, slippery and deceptive and seductive; defeating it, though, was never simple.

The troops came then, storming the house. The door

flew from its hinges, and men came through the living room window. Most of them were human, just doing their jobs. Maybe this was a black ops strike team that Lucifer had managed to hijack, or perhaps these guys were mercs. Malak had tears in his eyes as he leaped into their midst. He would not kill these men.

With a submachine gun slung over his back and the quarterstaff in his hands, Malak counterattacked.

The commandos wore all black, even their faces darkened with paint.

Some came through the back door, spreading out along the perimeter of the room, while others entered windows from bedrooms down the hallway. Most of them were armed with compact weapons, machine pistols with high rates of fire, devastating at close range.

The men were not prepared for the speed, surprise, or violence of action which Malak unleashed upon them without hesitation.

He bounded from his position near the front door, toward his right as the first of the soldiers raised a weapon in Malak's general direction.

Malak cut back to his left, closing the distance between himself and his attackers, and he dove toward the floor, the first burst from an automatic weapon tearing through the house, rounds ricocheting from the concrete walls and knocking down paintings on the walls, shredding a lamp, and blasting the glass table to bits.

Malak, in mid-air, tucked the staff under one arm, landed on the other hand, and launched himself up and forward feet first into the nearest man. He kicked the man in the face, arched his back, and landed on his feet again, already swinging the oak staff.

Wood cracked against bone, and another soldier went

down, the tip of the staff blurring into his jaw. Malak spun, whirling with the weapon, and the opposite end caught another soldier in the throat; he fell, silent and clutching at his trachea.

The fourth soldier managed to get off a short burst. He'd back-pedaled toward the far wall. A round caught Malak on the side, inches above his waist, and he had the feeling of being kicked. His forward momentum carried him ahead, and he smashed the man in the groin with the staff, an upward blow from below with all his strength behind it. The man's feet left the ground, and he fell in a heap on the kitchen floor, his mouth opening and closing like a beached fish.

Two canisters the size of soda cans clanged onto the floor. Malak dove out the back door. The concussion sent shock waves through the house, blowing out the unbroken windows in the kitchen, knocking the back door off its hinges.

He heard distant police sirens. The commotion had woken the neighbors up.

Malak sprinted along the back wall of the house, staying low, and then cut around the side. At the corner, he looked out at the driveway. There were two dark SUVs parked at angles in front of his home. He couldn't see any men out there, which did not mean they weren't there, crouching behind tires, trying to acquire him with night vision scopes.

He climbed through his bedroom window, and his feet crunched on the glass of the floor. He moved toward the door. He heard voices from inside the bombed out living room. He put the staff on his bed and gripped the H&K in his hands as he edged down the dark hallway.

A soldier entered his field of vision, and Malak shot him in the legs. The man fell sideways, screaming and firing his weapon.

Malak retreated and dove back out the window he'd

just come through.

He crawled through the bushes at the side of his yard, feeling spiders and insects on his hands as he moved. He kept his head down, glad for the overgrown holly bushes and live oak trees. His movements were slow and deliberate. He wanted to cut behind those vehicles in the front yard.

The wound in his side was healing, and it tingled and burned as his body mended itself. There was still that crawling, humming sensation in the back of his head, and he knew he still faced something that was not human.

A figure stepped from one of the vehicles, his body silhouetted against the headlights, and Malak knew *it* was looking at him.

Malak leaned into his scope and brought the shadowy figure closer. He put the crosshairs on center mass and gave the trigger a gentle squeeze. The weapon kicked his shoulder, the recoil negligible, and he fired again. The figure was gone.

His position no longer tenable, he ran full out for the vehicles, staying out of the direct light. There were shouts from the house behind him and off to his left, and he heard several shots. He made it to the nearest SUV, and saw no blood or body, and he kept moving until he was behind the truck. He went prone and fired at the front door from beneath the truck. Another man went down.

He did not know how many of them there were, but he figured he'd taken most of them out. Maybe he could escape in the SUV. Or maybe he should continue to stay and try to finish this one small fight.

He rolled sideways and changed magazines, then came to his feet again. The police sirens were getting close. Neighborhood dogs were barking like mad. He hoped people were smart enough to stay inside and out of the way. Lake City was not the kind of place where firefights with automatic weapons happened.

"Hello, Malak," said a quiet voice in his ear.

Malak attempted to spin and discovered he was paralyzed. He could not breathe, move his eyes, or even twitch. He fell to the ground like a stone statue, landing with his limbs fixed in position. His vision was blurred with wavy red and black lines. His face lay on the grass, mouth slightly open, as black boots sank into the soft ground inches in front of his face.

"I was hoping you'd be willing to talk to me in a reasonable fashion, but I'm not terribly surprised. It's a shame about that man you shot. He had small children."

Malak could not reply. He prayed.

"After all that you have been through, all that you have seen, you still cling to the belief that God cares. Shortly, you will find that your faith is misplaced. I intended to give you a place at my side, but you made your answer clear. In the coming years, I want you to remember this moment, when you are miserable and cold and everyone you care about is rotting in the ground. When the future stretches out before you, endless and desolate, and you are alone, wandering and defeated."

The cops were almost there. Malak heard engines gunning and tires squealing.

"You are an abomination. Weak, self-important, and finished." He laughed. "Did you really think I'd waltz into your living room and let you kill me? That's precious. I can't read minds, but I don't need to. Unlike you, I am free to move about this world as I choose, maintaining my human form. I will be in Beijing before the police find your dead body. But before you die again, I want to thank you personally for helping me do what needed to be done. You have been instrumental in bringing about my time. Think on me and smile, Malak. Or cry. I don't give a damn."

Darkness came for him, and Malak hoped that when he opened his eyes again, there would still be time to stop what was coming.

CHAPTER TWENTY-ONE
SONNELION

Baghdad, 844

"I have been searching for you," the Caliph said in Aramaic. His delicate hands perched on the armrests of the throne, and his feet were crossed, face relaxed but intent.

Malak had been in the presence of Caesar and other Caliphs. There was something unsettling about this man. He exuded danger and power in a way Malak could feel in his bones. It was a malevolent energy, an oily, crawling thing Malak had never experienced before.

"I should think I was easy to find. I've been in the same home for many years."

"Hmm. We have been searching for you for considerably longer than that."

"How can I serve?" Malak said. He kept his face neutral, paying attention to the twelve palace guards, the two exits from the room, and the burning eyes before him.

"There are many rumors concerning you," the Caliph said. "That you are both a Jew and a Christian, that you work miracles. Tell me, Malak, whom do you serve?"

"I serve the One God."

"Do you?"

"Yes, I do."

"You believe Allah is just and merciful, then?"

"God is good."

"Do you believe you are His messenger? That is what your name means, which of course you know. Do you consider yourself to be an emissary of God?"

"I do not presume that title, your Highness."

"We shall see. A test, then." The Caliph raised his finger from the armrest of the throne, a casual gesture, dismissive, arrogant.

Guards brought Nasir's family into the throne room at the tips of spears. Nasir looked terrified and angry at the same time. His grandchildren clung to sobbing mothers, faces buried in robes.

"We shall see whether your God is more powerful than mine."

"Do we not bow to the same God?"

"I bow to no one, *messenger*. You see, there are many religions. This is a good thing. It keeps men fighting and killing, preparing the way for the return of the Prince."

"I do not understand. How does this serve God?"

"You will learn the answers in the end. I want you to see this before I imprison you. I want you to feel your weakness. To understand that your precious God has long since abandoned you and mankind."

Malak prayed while he prepared to attack, visualizing each move in his mind. He felt the cold blade on the back of his neck. He would disarm that guard and attack the Caliph, force him to order his men to stand down.

"Kill them," said the Caliph, cocking his head to the side. Waiting. Curious.

Still kneeling, Malak drove his elbow backwards into the groin of the soldier behind him. He reached over his shoulder, grasped the man by his wrist, and flipped him onto the floor.

Screams. He could not look back.

He picked up the soldier's sword and launched himself at the Caliph, taking long strides, the blade at his shoulder.

"Tell them to stop!" Malak roared, closing the distance to the Caliph. The bearded man's eyes flickered with interest, an amused detachment in his demeanor, not an inkling of fear on his face.

Malak recognized Nasir's voice, begging for the lives of his family, "Please, no, they are innocent. They..."

Wet choking sounds. Consumed with rage, Malak swung the blade with terrible fury.

Time stopped.

The Caliph and everyone else in the room froze in place, yet Malak was still moving. He paused before the Caliph and gazed around the room.

Nasir was falling, yet not falling, his body impossibly suspended in the air, robes hanging to the ground, and drops of blood hovering a few inches from the floor. Two children lay in heaps at the feet of soldiers.

Malak disarmed the soldiers, prying the blades from their hands, their fingers breaking free like ice sickles. There was no sound when Malak tossed the weapons into a heap, no clang of metal or slap of sandal upon stone. He spun back toward the Caliph.

A tall, elegant man in white robes stood in front of Malak, radiant and wielding a long sword shimmering with a blue fire like lightning on a dark night.

"You prayed and I came," he said to Malak. The man's eyes were a startling blue, and his smile was sad.

"Who are you? What is happening?"

"I am Gabriel."

"The angel. You appeared to Mary and Daniel." It sounded ludicrous when he spoke the words, yet under the circumstances, it was more than plausible.

"Yes."

"I don't understand."

"I know. The thing which took your friend's life has many names, but I know it as Sonnelion. It is a prince of hell. It feeds upon anger and violence, seeks to plunge men into war. It serves Lucifer, and it craves your allegiance. It wants you to hate."

"It has succeeded, then," Malak said. He wondered if he should kneel before this angel, if indeed that's what it was. He was mourning the death of his family, still shaking with anger.

"You heard my prayers? You're a little late."

"No. I did not hear you. The Lord sent me here, now, and I am precisely on time. I am sorry for your grief. Nasir was a good man."

Things were happening too fast. Malak felt shock, grief, adrenaline, and remorse. He needed answers. He had questions about...everything. He had a hard time forming lucid thoughts.

"What am I, Gabriel? How is it that I continue to live?"

"You are an enigma. Your destiny is your own, it seems. I do not have all the answers. There was a war in heaven, and many angels rebelled against God along with Lucifer. Some now walk the earth as demons. Your role is unclear to me, but it seems you are pivotal to the future of mankind. All things work according to His good, yet some paths are easier than others. Unlike me, you possess free will."

"How can this be?"

Gabriel's musical laugh filled the throne room. "How can *anything* be? It is God's will. It is good that you ask questions, Malak. You are a seeker of truth. I do not presume to know what path lies before you, though I am certain it will not be an easy one. Your choices send ripples through time, shaping a myriad of possible futures."

"But the children... why? If you had gotten here a few

heartbeats sooner, you could have saved them. It doesn't make sense."

"I cannot know the answer to that question, Malak, and for this I am deeply sorry. My role is not to question, but to obey."

"Is my role, then, to ask questions? Am I allowed to wonder, or shall I be doomed to face the wrath of God for my doubt? I try to be a good man, yet I struggle with senseless tragedy, rampant evil in the world. I despise it."

"Question and fight, then. I am called away. One last thing, Malak. A gift from me to you. Remain still."

Gabriel flowed, a blur of light, and appeared in human form directly in front of Malak. The archangel touched Malak on the forehead with his forefinger, and peals of thunder reverberated in Malak's mind and soul.

Then the angel was gone, and things were moving again, and sound filled the palace. Malak turned to face the demon. Time resumed its normal course.

The Caliph growled at Malak, an animal sound which shook the room. Malak struck with his new knowledge, this gift Gabriel had imparted to him.

He spoke ancient words of wrath and fire and power flowed through his body. He was a conduit, connected to a bottomless well of energy and strength. The concussion reverberated through the palace, and the walls shook and the ceiling rained sand and pebbles.

The demon was gone, banished, skulking back to hell where he belonged. The other people in the room were staring at Malak in wonder and horror, mouths agape. The Caliph's body lay slumped on his throne, an empty shell.

Malak strode from the room, and the guards parted before him. He left the city alone and struck out for the desert.

For the first time in his life, he had a better grasp on his purpose in the world. If a war were still raging, then he would do what he could to do battle with the forces of evil. He could not know what paths lay before him, only that he would strive to be a force for good, content no longer to shrink away from a conflict that threatened to destroy humanity.

As a towering sandstorm descended upon the scorched desert, Malak lowered his head into the biting wind and walked toward the sea. He pulled his scarf over his mouth and nose while the sand and wind blasted him. His eyes stung, and his face was streaked with tears. He was numb inside.

While he had a newfound purpose, he also felt used, manipulated. He attempted to reconcile his understanding of God with the feeling that his own life was not his own. The sense that his free will was an illusion, and that the Creator was a puppeteer with a mean streak. Malak did not like the dark paths these thoughts took him upon. If God cared for his children, how could he possibly allow such evil to walk the earth? How could the creator have given rise to evil itself? If God is utterly holy, then where does evil spring from?

The wind raged, and Malak could see no more than a few feet in front of him. The desert was alive, tearing at him, mocking him, conspiring to consume him.

"What do you want from me?" Malak howled into the storm.

If he were a mere pawn in an eternal game played between God and the Devil, he did not want to play. His entire existence felt unjust. He was betrayed by the God he loved and tried to serve, abandoned along with the rest of mankind.

He realized he'd stopped walking some time ago.

"I quit," he said. "I am finished."

He sank to his knees while the sand and wind swirled around him, and that death came as a relief.

CHAPTER TWENTY-TWO
THE ENEMY

Now

Malak knew from the smell where he was. Smoke and fear and seething anger bottled up in one city, love and hate combining with history in a noxious perfume of religious fervor. The staccato of gunfire echoed somewhere close. He blinked and rubbed his eyes, his hand coming away bloody. His back lay propped against a concrete wall, combat boots splayed in front of him. Across the street, wrecked buildings smoldered. A pick-up truck blazed in the center of the road, two charred bodies roasting in the cab. He wanted to get the hell out of here.

A face peered from behind an apartment building, vanished before Malak could get a good look. The wall shook and bits of concrete rained down on his head. He wore fatigues, and an assault rifle lay on his lap. To the casual observer, he no doubt appeared to be dead or dying.

How much time has passed?

He was out of practice with the dying and resurrecting. He felt the usual vertigo and a gut-wrenching sense of loss. The sun was hot on his face, and he squinted into the shadows. He'd lost count of how many times he'd died in this city, this spiritual ground zero.

Mortar shells shrieked inbound, and Malak felt the hair on the back of his neck rise. He hated artillery. The rounds thumped into buildings beyond his line of sight, the rolling concussion a thing he felt in his bones. He heard sirens and wondered if they'd been blaring the whole time.

Jerusalem had a certain energy like no other place in the world, a pulse which throbbed with joy and anguish. Helicopters thudded through the sky in the distance like locusts in formation. Two Israeli fighter jets streaked overhead, mottled brown F-16s. Probably headed to drop ordinance on the Palestinian mortar crew. *For all I know, there's already a full-blown war happening here. Syria? Iran? If it's started, this city may be nuked any second.*

He pushed himself to his feet and ran for the nearest building. It looked like it was a low-rent apartment, but in the condition it was in, no one would ever live there again. The roof was caved in, and the walls had ragged holes torn into them. Helicopters were getting closer, somewhere behind him. He sprinted. Someone ahead was shooting at him. Great.

He wore an Israeli uniform, so he guessed that he was in a part of the city occupied by Palestinians. The shooter was firing a Kalashnikov on full auto, an unmistakable sound, and rounds snapped over Malak's head and cracked off the road. He made it to the rubble and pressed himself against the crumbling wall.

The gunfire ceased, and he heard several voices from down the alleyway separating two buildings. They were close.

"Hey," Malak shouted in Arabic. "I don't want to hurt you. Why don't you stop shooting at me?"

"Screw you!"

"I don't suppose you'd tell me what year it is?"

A grenade landed a few feet from Malak. *All right, then.* Nothing happened.

"You forgot to pull the pin, geniuses. Now look, I'm going to leave. Quit trying to kill me, and good luck with the Uprising."

An enraged howl emerged from the alley. A chorus of

anguish, followed by futile gunfire.

"Die, Jew!"

Malak decided to go the other way, having no desire to find a pointless fight here. For some reason, he thought about Somellion, the demon he'd vanquished more than a thousand years ago, yet who was no doubt cackling and reveling in the chaos now.

The fighters surprised Malak. They charged, five of them. He heard urgent steps on the street before they rounded the corner. They weren't going to let it go. They never did.

Malak turned to face them, dropping the TAVOR assault rifle on the rocks, coming back toward the corner in a crouch, legs tensed, hands splayed.

The fighters rounded the corner with assault rifles at their hips, none of them old enough to buy a pack of cigarettes in the States. They wore jeans and T-shirts, and their skin was swarthy, like his own, their hair dark and their eyes full of fear and rage. Tightly bunched, not taking time to watch their spacing or corners, they announced their approach with shouts and sloppy bravado.

He blurred into their midst, his elbows smashing, knees striking, hands arcing in a symphony of destruction, a melody of violence which has its own rhythm, a music elegant and terrible. Malak knew the song in his soul, a concerto worthy of Mozart with the same sort of bursting creativity. It was over in a few seconds. One of them was still standing, an AK pointed at Malak's chest.

The kid looked like he wanted to shrink into himself. Eyes wild and white and nostrils flaring and terror coming off him in waves, weapon shaking, and a Disney World shirt soaked with sweat. He was the youngest of the bunch.

"Shoot," Malak said, smiling.

"Death to the Jews. Death to the infidel."

"Right."

"I will kill you."

"You could. What year is it?"

"You killed my family. I will shoot you in the balls, then cut off your head."

"Yes."

Malak stepped forward until the barrel of the weapon was at his chest. The kid stepped back.

"You are insane!"

"You have no idea. I didn't kill your family, by the way. And I'm sorry they died." Malak stepped forward again. One of the men on the ground groaned. Somewhere in the distance, a bomb landed and people ceased to be.

"You are the enemy."

"Am I? How do you know that?"

"You slaughter innocents. You killed my family. You are the devil."

The kid was terrified and working up his courage. Malak could see it. A teenager screwing up his resolve, deciding to be angry, remembering how he was wronged, justifying whatever happened next. The anger feeding on itself.

"I didn't kill you, did I? Or your friends. And I could have. Maybe you know that, and maybe you don't. But I could have."

"Why? Why didn't you kill us?"

"Because I'm not the enemy."

Malak reached out to embrace the child because he thought that was the right thing to do. Because he wanted to show the kid something important.

The round pierced Malak's right lung and put him down. The angry man-child stood over him, working his face into a sneer. In suburban America, it might have been the defiant anger of a kid deprived of his video games, petulant and selfish. In the West Bank, there is a rage that runs deep and true. In Tel Aviv, it's there, too, and in Detroit and Washington and every place people exist and try to pretend that things are fine when they're not. That shot waiting to be fired heard around the world.

"You are the enemy. You have always been the enemy. And now you will die, just like you should. Like I said you would. Jew." He spat on Malak's face, a thick, wet thing sliding down the cheek.

"My baby sister, not old enough to walk, killed by your bombs. My older brother disappeared the next week. Taken." He kicked Malak in the face with a small foot. "Soldiers just like you. With your tanks and planes." There was a lot of blood on these streets, and some of it belonged to Malak.

"What is your name, boy?" Malak groaned.

"Mohammad. And why don't you just die?"

The kid looked like he wanted to cry, but he kept being angry. Good for him. That's an honest kid. There are things to kill for and things you kill yourself for, and sometimes they look the same, and people seldom know the difference. This kid got it, maybe, at the end.

"I wish you'd see. Hell, this hurts. Don't you see it?"

It got dark then, and that death wasn't so bad, as deaths go.

CHAPTER TWENTY-THREE
THE ROCK

The Pacific, 900 A.D.

When faith is the bedrock upon which a life is built, the loss of it, when belief crumbles to dust, reduces a man to bitter, abject desolation. Malak died in the sand, and in the sand he was reborn.

Waves crashing, the sun blinding, and the ocean a pale welcome blue, he plucked a crab from his chest and pulled yellow seaweed from matted hair and beard, pushing himself into a seated position. Coconut palms stretched toward the sea along a pristine white beach. At his back, a steep mountain lush with green jungle rose toward the cloudless sky. He'd never been any place like this before.

"Is this heaven? My reward? It looks a little lonely," he muttered.

A seagull landed a few feet away and twittered at him. The crab scuttled along the surf line with one oversized claw, and one tiny, ridiculous one, the big claw raised like a shield.

"What do you want from me?"

The breeze, balmy and sweet, ruffled his long hair.

"Remember our last talk? I quit. I'm not doing this anymore."

The palms rustled and the waves broke upon the reef line and lapped the shore, a steady rhythm of foam and clear water, more than a whisper, less than a conversation. Peaceful, serene.

Malak was not in the mood. He thought about the

family he'd lost, the screams of children still echoing in his heart. The demon he'd faced, a thing which he had never known walked the earth until he'd felt its unholy power. To him, it was yesterday, though he had no idea how much time had elapsed between Baghdad and wherever this was. Whenever he was.

His existence was unfair, he decided. Every life he'd lived felt futile, as did life itself. The friends he'd seen die, the blood he'd spilled with a blade... There seemed to be no sense to any of it, within the context of a loving, living God. *Especially* given that reality.

While he had experienced great peace, the times of turmoil and war overshadowed this, and he saw that both he and mankind were no closer to figuring things out than they were centuries ago.

The crab skittered toward a hole in the sand, and the bird hopped over to the crab and skewered it.

The crab, Malak mused, does not pity itself, even as it dies, any more than the bird gloats over the killing and the meal. Men are different. Perhaps emotions only make living harder. For the crab does not expect to live any more than the bird believes it will eat, and the fact that these desires conflict keeps neither awake at night. If the crab assumed he'd be protected, living the crab-life, surrounded by hungry birds, yet confident in his continued prosperity, he would get angry when that beak pierced his shell.

"What's the point? Clearly, there isn't one. When I believe, you destroy. You are God. I can't deny that you exist, not after the things I've seen. But you are not what you should be. You're a cheat in the marketplace, full of sunshine promises and whitewashed smiles, who then vanishes when it turns out you sold a lie, a cracked jar. You have no integrity. That you exist does not make me love you."

He knew that these words were the worst sort of blasphemy, and his lips burned a bit with the speaking of them, and his guts tightened up, his body rebelling against his mind.

He walked along the beach, letting the water slide over his bare feet, feeling the sand between his toes, and the warm sun on his neck. He walked for perhaps an hour or two, and wound up where he started, circling back to his first footprints. The bird cocked its head at him and laughed in the way that birds sometimes do.

He was on an island.

Malak plopped down in the sand and watched the sun slide below the ocean, streaks of pink and yellow and purple painted upon the vast sky, and the face of the waters shimmering orange against the dancing white of the breakers and the deepening blue of the sea. The day dying, the night born.

He did not move, watching the first stars appear, punching through both light and darkness, becoming a wondrous myriad of diamonds strung, melting into the sea. All the while, the waves hushed and frothed, luminescent and soothing.

He decided he would explore the interior in the morning, and that if he wanted to quit living and dying for both God and man, this would be the perfect place to do it.

That is exactly what he did.

He would come to call the island "The Rock," and although he couldn't know it then, it would become a place of solitude and wonder and joy. It would be a refuge, the only place he was born again more than once; often, as he was dying, he prayed he would wake up there. It didn't happen often enough for his liking, but when it did, he'd feel the sun on his face and the thirst in his soul and hear the music of the ocean, and he would smile, even as he shook off the last death.

It took time to figure this out. Malak was hard-headed, and immortality proved no solution to being stubborn.

Water was a problem, and it was only through dumb luck that he figured out that coconuts held life-giving water within their hard shells. During a storm, a green one fell next to him, and he heard the liquid inside. After wasting the precious liquid on the first few attempts, he learned how to remove the outer husk and pierce the shell within, drinking heartily. He also learned to drink from plants after a hard rain and started collecting his coconut shells to gather water during the rainy season. Despite being stubborn, Malak was smart, tough, and adaptable.

He ate fish every day, and the flesh contained water. At first, he speared them, and as time went on, he learned to dig alcoves reinforced by coral and lava rock, letting the tide bring the fish in, where they would be stranded after it receded. He added nets formed with vines from the jungle to make this more effective. There were abundant fruit trees on the island, as well, and when it did not rain enough, these saved his life more than once. The island provided.

He was gifted and cursed with what would later be known as a didactic memory. He forgot nothing. He could recall the taste of food he'd eaten in the Ludus or Lindisfarne on any given day at a specific meal, along with the ribald or Godly conversations which ensued. The more alone Malak was, the more he retreated into the past, finding comfort and solace with friends long dead. Hearing their cries, at the end. That was the thing.

As good as his memory was, these conversations were all one-sided, more akin to eavesdropping. He could not speak to his comrades any more than they could talk to him on this deserted island. The moments were what they were, unaltered and done, and even though Malak wished to speak into the past, he could not. What was done was done.

He exhausted these memories, and that soul-shrinking loneliness came back. It was a poverty of the soul.

He needed to get off the island because he was going insane. Also, he was bored. He'd been there for more rainy seasons than he could count. At least twenty years. He had every cause to believe that the easiest way off the island was to die.

At dawn, after a long night of dead conversation, he set out into the ocean.

He swam beyond the breakers, the waves smashing into the coral below, his blood blooming in the clear water, warm in the way that Lindisfarne was not, wild and teeming with life and death.

The first time, he made it beyond the reef. He swam until he was exhausted, swept by the current out into the open ocean. He choked on salt water and sputtered and stroked. Things stung and nibbled at his extremities. The moon rose high and bright, and he was far from land and man. He rolled onto his back while a thunderstorm crashed a few miles away, lightning arcing from horizon to horizon, white and ragged, waves building, his body carried up and down, as alone as any man can ever be.

"Here I am! Kill me! You don't care, so let's get it over with!" He gulped a cresting wave, the water stinging his eyes.

The first shark took his right leg above the knee with one bite. It felt like a hard shove, followed by tingling and pain and ironic, gulping laughter. The next shark chomped him in the torso and took him down for a while, a plunge into the dark, where his ears hurt and his lungs burned and his guts were on fire below the sea, and Malak decided that there were better ways to die.

————

He felt the same sun, heard familiar lazy waves, and saw the same damn bird making angry tracks in the sand when he opened his eyes again.

"Really?"

He experimented with ways to kill himself for a season. Drowning, starvation, fire, and the ever-faithful sharks. None of it worked. He wound up back on the beach.

And so began the conversation that mattered. The one he was meant to have.

Certainty is often a thing men profess, yet do not possess, a sad kind of striving which is a part of being human. There is a different sort, though, the burning certainty built upon lies and fortified with a true and pure passion, weaponized by experience and injustice. Evil lives in certainty.

God dwells in the truth.

Right and wrong exist, yet those absolutes are manipulated, shaded, and distorted to unleash atrocities. The "final solution" was the worst thing humanity came up with, with the trains and the gas and the systemic extermination of human beings. Millions of lives lost. Hitler, Stalin, Pol Pot, and ISIS knew how to use certainty as a weapon.

A man can choose between right and wrong, and so can a community, a religion, a nation. Before Hitler and ISIS, there were the Crusades and the Inquisition.

During the Crusades, Malak found evil, or perhaps evil found him.

CHAPTER TWENTY-FOUR
THE TRUTH

Now

Malak laughed, the ocean a gentle sigh, the water cools upon his toes. A seagull, winged and black beaked, danced a few feet away. The crab scampered somewhere close, no doubt. The Palestinian boy's face was still seared into Malak's mind.

While he generally liked coming alive in this place, today was different. He was running out of time. *Mankind's hourglass down to the last grains, while I lay naked in the surf.*

He swam out onto the shallow reef, noting the torpedo shapes circling below the pristine blue water, and he rolled onto his back, staring at the sky, where tremendous thunderheads piled on top of each other off to the east.

This island remained an enigma, one of many mysteries he'd not yet come to understand. He'd searched for this place more than once. In the early Nineteenth Century, he'd been part of a crew which sailed these waters, and he recognized the smell, the certain sheen that the ocean here had. Despite making way for several years and landing on countless uncharted islands, he'd not found it then. More than a century later, he'd culled through satellite images, narrowed his search to swaths of islands, and thousands of square miles and chartered a yacht. There was an almost magnetic pull about the place, yet he never found it, no matter how hard he tried and despite the millions of dollars he spent on his personal exploration.

After Google Earth came online, he culled through

every image, before finally relinquishing the quest. He wondered where and when it was and spent many hours contemplating the ramifications of a place which existed somewhere out of time and space. It was the closest thing he had to what humans called home.

The darkening clouds flashed and lowered, and the waves picked up. He backstroked his way to the beach and padded up to his cave to pray and think, scooping up a coconut and smashing it with his bare hands to drink the sweet liquid within.

He was here for a reason; that he did not know what that was did not matter. It would be made clear, in the way that things like this were. It might take time, and there was no use raging against it. He started a fire, using a kit he'd fashioned more than a hundred years ago, in its place beside the fire pit exactly where he'd left it, the coconut tinder dry and perfect, and he recalled what he called in his own mind, he considered "the conversation."

He'd been a creature of faith for centuries before he had encountered the living God. He was certainly a Christian, by any definition of the word, long before that day on this very island a thousand years ago. He remembered now, turning it over in his mind.

———

He was broken then, for even Angels weep. It was only in his brokenness that he could find what he needed to find. Perhaps it was his very strength which had prevented him from this encounter, a thing that could almost be pride, although Malak had never seen it that way.

Dying and being reborn on the same island over and over again felt like a curse. He wondered if he was in hell, paying the price for the blood he'd shed. As anger fled him, hopelessness found him. He meditated upon the scrolls he'd studied, the stories he'd heard, reciting long passages of the Torah. He lingered over the lives of Moses and David and Abraham, seeking some truth he was certain which eluded him. The words of the Apostles reverberated in his soul, and he sensed he was drawing closer. The Sermon on the Mount slayed him.

"Blessed are the poor in spirit, for theirs is the Kingdom of Heaven."

"Well, God, here I am. Crying out for you. Where are you?"

"You are the salt of the earth. But if the salt loses its saltiness, how can it be made salty again? It is no longer good for anything, except to be thrown out and trampled underfoot.

"You are the light of the world. A town built on a hill cannot be hidden. Neither do people light a lamp and put it under a bowl. Instead, they put it on its stand, and it gives light to everyone in the house. In the same way, let your light shine before others, that they may see your good deeds and glorify your Father in heaven."

God did not appear to Malak in a burning bush or an orb of light on the road to Damascus; there were no trumpets sounding from heaven, and the earth did not shudder under Malak's feet. He experienced a seismic shift within, shifting and grinding and opening. The sort of quiet change which appears to be subtle at first, but which roars and thunders as it manifests itself, charging through time. The kind of change which changes *everything*.

He touched something vast and wonderful and holy and so far beyond him that to say he was humbled is like the grain of sand proclaiming the ocean large. God met Malak on that island, and more than anything, what Malak felt was love, brighter than the sun on the hottest day in the desert, warmer and more sustaining, the fount of life itself, the source of all. The Alpha and the Omega of Genesis. Within this love, bound to it, there was hope. There was light and exhortation and purpose, and a deep peace, a new faith akin to knowledge yet more powerful, for it transcended physical facts and eclipsed centuries of learning.

The truth found Malak, and God was the truth.

Malak lay prostrate on the sand, with joy on his lips and a singing in his chest, every bit of his being filled with awe.

The world tilted then, and Malak was somewhere else from one moment to the next, and it was the only time it happened that he drifted without dying. In the coming years, he would need to remember and savor those moments he'd spent in the undeniable presence of his creator, for the world has always been a mean place.

———

Now, more than a thousand years later, and back on the Rock, Malak knew he needed a battle plan, but he required much more than that. He was certain that he'd been brought here to be reminded of some things that he had not forgotten, but overlooked, which is almost the same thing. While he'd asked Ariel his purpose, he'd been asking the wrong question to the wrong entity. He *knew* his purpose; what he did not know was how he could achieve it.

Trying to be the light in the world can lead to a deeper darkness when men deceive themselves into believing that what is wrong is right and what is right is wrong.

He did not want to make that mistake. Not again.

Malak needed to return to the world, and he hoped that God would forgive him for wanting to return to a place he knew almost as well as the Rock. A city of birth and death, the cradle and the grave for mankind and three of its religions.

Darkness fell, yet the sky was bright with stars and galaxies when Malak strode into the ocean and swam with fervent strokes through the breakers and to the open water beyond. As the first light of the day kissed the placid sea, he was thankful when the creature from the dark places below took him by the thigh and plunged, powerful as a freight train and unswerving as it hurtled into the cold deep.

CHAPTER TWENTY-FIVE
THE LANCE

Antioch, June 1098

Malak came to life among the dead. He regarded the narrow alleyway where bodies lay broken, stinking, and corrupt. He staggered over the lifeless heaps, dried blood staining the rocks beneath his boots. Women and children, eyes open and blue white. Malak reeled with revulsion and outrage.

He wore more layers of clothing than he ever had: a linen shirt beneath a vest of chain mail, and over that was a grimy, blood-streaked smock with a cross, stitched in red cloth. The alley was shadowed by smooth rock walls, buildings two and three stories tall pressing in on both sides, and he wanted nothing more than to escape. He heard cheering not far away. He'd come to loathe that sound.

The stench was almost, but not quite, bearable when he emerged into a courtyard, and a wider boulevard choked with armed men. Thousands of them. The reek of sweat and starvation and zeal doing battle with corpses around the corner.

A monk was speaking at the doors to what looked like a great church, holding something up above his head, while the men howled and beat their chests and cried out to God. Malak sank to his knees and closed his eyes, the feeling in him that what he was about to endure would be worse than anything he'd ever known.

"The Lance!" The monk shouted.

"The Holy lance!" the soldiers cheered.

"The infidels cannot stand against us. For God is with us."

More shouting, which made Malak want to crawl inside a clean cave of rock and solitude and crashing waves. People cheered, and he felt apart from them.

No retreat. Nowhere to go.

The collective thumping of chests and banging of weapons, jangling and cruel and sweaty, assailed him. Dangerous. Mean. Deceptive, fervent.

Evil slinks over walls, bones, and men, while nations congratulate themselves. The *sound* of evil is cheering and adulation and marching boots, joy and hatred and certainty becoming one thing, one abomination. History recognizes evil after the fact. And then it's too late, for it has been defined by those who listened and didn't give a damn.

"Though we be outnumbered," the monk went on, "God shall pry victory from the greedy hands of defeat. Jerusalem will not remain in the evil hands of the pagans."

Malak looked around, paying attention to the distant walls, the citadel. He was certain he wasn't in Jerusalem. Close, maybe, but this wasn't the same city.

"I told you," the monk intoned, "that my vision was true, and from God. No army can stand before His might. I give you proof."

Probably the monk was jumping up and down and shaking the thing he claimed he'd discovered. Maybe it was true, maybe it wasn't.

Malak felt a heavy hand upon his shoulder.

"You must be deeply pious," said a deep voice with some sand in it. A hint of amusement. "To pray on your knees at a moment like this."

Malak stood and met the man's eyes. The knight appeared to be of middle age, bearded and strong, and not as gaunt as many of the others who thronged the street.

"I give thanks to be alive," Malak said.

"As well we all should. I don't think I know you."

"I am Malak."

"Of?"

Malak froze, trying to discern the meaning and context. A thing he never really got used to doing, despite much practice.

"I am Robert of Flanders," said the man with piercing eyes and faded armor.

"Of course, sir," Malak said, allowing a smile to come into his eyes. "I have heard of your great deeds." He hadn't, but he was sure he would. "I am Malak of Lisdenfarne."

"Ah yes. I hear you fought well," Robert said.

"I'm sure the tales were exaggerated."

"A pious man, indeed. Have you your horse?"

"I have only what you see. And God, who is always with me."

"Indeed. Well, since you lost your horse, you will fight with me on the morrow. I need a pious man at my side. There is something about you. And you look like you could use a good meal, like the rest of us." He laughed. "Fasting while we are starving. This monk is either the smartest man alive or the most foolish."

"Yes, sir," Malak said.

"Perhaps you will lend me some of your faith. Come find me tonight, and we will break bread together. Tomorrow we may die."

"Thank you, sir."

Malak wanted to be alone. After years of seclusion on the island, where he'd dreamed about laughing and drinking and eating with humans, when confronted by the reality of human contact, he felt wrong. It was more than awkwardness of the social sort, it was a contemptuousness of the soul. Something awful was gathering in the arid air of this place. Evil was a storm that was not below the horizon, but one which was already here, invisible and insidious. Raging and building and about to unleash itself upon men with swords and mothers with infants.

He did not know what it was or how to stop it. He wandered away from the masses, the walls, and people and the lies crushing him. Still, he learned some things which were true.

The people spoke a variety of languages, but of course, this did not matter to Malak. There were Christians who had lived in Antioch side by side with the Muslims, but who had been expelled as the invading army approached. Many Christians were executed. The Franks, as the Muslims called that first wave of first crusaders, were a tattered, diverse, and desperate army. They'd taken Antioch after a siege lasting eight months, only days before when an Antioch commander betrayed his city.

The starving army flooded the city. Thirsty, too, yet not merely for water. It was blood that seemed to slake the thirst, and only for a time.

There was no refuge for Malak. He walked with small, careful steps, and he listened.

Peasants and nobility alike had traveled three thousand miles on a quest to retake Jerusalem from the Turks, and this great city was crucial to obtaining that victory. This city was Antioch.

He wound through the streets and climbed steps on the south of the city to the great wall which encircled Antioch. From this vantage, the city was beautiful, resting in a valley, houses and minarets climbing the slopes around him, and the great citadel on the foothills of Mount Sylpius. He strode along the walls, noting the towers and gates and the depleted defenders. To the north, the tents and dust of the Turkish army lay like a stain upon the land.

He gathered that some of the crusaders were motivated by genuine religious passion, which, in Malak's opinion, was seldom a good motivation for much of anything. There were groups of both knights and peasants who prayed openly and discussed God's providence. Some clung to beads around their necks, others held crosses.

Some looked upward with their eyes closed and their hands held out, and many of the ones that did that appeared to be the bloodiest. Creases in the armor caked in shades of red and brown and evil. Basking in the redemption of their sins and what they had been told was a war for God. The drying blood upon their hands was sanctioned, sanctified, and forgiven. A loathsome exultation in it. Gratitude for the opportunity to kill without consequence, rather than hatred for the need to kill.

Some men looked shattered and lost.

Malak was still working it out, but he'd felt God touch him, and he figured that God didn't want much part in this, whatever this was.

He knew about killing upon demand.

There is necessity, there is war, and there is murder. For the soldier who follows orders, the lines are not the same. The soldier is trained to kill.

The dreams come or they don't for a combat veteran, and it has nothing to do with what was right in the killing squeeze. A farmer is generally no match for a trained and conditioned veteran.

We need heroes who will stand at the gates. The men who battle should not be reviled, but revered. They stand and fall so that we may not kneel.

He also believed that religion and God were nothing alike. Passion for one does not resemble faith in the other. Religion wounds, while God heals. Religion is an invention of men. God is God.

Families huddled together, children running around shirtless and laughing through streets drenched in tragedy. There was a kind of hope in the air at odds with everything Malak could see. Tension, too, the kind which precedes a coming battle. The men sought courage, fighting and shouting, and proving how tough they were, while the women prayed in silence and stared out onto the street.

Yet how much blood have I spilled? If I strive to be God's instrument, then what sort of weapon am I? I play the song of death more often than that of life, and I'm placed wherever I'm placed by Him. What, then, is God? If He does not want blood spilled in His name, then why make me? Why bother?

————

The phrase "Holy War" had not yet made its way into the vernacular of the medieval world, and they were words Malak would never understand. He could recite the entire Bible, and he figured he understood most of it. Back in 1098, the Bible wasn't the Bible, but he still remembered every word he'd ever read. The Gospels, as the modern world would come to know them, and the entire Old Testament.

Malak felt the truth of the stories and the texts, and he'd felt something deeper which lay beyond that, and he'd also had an encounter that destroyed and illuminated him from within. Malak, the itinerant scholar and warrior, knew he had a role to play. He didn't know what that was, and that was part of the problem.

————

That night, he ate with Sir Robert of Flanders at a wooden table laden with fruit and bread. They dined upon goat meat and bread and drank weak wine. The conversation at the table was subdued rather than raucous. Sir Robert struck Malak as a man of faith and conviction, and his retinue of knights appeared more competent and less blood thirsty than some of the others Malak had encountered earlier in the day. Malak listened, keeping to himself, nodding and offering terse replies to questions. Better to speak little and understand more.

"I fear we will never see home again," one knight said. Taller than the rest, long haired and gaunt. "And even if we do, I wonder how we can forget the things we have seen. When I close my eyes, I see blood."

"Perhaps," Sir Robert said, "it will be better if we fall on the field. I have made my peace. Home is a distant dream now, not real. The Saracen army beyond the gates, that is real."

Talk turned to the tension between factions of knights. Count Raymond, Malak gathered, was not well liked by Sir Robert and his men.

"Raymond is greedy and cruel," Sir Robert remarked. "His faith is as false as his tongue and just as corrupt."

After the meal, the men slept on the floor, and Malak fell asleep to the sound of snoring and occasional fits of shouting from men haunted by visions of the past.

Tomorrow, they would ride from the gates to greet the vast enemy army.

CHAPTER TWENTY-SIX
SYMPTOMS OF MADNESS

Now

Malak squinted against brilliant sunlight reflecting from an endless plain of pristine snow, raising his hand to shield his eyes. The air was crisp and clean and still, and there was a sweetness to it, and the sky was that perfect cloudless blue of the morning after a storm.

He stood beside a recently plowed black top road, a snowbank taller than he piled behind him. He hoped he was in the United States. He'd seen places in Siberia, Canada, and the Baltic nations that looked like this.

He took a deep breath, savoring the sharpness in his lungs. A dark speck appeared on the road, cresting a ridge several miles away.

He took stock of his attire, which was often a good clue to where he'd drifted to. He wore jeans, winter boots, a wool sweater, and a lightweight yellow parka. He patted himself down and felt no weapons. No idea where he was, beyond the fact that it was cold and flat. The approaching car grew larger.

He felt it before he heard it.

A deep rumble, a vibration in his bones and in his soul.

A grating sound, the massive doors of fate opening and closing, heralding the loss of billions of lives and civilization itself. The sound of mankind slaughtering itself.

The top layer of fresh snow around him danced a small thing unremarkable under most circumstances. The wind, perhaps. An errant breeze.

Dread and urgency clenched Malak's chest. Smoke and fire bloomed a mile or so away.

The missile rose with ponderous dignity, gathering speed and altitude, a gray plume in its wake. It shrieked upward, and the contrail got smaller, and the rocket was gone, hurtling into space.

Malak counted five missiles climbing. He checked his wrist and was glad in an ironic sort of way that he wore a watch.

He wept. Time had run out for mankind, and was now measured in minutes rather than millennia.

A Minuteman III intercontinental ballistic missile would reach its target within thirty minutes. The retaliatory strikes would be swift. Malak knew that China and Russia deployed submarines with the ability to nuke American cities within ten minutes. Long range bombers would already be aloft, dealing death to millions. Mutually Assured Destruction becoming a self-fulfilling prophecy.

The world was dying.

Each ICBM could carry multiple warheads, though the nuclear summits in the nineties outlawed MIRV systems. How much death was inbound?

The car pulled up beside him, a baby blue Volvo station wagon loaded with kids and suitcases, boxes strapped to the roof.

The driver already had his window down. Bearded and grinning, he leaned out and offered his hand to Malak. A plump blond waved from the passenger seat.

"Welcome to the end of the world," the stranger said. "We've got room. Climb in."

"Thanks," Malak said in English. North Dakota. Maybe Montana. Good. He squeezed into the back seat next to a happy child of five or six and a sullen teenage girl. The car rocketed forward before Malak closed the door.

"Maybe they hit back, maybe they don't. Heck, they might have launched a preemptive attack, and then we'll all burn before we know we're dead."

"Thanks," said Malak. "Really." What do you talk about during the last minutes of civilization? What do you say?"

"What were you doing out here?'

"Just a little lost."

"Well, today is your lucky day."

"Really?" Global nuclear war had an unlucky ring to it.

"We found you, didn't we? I'd say that qualifies." This from the happy blond wife in the passenger seat. Beaming at him. "God is good all the time. The rapture is at hand. Pardon our bad manners. I'm Jolene, and this big lug is Jimbo."

"I'm grateful," Malak said. The five-year-old with blue eyes lit up and offered a fist-bump, and Malak had to smile. The teenager with long hair smirked sideways, rolled her eyes, and looked annoyed with her phone, which, Malak guessed, would soon be a useless relic of the past.

"May I borrow that phone?" Malak said.

"Whatevs," she said.

"Much obliged," Malak said to the surly kid. "You might want to drive a little faster, by the way."

He dialed the number from memory, praying and calculating. The missiles he'd seen launch would be somewhere over northern Canada by now, approaching the Arctic Circle, hurtling through space at speeds exceeding 17,000 miles per hour. If the Russians had launched a first strike, then they may well have targeted these silos. If that was the case, then they were probably all dead already. A Russian SS-18 Satan could carry up to ten multiple independently targetable reentry vehicles (MIRVs). Each of those warheads would carry a payload of 500-700 kilotons. Some of the larger Russian missiles could carry a payload of 20 megatons, unleashing a blast radius of 10 miles.

Kelli answered on the second ring. "Boss?"

"What's the situation?"

"The team made it to the bunker. Three U.S. cities were attacked, Russia is denying responsibility. There's been an exchange in the Middle East. Things are—" her voice devolved into static, and the line went dead.

Malak dialed again, but the phone only beeped angrily at him. He looked out the window, wondering if he would see the flash. His team was safe for now, but that was small solace.

"Where are we?"

"North Dakota. Heading for the Canadian border," Jimbo said. "We left almost a week ago. Honestly, I didn't think we'd make it this far."

"You did well," Malak said. Of course, he'd driven his family smack dab into the middle of one of the worst places in the world to be at the moment.

Malak decided to keep quiet, trying to minimize his intrusion on this family during what would likely be their last time together upon this earth. He wondered what they were thinking about. They seemed at peace. Had they led lives of joy and love? These children never had a chance. Even if by some miracle they lived, their world would never be the same.

He checked his watch again. The Minuteman missiles would be entering the atmosphere, locking onto targets on the other side of the world. What of those children? Those innocents? Death descending from the heavens. *Lord, please spare us.*

The snowbanks flitted by, along with leafless trees,

and the sun continued to shine bright against the deep blue sky. The miles slipped past. Malak patted the young boy on the head. The girl was sleeping or feigning sleep, earbuds on.

Maybe, just maybe, they would make it through the gauntlet.

CHAPTER TWENTY-SEVEN
CRUSADER

Antioch, June 1098

Morning broke to the sound of clinking and scraping and muttered oaths, that ageless music of men preparing for battle. While he'd slept, someone had laid out an array of weapons and clothing for him.

In the dim room filled with knights, he pulled on heavy chain mail, which draped down to mid-thigh over a linen smock. Over the chain mail, he donned a white tunic emblazoned with a red cross. He girded his waist with a woven belt and placed a jeweled dagger into its sheath. He hefted the long sword, unused to its length and weight, and put it back on the floor before examining the other items.

A lance, wooden with a wicked barbed metal spear at the tip, would be his primary weapon on horseback. He lifted this, feeling the balance. He placed a helmet on his head, and it felt wrong and limited his field of vision. He took it off and resolved not to wear it. He lifted the shield, a roughly triangular thing, curved to conform to his body, flat at the top, constructed with metal, leather, and wood, slipping his left forearm into the grips. The shield was surprisingly lightweight and longer than what he'd grown accustomed to as a gladiator.

There were other items along the walls and beside his pallet which he decided not to carry. Maces and flails, crescent shaped axes, and heavy iron war hammers.

Sir Robert tapped Malak on the shoulder. "Stay close,"

he whispered. "We ride with six divisions today. Bohemond is in command and will remain in reserve with 200 knights. Godfrey will hold the center. Raymond rides at the front with his men, and he will have the Holy Lance. If nothing else, it gives the men hope."

In the gray dawn, he followed the men into city streets thronged with soldiers. Tattered peasants wearing rags and wielding clubs rubbed elbows with nobles in glittering armor and colorful standards. He remained with Sir Robert's men, and they went to the stables, where Malak met his horse.

"Gabriel belonged to a friend, a great warrior who fell in battle during the siege," Sir Robert said. "He will serve you well."

Malak patted the magnificent horse on the nose and stroked his white mane. He swung into the saddle, placed his sword in its sheath, and held his lance upright. He rode toward the nearest gate, where knights gathered atop enormous warhorses, stomping their feet in anticipation.

Along the walls, archers took positions. Some held crossbows, while others gripped longbows, quivers at their backs. Barrels of arrows lined the walls. The smell of hot tar mingled with sweat and fear and lingering death.

Some men banged swords against shields, others pounded spears onto the street, and the air hummed with fervor and energy.

Trumpets sounded, and the gates opened.

The cavalry surged ahead into the morning sun. Malak marveled at the fluid strength of the beast beneath him and found himself succumbing to a sort of euphoria. Banners of red and yellow cracked in the wind, and the crusader army streamed from the gates of Antioch. Godfrey's men were some distance to his left.

High in the saddle, his shield and reins in his left hand,

and his lance held in his right hand, Malak trotted at first, then galloped, surging with the wind in his face and a gathering strength in his soul, his heart hammering.

The Turkish army waited less than a mile away, a long dark line of infantry armed with spears. Great siege engines rose from the ranks. As Malak closed the gap, enemy cavalry wheeled from his right flank, coming hard. Behind the enemy infantry, archers unleashed a volley thick enough to darken the sky.

Arrows fell among the men with a sound like a strong wind through a still forest. Horses screamed, a terrible agonized sound, somehow worse than that of the dying soldiers, perhaps because the horses were innocent, and blood flowed from man and beast alike.

The knight directly in front of Malak slumped in his saddle and toppled to the ground, a feathered shaft protruding from his eye socket, his face a rictus of pain.

Sir Robert changed course and charged directly into the approaching enemy cavalry. Arrows continued to rain, and Malak lowered his lance.

The oncoming Turks wore conical helmets and held smaller, round shields. Malak sought his first target, fighters on the field drawn by death and an unspoken agreement that one of them would soon fall.

The clash of spear upon shield rang out on the valley floor all along the line as the two armies crashed into one another, and there was a kind of flow to it, that river of death, that tide of destruction, with pockets of men separated and surrounded on both sides. Chaos swirled and raged on the field of battle.

Malak lowered his lance, imitating the men around him, bracing for impact. He guided the horse with his knees now, and Gabriel responded to a slight shift in Malak's weight, almost eager, it seemed, to join the fray.

The bearded Turk shouted, his spear leveled at Malak's chest, low in the saddle and leaning forward, and pounding at full speed. Malak pivoted astride the saddle and tensed his shoulder, anticipating the heavy blow to his shield. The impact rocked him where he sat, but his arm was strong and his back was ready, and his right hand was already in motion.

Before the Turk had time to react, Malak's lance flashed across the space between them, the tip of the spear finding the soft spot in the throat, punching through flesh and bone with the momentum of the horse behind it, tearing the man from his horse, and for a moment he dangled half way down the length of Malak's spear, writhing, feet bouncing on the ground and gouts of blood spraying the air and flowing onto his chest.

Malak lifted the man higher with inhuman strength and yanked savagely, ripping the spear out, tearing the Turk's head almost completely off, the spine shattered and bits of sinew and viscera wet and red.

Malak pushed the horse ahead and lanced another man through the back. Enemy infantry ran among the knights, slashing with swords. Arrows chunked into Malak's shield, and he felt a burning sensation on his neck, and then the warmth of his own blood.

Malak found himself separated from his fellow knights, cut off among enemy foot soldiers. He leaped from his horse and drew his sword.

Shouting and screaming and the clang of metal upon metal became one noise, a symphony of war, a cacophony of death and destruction. The trampled earth was already littered with bodies, and Malak was aware of birds circling high in the sky, waiting out the battle for the time they could swoop down and gorge upon the living and the dead.

The attackers thrust angry blades at his chest, and Malak used his shield as a bludgeon, taking the blows and striking back with all his strength, pummeling two enemies at once with his left arm, smashing them in the face with enough force to shatter their necks.

The long sword in his right hand came alive and blurred, severing a man's arm at the elbow with a down stroke, his right foot dancing forward, striking again with the shield, then following through with a thrust to the belly of the man, the tip of the sword twisting and skewering, wrenching the crimson blade back out.

Malak laid waste to the Turks around him, spinning, parrying, slashing, and stabbing with maniacal ferocity. Torn bodies lay at his feet, and he hacked into the retreating mass of men, implacable and savage, and there was no mercy in him, no fear, only death.

His foes backed away, eyes white, nostrils flaring, desperation and terror and something akin to awe on their faces, even as Malak cut them down.

From the ground, he could not see where the rest of Sir Robert's knights had gone. Horses and banners flashed through brief gaps in the hand-to-hand fighting, only to be swallowed by the shifting lines. Wounded men crawled and moaned, bleeding onto the trampled, stained earth. Malak twisted his ankle on a mangled man and fell to one knee.

A few Turks lunged at him, emboldened by his momentary vulnerability, and they seized the opportunity with screaming and blades slicing the air.

Malak ducked below the top of his shield while one sword arced close enough to ruffle the hair on the top of his head, and two more smashed into the front of his shield, the vibration sending a shock through his left arm.

"Kill the devil," one of them roared.

"Die!" screamed another.

"Allarraagh!" Howled a third when Malak's blade cut into his testicles and then through his abdomen, cold metal slicing warm flesh, exiting beneath the rib cage and splitting the man in two. Malak surged to his feet, smashed with the shield, and propelled his body like a battering ram into the attackers. They fell onto their backs, swords forgotten and arms flung upward to protect themselves from the inevitable killing blows, which Malak delivered with practiced and swift efficiency.

There came an odd sort of lull in the fighting around him, as the killing tide swept onward and the Turks fell back. Behind, Turkish infantry ran his way, many without weapons. They streamed past, giving him a wide berth in the way of a river around a rock.

He stood, an island in the sea of slaughter, chest heaving, blade slick and dripping, his previously white tunic soaked in blood. The wound on the back of his neck was sticky and tingled.

He felt a gentle nudge and turned to see Gabriel, that beautiful white horse, standing patiently at his shoulder. Malak swung into the saddle and surveyed the field. Behind him, the city walls remained unmolested, and the crusader infantry pressed into what was left of the ragged lines of Turkish foot soldiers. Ahead, fighting continued in earnest. Malak spotted Sir Robert's banner off to the right and urged Gabriel into a knot of enemies. Malak cut downward with the long sword, leaving broken men in his wake.

Robert was in trouble, and Malak watched as Sir Robert's stout horse was cut from beneath him, enemies swarming and overwhelming him, a coordinated counterattack gaining success and momentum.

Malak was close enough to see the fatigue and resolve

in Robert's eyes when the glory descended, that wondrous sensation of unstoppable strength and certainty. It was the same moment he felt the itching, crawling presence of a demon.

For the first time in his existence, he was ready.

Burning, he jumped from the horse and stood beside Robert while unsuspecting Turks flung themselves into his path. They died with unleashed screams on their lips and shocked agony on their faces before a wrath terrible and unyielding. Bodies erupted into flames before they swayed and teetered and toppled, missing heads or limbs.

Malak locked eyes with Sir Robert for a moment, clutching rosary beads in his left hand and an exhausted blade in his right.

Malak grinned at the knight. Sir Robert crossed himself.

"God is with us," Sir Robert panted. "Angels are at our back."

"There are no angels here," Malak said.

The demon came strong and fast, running for Sir Robert while the oncoming Turks parted before his advance, making the way for a champion. It hurtled into the clearing of men and stopped short ten paces in front of Malak and Sir Robert. It looked like any other man on the field. Swarthy, bloody, and mean, emanating power and cruelty in a way men did not.

Malak spoke words of power while he engaged his foe with sword and dagger, and the earth trembled beneath his feet when their blades clashed.

Arrogance yielded to doubt and fear on the demon's face when Malak pressed his attack.

"What are you doing?" the demon huffed, parrying and diving and coming up light on its feet.

Malak darted ahead, dagger in his left hand, sword

weaving in his right, speaking ancient words. The light around him was strong now, blue and hot like a brilliant star, his faith a shield. Beating the enemy back and into submission.

"You are a fool," it said, launching a blistering counterattack. Lunging and smashing. "You can't win. Why fight?"

Malak fought back with grim focus and relentless fury.

The words were almost finished, though this time Malak was certain he did not need them, for there was an external power flowing through his arm. The demon fought like…a demon. Quick and deceptive and mocking and urgent. Malak swatted his foe's sword aside with a powerful downward blow, stepped close, and buried the jeweled dagger into the demon's neck. The demon sprawled onto its back, and Malak kicked the sword from its hand.

"Traitor," it frothed, barely a whisper.

"No," said Malak, before his blade swept through the demon's neck.

The fading glory was replaced by weariness, a heavy burden of guilt, and a certain shame. He felt outside himself, a passive observer, while the battle washed over him. The cries and shouts and song of steel on steel seemed muffled and far away. Sir Robert was shouting something into Malak's face.

The horse was beside him then, and Malak climbed into Gabriel's saddle, carried back to Antioch, where an old man removed an arrow from Malak's shoulder and tended to a deep gash on his neck, the barber muttering to himself the whole time.

"Rest," said the wisp of a man. "You're in God's hands now."

The Crusades were like that. Malak slept, but he didn't quite die.

CHAPTER TWENTY-EIGHT
ARMAGEDDON BEGINS

Now

For a time, it seemed that the blue Volvo was a ship in a sea of white, thousands of miles removed from the rest of humanity. They had yet to see another car. When Jimbo tried to turn on the radio, all he got was static. Nobody had a working phone.

The family was strangely serene. Jimbo and his wife sang songs, and the car kept cresting the low snow covered hills. "We should be getting close to the next town," he said. "We'll get some fuel if we can." Both of them continually looked up and out the windows. Maybe looking for incoming bombs, or mushroom clouds, or perhaps looking for Jesus to come down in a blaze of trumpets and glory. Malak did not ask.

A dull thunder pursued them from behind, growing in volume. Malak turned his head with cold dread in him.

A pair of sleek black helicopters swept low on the road to the south of them, coming fast and sending up swirling snow with their rotor wash. They circled the car and landed a quarter mile ahead, while Jimbo continued forward.

"Better stop here," Malak advised. "No matter what happens, get your family as far to the north as you can, okay? Wait until I'm gone."

"Who are you?" Jimbo said.

"Let's just say I'm not someone you want around. How long has your boy been sick?"

Jimbo's eyes widened. The little kid grinned at Malak

with big, innocent baby blues.

"We found out last year," Jimbo said, stuttering. "We don't talk about it. No need. Not now, especially. How did you…"

Malak put his hand on the little boy's forehead and took the cancer from him, a tumor that had wrapped around the back of the child's brain.

He opened the door and stepped into the icy air. "Godspeed," he said, thumping on the roof of the idling vehicle.

He walked to greet the men who stepped from the birds in the middle of the road. Those were some good people, he thought. These up ahead won't be. Maybe CIA, though Malak found it hard to believe the government could have been that efficient in tracking him.

As he got closer, he could see that the men were armed with submachine guns.

If they'd wanted him dead, they would have killed him already. They clearly had something else in mind. Malak's biggest concern at the moment was for the family behind him. There was no telling what these guys wanted or what they were capable of. Malak put his hands on top of his head and came to a halt. The rotors were still spinning, and the wind was ice on his bare cheeks.

A man in fatigues hopped from the nearest helicopter. Malak recognized John, the spook who'd started interrogating him after the kerfuffle in Saudi Arabia.

John waved to Malak and turned heel, walking away from the helicopters into the fields, presumably so that they could talk.

"You're a hard man to find," John shouted when Malak caught up to him. The snow was up to his knees.

"Apparently not as hard as I'd hoped," Malak said.

"Did you mean it?"

"What?"

"Did you mean it when you said you were on our side?"

"You know the answer, I think, or you wouldn't be here. Yes." Malak chuckled. "Well, let me qualify that. Probably, yes. That depends on which side you're really on."

"The United States of America. That side."

"Usually, that's the side I've been on," Malak said, unable to resist. John was stone faced. Maybe this wasn't the best time to be a smart ass, with the world coming to an end. Still, this guy had put Malak through some pain, so he'd have to work for it, at least a little bit.

"I'm a citizen, and a combat veteran," Malak said. "You probably wouldn't believe my service record if you could see the whole thing."

"You might be surprised by what I would and would not believe. I'd like you to come with me," John said. "Your country needs you."

Malak wanted to tell John that in this war, the lines of good and evil had already been drawn and that they weren't confined to nations. That he'd lost two toes from frostbite at Valley Forge and an arm at Bull Run, a friend on the Trail of Tears, and something worse at Mei Lay.

"Brief me on the bird," he said instead. "I'll want to work with my team."

"That's already handled," John said.

———

As bad as things were, it could have been worse. Malak culled through an intelligence summary John provided on an iPad, complete with diagrams of fallout patterns, fleet movements, and real-time satellite photos of Russian and Chinese missile silos.

The photos of New York, LA, and Washington, D.C. left Malak with a hollow feeling. Each city had been struck by a nuclear weapon, apparently by Russian missiles. The fires still raged. Millions of lives were already lost. Most of Congress was dead, killed during an emergency session. The President was dead. The Vice President and Secretary of State were still alive, somewhere.

Malak asked John a few questions over the headsets they both wore while the helicopter flew toward an undisclosed location somewhere in the Rocky Mountains. John let Malak read.

The world was burning, as war engulfed the planet. India and Pakistan were engaged in a fierce aerial battle, and both nations were poised to launch nuclear weapons at population centers along with hard military targets.

Iran attacked Israel. The Saudis were staying out of the fight, despite desperate pleas from the United States.

China was in the process of making a land grab in the South China Sea, taking over atolls in international waters and menacing the Philippines and Japan. Chinese warships menaced Japan and the Strait of Taiwan.

North Korea invaded South Korea, and the DMZ was a shattered moonscape. The USS Ronald Regan provided air cover and bombarded the Korean mainland with cruise missiles. U.S. fighter jets engaged Chinese and North Korean aircraft.

The next hours and weeks would determine the fate of the world. If clear heads prevailed, there was still a chance to avert a global nuclear war.

Malak wanted to believe in mankind, but his faith was betrayed and misplaced. He had lived and died and fought and mourned. The selfish nature of man never changed. Rather than swords and spears, men now claimed the power of the atom, wielding destruction in a flash and the push of a button with an ease and dissonance which the thrust and twist of the blade could never know. Disconnected from reality. For money, vice, power, or love, there is murder, and it's always wrong.

Perhaps that was the problem with men from the beginning. The distance of a bullet, a bomb, or a drone made life easier for those who didn't have to do the killing. Phrases like "collateral damage" and "strategic objectives" replaced fact and morality and shattered bodies, and the scale grew larger until men didn't care anymore about what the words really meant.

CHAPTER TWENTY-NINE
HOLY WAR

Jerusalem 1099

The crusaders, who for the most part called themselves pilgrims, were not all bad, nor were they all good; they were men. Some were prone to chivalry, heroism, and kindness. Too many, though, were led by evil. When Jerusalem fell and the army streamed through the broken city, the worst in mankind boiled to the surface.

In the days following the battle of Antioch, Malak almost walked away from the conflict. Later, he wished he had. He was swayed by the tales of atrocity committed against Christians by the Muslims. Blood begat blood, an anguish which multiplied and spread, receding at times while it hid and lingered in dark places, only to seep into the world again.

The end of the world began with a spear, continued by the sword, and concluded in a blinding flash. Jerusalem, a city revered for its Godliness, killing the world with the lack of it.

It was only much later that Malak reflected upon this truth, when he saw not only how destructive the clash of three religions had been, but also when he could see the way his own actions had reverberated throughout history.

For a year, Malak lived in Antioch among Sir Robert's knights. The various nobles bickered and positioned themselves for greater wealth and power. Godfrey, whom Malak met more than once, struck him as a decent man, while some of the others in that game of thrones were blatantly self-serving and loathsome.

Malak roamed the streets and alleyways at night, listening, learning, and sometimes teaching. He gave bread to the beggars and healed leprous children, his face hidden beneath a cowl, anonymous and shrouded in shadow.

He spent a good deal of time with some of the remaining Jews at the synagogue. They tolerated his presence at first, having little choice because of his stature, yet a few of them became men he called friends. His ability to recite the Tanakh afforded him a certain grudging respect from even the most zealous and embittered.

David, an old man with a tangled gray beard and merry eyes, was Malak's favorite person in the city. He spoke with a voice hardly more than a whisper, yet his words were infused with the kind of gentle truth and light that compels men to lean close and grow quiet to hear.

"Alone, a man has no chance. He is nothing. Why, then, do we fight?"

"We fight because we must," said a fervent young man. "And we are never alone, for God is always with us. Does God not command that we defend our beliefs?"

"Are we not men?"

"We are *chosen* men."

"What do *you* choose?"

"I choose to fight."

"Often the heaviest bonds are those we place upon ourselves. A man who yearns for battle has lost the war that matters."

"Maybe," Malak interjected, "but there are times when a fight is needed, whether it's wanted or not."

"True," David whispered. "But wanting leads to having."

"Why do we not have peace then? God is holy and sometimes calls us to war."

"Exactly," the Rabbi said. "A holy war is one we wage upon ourselves; crusade, Jihad, or whatever it's called. In the end, it's nothing more than collective suicide and murder of tomorrow. There is nothing holy about a holy war."

One year later, the old man David was dead, and Malak was storming the walls of Jerusalem.

Holy war, Malak decided, is a blood sacrifice upon an altar forged by man in the name of a weeping God. *We kill ourselves with intolerance. We destroy our future through ignorance and the justification of violence, which spawns in closed spaces where light and truth fight and fail to penetrate the murk and shadow. Minds, souls, and nations, succumbing to hate. The hungry dark consumes fact and hate with the constricting coils of self-righteousness, religious certainty, and rivers of cascading consequences which run red through millennia.*

He came to believe that holy war is one we wage upon ourselves; crusade, jihad, or whatever it's called. It's nothing more than collective suicide and the murder of tomorrow. There is nothing holy about a "holy war."

———

The crusader army arrived at the walls of Jerusalem on a hot day in July. Malak witnessed men fall to their knees, overcome with joy at the sight of the holy city. Their quest was almost finished, and laying eyes upon this land was something they'd dreamed about for many years.

Malak remembered the last time he had been here; the screams of old friends seemed to echo from the walls.

The trees had been cut down by the Muslim defenders in order to deprive the Franks of wood to build siege engines. The land itself was scarred, baking in the sun with ripples of heat rising from the rocky ground, drained of a certain color, as if nature retreated into itself here, the full spectrum lost in clear lines of black and white. The walls of the city were tall and strong and reflected the sun.

Malak wandered. Rumors spread about his deeds in the battle of Antioch, and he decided to lose his armor and name and take the anonymous mantle of a foot soldier. He wore a light leather vest, carried an old, badly balanced sword, and a dagger. He decided that when the battle began, he would find better weapons on the ground.

He talked to Christians who had been living in Jerusalem before the army arrived at the gates. They were not happy, being displaced, expelled from the city they called home. Many were angry with Malak and told him to walk away. Some of them confirmed that the Caliphate was brutal toward Christians within the city walls, and he heard tales of beheadings and acts of rape.

The Europeans built siege towers from a fleet of resupply ships, and the men rejoiced. It was a miracle, they said. The towers took shape, hulking behemoths with ramps that would drop down when the tower was close enough to the wall.

Malak stood beneath one of the towers while the builders were finishing it, gazing up at it. It was impressive, a marvel of human ingenuity.

"Stinks, doesn't it?" said a man with a hammer.

"Yes. Why is that?"

"Vinegar. The animal hides are soaked in vinegar. That way, when they shoot flaming arrows from the walls, this thing won't burn. That's what they say, anyway."

"Ever built one of these before?"

"No. I'm just a carpenter." He laughed. Malak noted that the man used the word *nahgahr* to describe his profession, a Hebrew word. He looked exhausted, sweat running down his face, his beard matted and wild.

"I do what must be done." He pointed at the men up

on scaffolding above them. "You know how it is. I'd rather build something *beautiful*."

"Well, thanks," Malak said, hesitating. "I don't want to get you into trouble."

"It's almost time for a break," the man said. At that moment, there were shouts from the siege tower. "See? Would you break bread with me?"

"Certainly," Malak replied. They sat in the shade beneath the tower.

"I don't have much," Malak said. "Take what you like."

"Thank you, brother."

"Where are you from?"

"I was born not too far from here," the man said. His eyes were not tired, and there was a shy sort of smile about the man that Malak instantly liked.

"What is your name?" the man said.

"I am Malak. I was born here, too, I suppose."

"Ah. Yes," he said, smiling still. Nodding his head as though Malak had said something deeply profound. He waved toward the city walls, shimmering behind walls of heat, wavering over the torched land.

"Malak, what do you make of this war? Your name means 'messenger,' so do you have a message? What might it be?"

"I, too, do what I must. I'm not fond of war. If I have a message, I don't know what it is. Run, maybe. Yes. That would be it. Death is never far behind me and always in front."

"Yet you choose to fight?"

"There are certain things you don't know," Malak said, handing him half of a loaf of bread, "and many things I don't either. What can we do?"

"You wear a sword."

"Yes."

"I hold a hammer and a piece of bread."

"Right. Though now you're not holding a hammer. You're eating faster than a monk after a seven day fast."

"You're right about that." The man laughed heartily and sighed. "At some point, though, perhaps it will be the other way around. Men are foolish."

"Sure. There are some things worth fighting for."

"Yes, there are, Malak. But most things are not worth fighting for. Love is—"

"Wait a minute," Malak interjected. "Don't tell me you've been listening to these knights talk about chivalry. They're nuts."

A sad smile. "Love is your best defense and your greatest weapon. It is the reason you and I exist. Sometimes people forget. If they remembered, they wouldn't need swords. There is a way, a truth, and a light where love triumphs. Where there are no swords. Because there is no need."

"If you knew what I know, I don't think you'd say that," Malak said, eating his last bite of dry bread, the aftertaste of olive oil still on it.

"In fact," Malak said through a mouthful, "if you'd met some of the bastards I have, or seen the evil I have seen, I'm certain you wouldn't wax poetic like that. No. The way is bloody and always has been."

"You are a great warrior, and I am but a carpenter," the man said. "I am glad that we have a moment today; you have a good heart. You fight, and sometimes you kill. That is a kind of destruction, would you not say? When you take a man's future? You have destroyed a man, have you not?"

"Yes," Malak grunted. Glad, now that he was finished with this meal. "More times than I'd care to admit. I wish I could be something else."

"Why do you not do it, then?"

"There's a lack of choice involved, trust me."

"Why?"

"I don't understand the question. I can't do anything else. When I try to do something different, I end up with a blade in my hand. There is no 'why.' It is.

"Love, regardless. Never is it too late to become the man you were meant to be. I must go back to work. You are a better soul than you think, Malak. You can choose to create rather than destroy. Trust me."

"Thanks," Malak said. He pushed himself to his feet and surveyed the land, threadbare soldiers arrayed like ants around the city, the tents flapping in the gentle breeze, the great walls, and the cloudless sky. Archers on the ramparts, little black dots against the glare of the walls and hills of the city beyond. Drifting to the fight at hand.

The man shuffled off into a crowd of incoming workers, an angry noble behind them shouting and swearing and sweating.

"Wait," Malak said.

The man turned, some twenty paces away, tired soldiers and workers stepping between them. The man smiled again.

"What is your name?"

The man cocked his head and grinned, setting his hammer down on a piece of wood. "Those who know me call me Yeshua."

"Wait!" Malak exclaimed. But the man was gone, disappeared into the crowd of dusty workers, and although he spent time looking for him, Malak did not see him again for a long time.

The battle began the next day.

CHAPTER THIRTY
THE PRESIDENT

Now

The Rocky Mountains thrust upward from snow-covered plains, ragged and beautiful, and through the helicopter cockpit, Malak admired the view. Many of the peaks lay cloaked in low gray clouds, and at times the sun hit the snow just right so that it seemed to be illuminated from within.

Malak didn't trust John. He couldn't figure out exactly what the man wanted from him, and the vague responses to his questions filled him with a sense of unease. He was concerned about his team, though, and this compelled him to go along for the ride. He'd learn the truth soon enough. He needed intelligence, and that was something else that John could provide.

"One of the advantages of a vast bureaucracy within the military-industrial complex," John said over the headset, "is that the left hand usually doesn't know what the right hand is doing. That can be a blessing and a curse."

"So?"

"So after our previous encounter, I got curious. You wouldn't believe what the new NSA quantum super-computer in Utah can do now."

"All right." He remembered Kelli talking about the computer with a mixture of awe and revulsion.

"The bottom line is this. I know what you are. And I know what *he* is, too. I don't have much of a budget, but what I do have is some friends in very high places. I've shown them the evidence, and they have been willing to give me a pretty long leash. Now that things are completely screwed up, they're willing to try anything."

"I don't follow." Malak wondered who *they* were.

"I set certain search parameters. This thing is as close to AI as it gets. Hell, maybe it *is,* and we don't know it yet. Anyway, it's much more than a simple code-breaker. What it does best is find patterns. It decided you were of particular interest. You and our mutual friend."

"Who might that be?"

"You know. No need to play dumb. After the incident at Dugway, the computer went into overdrive. Very fascinating stuff. I've got pictures dating back to 1911 with you in them. Him, too. I wonder how old you *really* are. The thing is, I know you're not human. You're an extra-terrestrial entity, maybe inter-dimensional, and I'm guessing that there are more of you. For whatever reason, you've been on our side, while the other guy has been trying to destroy the earth."

"I see."

John tapped an icon on the iPad, and a row of grainy black and white pictures popped onto the screen. He tapped the screen twice, and the pictures resolved and zoomed in.

"The Western Front, World War I. That's you in a trench smoking a cigarette. Normandy, right there on the beach. You again."

"Hmm."

"The computer looked for anomalies, lo and behold, at certain times, I find an aberrant electro-magnetic pulse that shows up in places you have been when there is violence. The computers, like I said, they're amazing, pulled satellite and aircraft surveillance data going back to the sixties. Vietnam. Cuba. The Soviet Union and East Germany. The Middle East, obviously."

"Let's say for the moment that you're on the right track," Malak said. "What do you want me to do?"

"I want you to stop this bastard, and I want to help you."

"How do we do that?"

"I've been looking for you, when he was the real enemy the whole time. You are the key to stopping him, I'm pretty sure. I can help you find him."

"Then what?"

"Then you do what you do. Take him out. Put him down. I don't know. You won't face him alone. Hell, we'll drop a nuke on his head if that's what it takes. Though something tells me even that wouldn't be enough. You tell me. How do we stop him? What are you?"

"You're not so far from the truth," Malak replied. "Unfortunately, I don't know how to stop him. He's intent on killing the world, you are right about that. He doesn't have to do much, though. Men do the work for him."

"We know you've been looking for him, though," John said. "Your hacker woman, Kelli, filled me in. Amazing lady, by the way. Smart as a whip. I've let her play with our computer. She's like an eighteen-year-old kid in a Ferrari. Whooosh!"

"Mostly, he finds me," Malak admitted. "He is stronger than I am. Much stronger. I want to help, but I'm afraid you will be greatly disappointed. Reports of my heroism tend to be exaggerated."

The bird dipped toward a rock face, bucking and shaking in the turbulence. Gray doors slid open, revealing a black cavern with blinking lights on the ground. The helicopter slowed and slipped into the cave. Malak smirked, finding this to be something of a cliché, the black-ops-site concealed within a mountain. It was real.

His team stood from their seats at an oblong conference table in a small room under the mountain. Kelli beamed at him, looking younger and more vibrant than she had in decades. Tiny Tim grinned while Syed offered a wan smile. Ben and Vladimir remained characteristically stoic and stone faced.

"Good to see you, boss," Kelli said.

"I'm relieved you are all safe," Malak said. "So. It seems we have our work cut out for us. John has filled me in, at least in broad strokes."

"And let me say," John cut in, "that this team you have assembled is top-notch. A real asset to the United States. Your country will reward you for your service."

Kelli rolled her eyes and sat back down. Vladimir's lips curled into a thin smile. Syed winced. Malak felt uncomfortable and claustrophobic. He didn't like being in a cave, and he didn't trust John, or the United States government, for that matter. He had plenty of reasons not to.

"We have the opportunity to change the course of history," John said. "To defeat perhaps mankind's biggest adversary once and for all. You are the tip of the spear."

"So, what," Kelli laughed. "We're like the Avengers? Are you kidding me? You're a clown, and I wish you knew what you were doing. Jesus. Worse than a clown. You whisk us away to your secret base, inside a mountain no less. What's next? Super Suits? Are you going to give us powers?"

"Kelli," Malak said through a smile, "give him a chance. This is weird, yeah. Maybe he's on the right side."

Long dark hair in a tangle and pale elbows perched on the table, Kelli rolled her eyes and sighed.

"So," Vladimir said, "maybe it's just me, but we see Kelli walking around after years of being in a wheelchair.

These are strange times, and we keep odd company. Perhaps what we have known in our hearts is confirmed. This is not a bad thing or a good thing. It is. So, now we deal with it."

"Look," John said. "I understand. I get it. Realize I'm on your side, and so is the United States of America. I can't stress that enough. Malak, you know how important that is, what that means. Tell them."

"You're better off with the goofy suits," Malak said. "I'm not fighting for the U.S., but I'll fight for *us*."

"That's the same thing," John said.

Malak folded his hands on the table and smiled and nodded his head.

He wanted to explain that fighting for an ideal isn't the same as fighting for something real. He wished that he could make this man understand the difference between fairness and law, religion and truth, might and right. But John was a *true believer*, a patriot, and Malak saw this and knew his words would be wasted.

His words would not convince John with a long and vivid discussion about starving in Valley Forge, or fighting at Antietam, the whole damn country of Belgium (twice), North Korea, Viet Nam, Iraq, Afghanistan, Pakistan, France, Germany, Somalia, Lebanon, Syria, and Yorktown. All for the United States. John couldn't have known what that was like, what sacrifices lay in the history he touted so easily, and that ignorance combined with belief made Malak cringe.

Ignorance, combined with belief, is how the world ends, Malak thought.

The new President of the United States walked into the room.

———

The leader of the free world was short and southern and reeked of politician, and Malak shrunk inside when he met that man's eyes. They were familiar, narrow, and false.

"Howdy," said the President.

Everyone in the room stood up, including a reluctant Malak.

"Thank you for helping the United States. A grateful people applaud you." He nodded and smiled, and his second chin grinned with him.

The man was of middle height, dripping with surly falsehood. Narrow-lipped and dark-haired in a grey suit adorned by the obligatory red power-tie and American flag pin, he stood at the head of the table.

"So," said the President, "You are my go-team. Is that right?" He grinned, and Malak wanted to punch the greasy bastard just because.

"I understand we have something of a celebrity in our company; someone who has *seen* some things. Good. We are glad you're on our side. Let me just say that it's a pleasure to meet you, Mr. Malak."

The President reached his hand across the table, and Malak took it. Took the nausea that rocked him, and still managed to grin back.

"Mr. President, it's an honor," Malak lied.

"I hear you've got some stories to tell," the President said, "but what we're most concerned about is the ones you've got left to write. I believe you are the key to the future. Does that sound about correct to you, or am I missing something?"

"I'd say we've all missed a great deal, sir."

"Don't bullshit me. You're supposed to be some kind of angel. I'm from Texas, and we don't buy into bullshit."

"Yes, sir." *How many times have I said that?*

"So here's the thing," said the President. "You aren't what I thought you'd be, so you probably ain't what you claim to be, and I'm good with that. My advisors made me come here because they know me. They know my beliefs. They get the truth. Show me a miracle. Don't disappoint me."

"What?"

"I read the briefing, and I want to believe. Let's cut to the chase. Show me. Now. Otherwise, you're just another charlatan."

Is he that foolish? Yes. Yes, he is.

"Mr. President," Malak said, trying to sound diplomatic and grave, "do you believe in God?"

"Well, of course I do. He's a whole lot smarter than me and you. He decided long ago that the United States would be the greatest country on earth."

"Did he?"

Anger flashed across the President's face. "Don't you know history or read your Bible? It's all there. Those who condemn Israel are doomed. Read the Old Testament. Don't mess with God."

Malak thought about Jerusalem and smiled, rather than ripping out that man's throat with his bare hands. He found the President to be nearly as repugnant as a demon and recognized that the man wielded unthinkable power.

"Rapture is coming, and America should be at the forefront," said the President.

CHAPTER THIRTY-ONE
THE CARAVAN

Jerusalem, 1099

The siege was short and the attack brutal. Catapults hurled great rocks into the city and against the ramparts. Muslim archers rained fiery arrows from the walls down upon the attacking army.

Thirsty and hot, the men on both sides of the walls dealt death while priests prayed.

Siege engines lumbered across rocky ground, pushed and pulled by sweating soldiers. One of the towers became hopelessly stuck in a ditch, but on the eastern wall, where Malak fought, Duke Godfrey's knights ascended the walls. The crusaders streamed into the city.

Malak followed behind knights and foot soldiers, joining the fray, slashing and hacking, often in tight quarters where the men were bunched together, sweat and blood and fear heavy on the air, and the stink of hot tar and smoke hanging over the city. The smell of war.

Screams of rage and pain mingled with the clash of steel and the roar of thousands fighting and dying. There was a certain sadistic glee in some of the men, a maniacal bloodlust and adrenaline-driven quest for killing, teeth bared like wild dogs, blades dripping, and armor speckled with red.

Malak was one of them.

Knots of defenders fought with brave vigor, firing arrows from rooftops and windows, halting the attackers for a time in streets and close alleys. The crusaders came like a terrible tide, pushing forward, sweeping over the Muslims and trampling corpses.

Near the Temple Mount, fighting was fierce and mean. Blood soaked the streets, thick enough that sometimes it splashed onto Malak's calves, a destruction terrible and tragic.

Malak watched a mother holding a lifeless child cut down from behind.

A father armed only with a shovel battled with three men while his woman cradled an infant and cowered behind him in a doorway. A knight hacked the man's neck, and Malak stepped toward the woman wanting to help, but then she was pierced and bleeding and lying on her back, and he couldn't save her.

Out of his head, Malak shoved fellow Crusaders from his path and attacked those three knights. He killed them without speaking, swift and deadly. Their heads rolled on the ground, lifeless eyes shocked and open, betrayed by one of their own.

Malak could not abide the slaughter, yet slaughter was his.

He fought against both Muslims and Christians, then switching sides to defend the innocent. An arrow pierced his left thigh, and Malak snapped the shaft just above the meat, clenching his eyes at the pain, hands sticky and red.

He continued to fight, losing blood and heart. When night fell, the fires in the city produced a sickly orange glow against the sky, and the smoke obscured the stars.

Morning came gray and cruel, and the Crusaders built vast pyres of bodies outside the city walls, pyramids of the dead, some almost as tall as the city walls, pitch dumped upon them. There were too many to comprehend.

When the torches lit the pyres and the oily stench of burning flesh snaked through the air, Malak gagged and strode away from the city, vowing never to return.

He did not have a particular destination in mind, only knowing that he had to get away. He left his weapons behind him at the Eastern Gate and trudged in that direction.

———

He was dozing in his saddle, the creak of leather and familiar scent of camel and horse and the blazing summer sun lulling him into a torpid haze. He no longer noticed the incessant flies or bickering shouts of the family plodding along behind him. The world seemed to be a single color, a combination of sight and smell and certain lassitude, as each day bled into the next sunrise. Sand, more sand, and constant thirst.

He felt her before he saw her. A quickening, a breathless kind of excitement. He knew. Felt lightning in his soul, there on that dusty sun-baked road a thousand miles beyond Jerusalem. He'd been walking and riding for six months, numb and tired, a crusader without a crusade. Though he'd been wounded and crushed, killed and stabbed, those hurts could not have prepared him for the anguish and pain *she* would inflict. He had been physically broken before, but he'd never experienced anything that compared to the shattered agony she left him with, a jagged, relentlessly ferocious dagger twisting in his heart that pursued him across the gulf of life and death. There was no way to outrun it, even through centuries.

Perhaps he was created to love; the loss of it killed him more than once. It was a betrayal and a lasting hurt he never truly got over, and even God himself did not fill the void she'd left in him. He was a killer, though. There was always that. And he hated it.

There was no way to know how it would turn out back then, and looking back on it later, at least on sunny days,

Malak would tell himself he'd do it all again anyway, that the pleasure was worth the pain. Most days.

Then she was close, piercing the day. Jolting him erect in his saddle in the way of danger close, but not quite, for the sensation was inviting and seductive and alarming at the same time.

She drew near from the east, and the dust cloud from her caravan bloomed along with that soaring feeling in his chest and the certainty that something profound and beautiful was on the way, inevitable, destined, irrefutable. True.

Some things are true only for a time, doomed to become lies. Love that cuts away pieces of your soul can feel like that, and later cause doubt about whether it was real in the first place.

The truth is that she did not love him the way he loved her. For a while, she did, and that's what made it so hard for those years afterwards.

He wanted to keep believing it and invented ways to make it true in his own mind. They were good together, shared what humans would consider to be a beautiful, long life at one another's side. They grew, learned things together that they could have known no other way.

She was the love of his life, and her soul was wrapped around his own. There was a deep peace in those years of sunshine and flowers, basking in the glow of affection and warm touch, and also the hunger in places he did not know existed, a need only she could satisfy. A need he never felt with anyone else on earth through the centuries.

Love wrecks men and history, someone said to him a thousand years later. If he'd known how it would end, it wouldn't have mattered.

The caravan he traveled with halted at a muddy oasis to water the animals. Low shrubs and a pathetic palm tree clung to the edges of the shallow hole. Malak wondered how many people had come this way, what stories lived here.

She grew close, that singing feeling in his chest urgent now.

A colorful group of weary travelers approached from the east, sandy and crusty. There were about thirty of them, mostly men. One of them broke off from the group and came at a gallop toward Malak's caravan. Malak wound his way around the mud hole to greet the stranger.

The man bounded from his horse and strode toward Malak. He was shorter than Malak by a hand, stocky with black hair and wide cheekbones, a regal air about him.

"Are you well?" the man asked.

"Well."

"Where are you coming from?"

"Jerusalem."

"Ah, yes," said the man with olive skin and shiny black hair, braids woven into his beard and dancing dark eyes. "We travel to Baghdad. It is a long journey. How is the road?"

"No real problems," Malak said. There was a group of unpleasant folk about thirty days' ride behind us. I doubt they will bother you now."

Malak smiled at the man, remembering the ambush and the brief fight that ensued. No, they wouldn't be trying to steal any more horses.

"I am Gur Khan," of the Khereid clan. I miss the mountains and lakes of my country. This place is not fit for people." He spat over his shoulder.

"I am Malak, and I agree with you. It is too hot and parched here. I don't understand why anyone lives here."

"Where do you travel?"

Malak shook his head. "I go east. That is enough for now. My companions are traveling to bring riches back to the

Holy Land." He chuckled. "I wish them luck."

"I am on a diplomatic journey," Gur Khan said with a crafty smile. "Perhaps I, too, will find the riches I seek."

Malak noted the curved bow attached to a colorful blanket draped over the gray horse, and, looking over Khan's shoulder, observed the alert bearing the other men in the caravan displayed. These were warriors.

Malak could not see her yet. He shifted his weight, an anxious sort of anticipation in him. The knot of men and horses shifted.

Golden hair shining in the late afternoon sun, she stared at him across the space of fifty paces, time seeming to spin out of control, a falling, reeling feeling in Malak's soul. An instant connection.

Gur Khan grinned at Malak. "She is something, isn't she? Absolutely hideous. She asked us to bring her to the west. She is the ugliest thing I've ever set eyes upon, yet she has a good heart. She is tall and gangly like a bird. White as new snow."

"Where did you find her?" Malak said. Heart thumping. He'd taken a long swig of water just moments before, but his mouth was dry. She was glorious.

"She found us. Wandered into our village in the midst of a hard winter, half-starved and frozen. One of my wives took pity on her and nursed her like she was a baby. She's a strong woman, I'll say that for her. Works harder than some men. Cooks, cleans. I'll give her to you if you like."

"I'm not sure what you mean."

"A gesture of goodwill between two travelers on a long dusty road. She will be no trouble to you, I can assure you. She doesn't complain. And she rides like one of us."

"A most generous offer."

"I will not be offended if you refuse, although it *would*

be rude. You don't know that, though, so I will forgive you. The truth is, she makes my men uncomfortable, so I'm not being as selfless as you might think. Let us camp and share a meal. Join me at my tent after dark and consider my offer. She and the horse she rides are my gifts to you."

The sun could not set fast enough.

———

Malak loved that woman with long blond hair, and they sang songs and made love, and she bore him a son. Losing her tore him apart in that ripping kind of way which leaves longing and bewilderment and lingering agony. She taught him some things, and he taught her some truths, and for a time, life was good.

She was never his. Women and angels belong to no man.

CHAPTER THIRTY-TWO
MARCHING ORDERS

Now

Malak stared at the President, who met his glare across the conference table. The air in the room tasted stale and close. Air handlers hummed, a sound beneath the sound of the world sliding into a dark abyss. The man in the suit with the America pin and red power tie smiled without humor, a condescending twist of the mouth, believing, perhaps, that he had won some sort of argument.

"Tell me what you mean by *rapture*, and also how you think America should be at the forefront," Malak said.

The President raised his eyebrows. "You've never heard of rapture? What sort of angel are you?"

"Please forgive my ignorance," Malak replied. "Enlighten me. And I never said I was an angel."

"When Jesus returns, the faithful will be raptured up into heaven. This happens at the start of Armageddon, and Christ will throw the devil into a lake of fire for eternity. It's in the book of Revelation."

"Actually, it's not," Malak said.

"You need to read your Bible," the President said, irritation and frustration written on his bland face. "But we aren't here to discuss theology. Maybe when we meet again on the other side, we can spend years talking about that. Right now, we need to discuss our next moves."

"Let me ask you something, Mr. President."

"Shoot."

"Do you want to stop Armageddon, or start it?"

"I'd say it's started already. It started when America was attacked by nuclear weapons. I ordered a measured counter-strike. If things escalate from here, then they do."

"Why am I here, then? What can I possibly do?"

"I want you to hunt down the sommbitch antichrist and kill him."

"I see."

"Don't be flippant. We know who he is now, and we are aware that he was operating right under our noses. His outfit was funded through NSA dark money. He's gone to ground, but we will get a lock on him shortly."

"You're wrong about him," Malak replied. "I will try to kill him, but he's not the antichrist. He's worse. Lucifer, if you can believe that."

"Hmm. We will see. If that's the case, then Christ will be here soon, and it won't matter much what we do. Until then, I want you to go after him. You've got whatever you need at your disposal. If you can't kill him, capture him, and we'll lock him in a vault and keep him there for eternity."

"It won't be that easy. Surely you know that."

"I have faith in God, and that's all that matters. Sometimes, though, God wants us to help ourselves. So that's the best plan I've got."

"Fair enough."

A man with a no-nonsense buzz-cut and a chest full of ribbons marched into the room and whispered urgently into the President's ear. The President smiled and nodded as he stood.

"The President of Russia is on the phone," he said. "We will talk again. Godspeed." With that, he turned and strode from the room.

Malak gazed around the table at his team. All of them

looked weary and skeptical.

"Well," John said, "I think we've got our work cut out for us. Kelli, why don't you join me in the operations room? The rest of you can grab some shut-eye. If anything comes up, I'll send for you. We can have you on a jet and airborne in fifteen minutes."

The remaining men talked about the state of the world, a depressing conversation. Fighting on the Saini Peninsula continued, with heavy losses on both sides. Israeli armor pushed into Syria, supported by U.S. aircraft. Tel Aviv and Jerusalem burned, with Iranian rockets streaking into the cities hourly. The Israeli missile dome defeated most, but not all, of the attacks. Reports of chemical and biological agents abounded.

In the South China Sea, the United States engaged the Chinese navy. Chinese bombers departed from newly constructed airfields on islands formed from coral reefs and attacked airfields in the Philippines. The Japanese lost two heavy cruisers, and U.S. submarines hunted the Chinese carrier group.

In Europe, NATO forces clashed with Russian units in Ukraine, Norway, and Sweden. F-35 fighter jets fought intense aerial battles with SU-22 aircraft. A Russian bomber group was shot down over the Arctic, as Canadian and U.S. aircraft scrambled to meet the threat.

Flurries of lightning cyber-attacks targeted communications and infrastructure, each side trying to blind the other. Much of the U.S. power grid was down, likely from such an attack.

It was unclear what triggered the global war.

"It's been building for decades," John explained. "The recent droughts in the Middle East, the rise of the Islamic State, the battle for oil in the Arctic and the South Pacific, all of these things came together. A perfect storm for humanity."

"It's out of control now," Malak said. "I don't see how this can de-escalate. It's just a matter of time before someone launches a full-scale nuclear attack."

"Maybe," John admitted. "But there is still hope. Our diplomats are talking to the Russians and the Chinese. They understand the consequences. No one really wants to kill the world. But nobody wants to lose."

"I hope you're right, but I fear you are wrong about that."

———

The sleek jet streaked from the cave and into the night, banked north, and climbed hard. The moon shone full and bright, and the clouds below shimmered silver and pale. Jerusalem waited on the other side of the planet.

CHAPTER THIRTY-THREE
LOVE

The Khangai Mountains, 1100-1139

In the shadow of the great mountain Bogd Kahn Uul, Malak lived and loved with the beautiful blond woman he came to know as Ariel. They dwelt miles from the nearest Kherite settlement, beside the Tuul River in a lush, primal forest of pine and birch.

In the fleeting summers, they made love on the banks of the river under a canopy of willow trees when the sun was kind and golden and the air was sweet. The water danced, and the breeze was cool on their naked backs while songbirds serenaded them, and with each caress, Malak felt a deeper kind of peace.

She was a gift, a blessing in every way.

In the winter, when the temperature plummeted and the ground froze and snow gripped the universe, their world shrank to a simple home constructed of timber and cured animal hides. The icy wind moaned and hurled hollow threats at them, and they laughed and held each other close, safe and warm.

"How did you find me?" she said beside a fire one night.

"Destiny. Fate. I don't know, love. God is good, yes?"

"Yes. I wish I could remember, though. Remember my own past. You are the first thing I recall, there on that beach in the north. I recall everything. The sound of the waves. The warriors attacking, dying. All of it."

"I know."

"Why are we different, my love? What purpose does that serve?"

"I wish I knew."

"The world is cruel, but you are kind and sweet. I want to stay with you forever."

Malak kissed her on the lips and nibbled her ear. "Such a perfect ear," he said. "And your nose. You have a fine nose." He tickled her.

"Stop; I'm serious." She giggled, then grew serious again. "Don't you think about these things? About the future? About the past?"

"Of course I do. I'm content not having answers. What else can we do?"

"I don't know. Sometimes we feel like a dream. Like I'll wake up and you will be gone. Sometimes I watch you sleeping and I wonder if you will just disappear. It seems… too good to be true. Unreal."

"Oh, it's real," Malak said, trying to change the subject, touching her where she was most warm and yielding.

"Oh," she sighed. "All right then."

———

Malak could never forget the atrocities he had seen or the blood he'd spilled, but there was healing and understanding in those years with Ariel, mingled with a certain forgiveness. For he needed not only to forgive himself, but to be forgiven. She helped him to find these things.

A few other families moved into the area, and a sense of community grew among them. Malak enjoyed the sound of children laughing. Sometimes they sang songs and broke bread together, feasting on roasted goat and drinking wine from skins. Malak shared his faith in a casual way when people asked, and over time, Christianity took hold in that small part of the world. Historians would later brand that pocket of religion as Nestorian Christianity.

Travelers and traders passing through the valley spread stories, and whispers eventually reached the halls of power in Constantinople and as far away as England. There were rumors of a king in the east called Prestor John, a mighty ruler with vast wealth who might come to the aid of Christian forces for another Crusade. But Malak knew none of this at the time, and it would be centuries before he learned that the legend he spawned was spun to incite war.

Within their small enclave, the people did not seem troubled that neither he nor Ariel aged. When their son was born, mothers brought food, fathers sent gifts of horses and bows, and the celebration was grand.

They named the boy Isaac, and he was a joy and revelation to Malak. He never dreamed that he would ever be able to father a child. Malak sang songs, cradled the infant in his arms, and took him on long walks in the summer mountains.

Malak hunted deer and fowl with his bow, and he raised horses, sheep, and goats. He envisioned his son grown and strong, taking long trips out into the steppes where the sky was vast and the air was crisp.

"How are we allowed to be so happy?" she sighed on a summer night beside the river, breathless and covered with a sheen of sweat. "It almost seems unfair. But God knows, I like it. We are blessed. Don't you ever feel guilty?"

"Not about you. Not about being happy. Never. No."

"Will you love me like this forever?" She smiled at him, running her fingers through the hair on his chest.

Malak put both of his hands on her cheeks, cradling her face, and touched his forehead to hers, holding her and cherishing the moment.

"Forever, my love," he said.

———

Isaac was not quite five years old when a feud broke out among neighboring clans. Malak trained some of his fellow townsmen and made sure that weapons were easily available. The troubles seemed to pass the town by. Malak helped build fortifications around the edges of the tiny village, just in case, and set up regular patrols by the men.

When raiders stormed his valley, Malak was in the forest. He heard the distant screams and saw the smoke.

Branches lashed his face, and the wind whipped his hair as he galloped toward his home. His heart hammered in his chest, and he felt a terrible, anguished sense of urgency mixing with rage, a burning anger hotter than he'd ever known, deadly and fierce. He'd never known fear like that, for he'd never had so much to lose.

The day darkened, and shadows turned sinister and mocking. The sun itself felt stripped of its power. Over the thump of his mount's hooves on the yielding ground, the clash of metal and the crack of wood pierced the still forest.

Malak broke through the woods into the clearing onto the gentle slope above the tiny village, where every home blazed and smoked.

In the middle of the destruction, a blond woman stood tall while she fought several men armed with long daggers, her only weapon a hoe. She kicked and spun, slashed and hacked. One of the men fell.

Hurtling down the hill at a full gallop, Malak raised the convex bow and loosed several arrows in quick succession, holding the horse tight with his legs. His shots went wide and high. He counted nine attackers. Beyond the village, smoke snaked above the trees, where other farms burned.

Closing the gap, he leaped from the horse and sprinted

toward Ariel. Smoke burned his eyes and caught in his lungs.

Somewhere close, his son wailed.

Ariel, bleeding from a wound in her shoulder, roared at her attackers, teeth bared, stabbing, parrying.

The other men in the village lay strewn about, bodies porcupined with arrows. He didn't see the women or children; they'd probably already been taken. Malak stopped long enough to place an arrow into a man's back before drawing his own blade and leaping into the fray.

His eyes locked with Ariel's for a moment, long enough to feel the despair and defeat on her soul. The remaining enemies attacked with renewed vigor, five of them close, two of them firing arrows from a distance.

Isaac's cries grew farther away.

The first arrow caught Malak in the belly. It was the sensation of being kicked by a horse, followed by spreading warmth and a tearing feeling inside. Worse than the physical sensation was the scream in his heart, the howling into the abyss because he knew what that arrow meant. He raged against losing everything, ached in every place that could hurt.

He hurled his blade, and it spun end-over-end and impaled an archer to a tree while Ariel screamed, her weapon knocked from her hands.

Malak prayed for power that never came, helpless to save her. A bearded man thrust his dagger through her back, the tip appearing in a bloom of crimson between Ariel's breasts. Her mouth opened in a soundless cry of anguish, and her legs sagged under her weight.

Ten paces away, Malak found he could no longer breathe, a shaft appearing with almost miraculous speed in his throat, and he choked on his own blood while the world spun. He clawed at the arrow with clumsy, slick hands while more arrows found his torso, and he could no longer stand.

On his knees, through the smoke and the blood, he heard his son cry for the last time, and Malak died again. That death was almost as bad as the first one.

CHAPTER THIRTY-FOUR
REVELATION

Now

Throughout his lives, Malak spent many years studying ancient prophecies. He'd read scrolls in Hebrew, Aramaic, Greek, and Arabic. His interest was not confined to Christian prophecy alone, and he was intrigued by the similarities common among the world's religions.

The Book of Revelation, perhaps the most famous apocalyptic collection of prophecy, was terrifying and mystifying. While the book contained many specific references and signposts, the timeline for the end of the world was very much open to interpretation. Mankind had been worried about the end of the world for as long as men were men.

Malak had one significant advantage when it came to understanding those dire predictions: he knew that the war was real. Demons existed, and so did God, and he approached the current mass destruction on the planet from this perspective.

What confounded him more than anything was his own role. The apocalypse would happen eventually, and it would be in God's time, not man's. Would it be long after men walked among the stars and the great diaspora of humanity throughout the galaxy, or sooner? Now, perhaps.

And if it was going to happen, what the hell was Malak supposed to do about it?

The more he knew, the less he understood.

———

"So, you are an Angel of the Lord," Vladimir said. "And we are going to try to kill the devil. The actual devil from the Bible. Is that right?"

Ben and Tiny Tim chuckled, and the aircraft encountered turbulence.

"We knew you were different," Syed said. "Help us to understand."

"I don't have answers for you, I'm afraid. I know it must sound insane."

"I'd say that's an understatement," Syed remarked dryly.

"How old are you?" Tiny Tim asked.

Malak regarded his friends. They knew him well, trusted him. They deserved to know. He told them. The flight was not long enough to go into detail, but he gave them the broad strokes. They sat in rapt silence, shaking their heads in disbelief from time to time.

"Ah, the things you have seen," Ben Cohen said. The former Israeli offered a rare grin. "To have witnessed what you have… I cannot imagine. A blessing and a curse."

"So you believe me?"

"What's to doubt?" Tim said. "The world has gone insane. Maybe we're the only sane ones left. Here we are on a stealth jet that looks like a UFO, bound for the Middle East while ICBMs fly. Kelli is walking again, and you're an angel."

"What I'm curious about," Syed said, "is the nature of things. The underlying nature."

"What do you mean?" Malak asked.

"You know I am Muslim. Is *your* God *my* God? Are you an angel or a devil yourself?"

"I do not know," Malak said.

"I believe there is only one true God," Syed said. "My question is this: how do we know we are on the right side?

How do you know?"

"You know *me*," Malak said. "You know I am not evil."

"Not on purpose, anyway. That doesn't mean you're not evil. If you do a thing that you think is good, yet many die because of what you did, are you innocent? Does the blood on your hands belong to you? Did Hitler know he was evil?"

"There is much blood on my hands," Malak admitted. "I don't claim innocence."

Syed shook his head, unconvinced. "What is the difference, then? If evil results from your actions, does this not make you evil?"

"Perhaps it does, my friend. Or perhaps the important distinction lies with intent. I strive to be good. I really do. It's never good enough."

"Well, I don't think Hitler recognized his evil nature, either. Or Stalin or Pol Pot. I think they saw themselves as heroes."

"Well, Syed, I don't—"

The jet banked hard, and Malak tumbled at the unexpected and sudden change of course. A red light blinked on the wall of the cabin, and the whine of the engines changed, more high-pitched.

The pilot's voice came on over the speakers. "We've got contact," he explained. "Strap in. Countermeasures."

The jet shuddered, and Malak wished the Spartan passenger cabin contained windows. He hated not knowing what was happening.

He held onto the straps over his chest, and the rest of the team did the same. The g-forces increased, and his limbs felt heavy. He wondered how fast they were going.

"My apologies," the Captain's voice crackled, "but we're not going to make it to Israel." He offered no explanation.

The next hour was tense, and no one spoke beyond the

occasional grimace or grunt. The sound of the engines changed again, and Malak's ears popped. He felt the plane bounce on its wheels, and he was glad. He'd never liked flying.

The ground crew opened the side door and brought a staircase on wheels up to the plane. Malak and his team descended onto the tarmac.

In the grey dusk, Malak saw dozens of warplanes, fighters, light bombers, and reconnaissance aircraft, red lights blinking. Crews sprinted back and forth, and trucks and forklifts carrying bombs serviced the planes. Pilots wearing olive flight suits walked around inspecting their birds, pausing now and then to peer at something and make notes.

Their pilot rounded the nose of the jet and offered a hand to Malak. "I'm Hawk," he grinned. "That was fun."

Hawk's eyes were merry and his skin was bronzed, his sandy hair cut high and tight. "I hope I didn't shake you up too much back there." Malak sensed great sadness beneath the easy demeanor.

"What happened and where are we?"

"Germany. Ramstein Air Force Base."

"Oh."

"Yeah. Right in the middle of a bull's eye. Not the best place to be at the moment, if there is any good place."

On the runway over Hawk's shoulder, an F-35 rocketed down the runway and lifted into the darkening sky. Hawk had to shout over the roar of the engines.

"They're running non-stop operations here. The Russians have the Ukraine. It looks like NATO is going to let them keep it. We're flying patrols over NATO airspace. Weapons free. This is crazy. End- of-the- world shit. I had to shake a pair of SU-24s off the French coast. No idea what the hell they were doing there. Fortunately, this baby is *fast*." Hawk patted the black exterior of the jet affectionately.

"Well, thank you," Malak said.

"Sure thing. Now we've got to figure out how to get you to Jerusalem. Somebody *really* wants you there."

"Why didn't we fly there? Did you take damage?"

"No. But there's too much traffic in the air. Especially further east. We've lost a lot of jets already. My orders were to land here, then await further instructions. I'm guessing you're in for one hell of a trip."

Malak had a sneaking suspicion what kind of trip it would be.

The SAT phone John had given him before they left beeped, and Malak answered.

"I'm assuming everyone on your team can swim," John said without preamble.

"Yes."

"Good. Your pilot will fly you to the coast. Our friend is still at the same location. We've got eyes on."

Malak sighed. He'd never been on a submarine before.

CHAPTER THIRTY-FIVE
THE BLACK DEATH

Florence, 1348

Malak lived in Florence for two years before he came alive. He existed but did not live. He was a broken shell, and he spent his time working at a variety of mindless jobs. He spent six months working on the docks of the Arno River, toiled in the wool district, and finally settled into a solitary life sweeping the stone floors of a cathedral. He went weeks without speaking, and the priests generally assumed he was a dullard. He slept on the street.

"Why don't you smile?" Father Giovanni would chide in his kind fashion. "You are young and healthy. Look at me. I am old and I have not seen my feet in ten years, yet I always smile."

Malak would shrug and put his shoulders into the broom.

"I *see* you, Malak. You are not who you pretend to be. I wish you could at least feign happiness. You might like it."

"I embrace my lot," Malak would mumble. Or, "I am humble and thankful." These short exchanges went on for almost a year. Eventually, Father Giovanni, resigned to Malak's silent thick-headedness, would smile, shake his head, and waddle in the opposite direction. That was all right with Malak.

In his free time, he walked the streets, an observer not connected with life. Children laughed, young people fell in love and married under canopies of flowers while minstrels plucked and singers sang. Portly merchants strolled the cobblestone thoroughfares wearing colorful robes of silk, and women swept past Malak, leaving the scent of flowers in their wake, exotic perfumes and fragrances he could only guess were meant to be intoxicating.

He was dead inside despite the life all around him. He formed no friendships, did nothing to help others. He watched from a distance, and if he began to feel, he crushed that emotion. He was like that cripple, Nicco, who sat at the steps of the cathedral shaking his can every day. The man's legs existed, but there was nothing in them. No sensation, no purpose. In Malak's mind, his soul was like that. Numb. Impervious to pleasure and pain.

He believed he was doomed to loss, for he'd lost the love of his life, his child, and every friend he knew. And it seemed that it would always be that way; that he was destined to grieve. It was better, he decided, not to feel anything at all.

Malak embraced depression and isolation with the vigor he'd once engaged in battle and life. He found that he was excellent at swimming in his own piss, allowing self-pity to define him, so much so that he allowed the warmth of it to lull him into dull complacency. He did not care anymore. Nothing to gain, nothing to lose.

The plague brought Malak back to life and killed one in three humans in Europe.

Florence changed almost overnight. It was a transformation from life to death, from hope to fear. The laughter ceased on warm nights, and the music died. Windows shut, doors closed, cries of anguish on the wind, the city seemed to constrict upon itself.

On a sunny morning, Malak found Nicco sprawled on the cathedral steps, stone dead, grotesque blackish tumors swollen on his neck. Malak hauled Nicco's body to the graveyard for paupers, unprepared for the sight and smell which greeted him.

Bodies wrapped in linen lay stacked like firewood next to a great hole in the ground filled with the dead. Flies droned and swarmed, and waves of corruption washed over Malak, sick and sweet and bitter, the scent of death mean and strong. He put Nicco's body on the ground and gagged, fighting down bile, hands on his knees. Some of those bodies were tiny.

There were too many to bear.

A priest with tired eyes stood before Malak. "Thank you for bringing this lost soul here," the priest said. He reached into his robes and tossed a coin to Malak. "God's judgement is upon us."

Malak stood tall and clenched his jaw, staring into the priest's eyes.

"Blessed are the meek," said the Priest. "The last days are upon us. Seek forgiveness." The man turned away, and Malak realized he was shaking. Shaking in his soul, straining at the chains.

He trudged back to the church, allowing himself to feel. Letting that pain in. Giving himself permission to grieve for the hurt. Hurting *with* them, rather than looking past them. Seeing their pain.

What he felt most was shame. He could have healed Nicco. He should have done more. That he was angry with God was no excuse. The selfish, numb existence he'd lived served no real purpose.

Tragedy can be a fulcrum, a pivot, and even a blessing. It's impossible to see while it's happening, and those years in between are killing years. Not everyone makes it out.

Bells rang, melodic and mournful, echoing through the streets, and Malak came to a crucial decision. He resolved to fight for mankind.

He knew he could not fight *against* God. But he could fight *for* humanity when God appeared absent, when wars raged and disease stalked the earth. He would use his skills, as a healer and a warrior, on man's behalf, rather than be content to observe.

Even though he'd lived longer than any human alive, he felt human again. Sensed the magic and tragedy mingled with regret and the fear which shapes lives and history.

Men could do great things if they'd just stop being men.

––––––––

The Black Death ravaged Florence with the relentless enthusiasm of a young man making love to the first woman he's tasted, who is supple and eager and inviting. The plague was insatiable, and death was its desire.

It did not love, it raped. It took. It reaped. The sickness reveled in tears, exalted in anguish, and penetrated rich and poor alike with joyful abandon, finding the city yielding and intoxicating.

It took priests, monks, merchants, wives, and children with equal gruesome glee.

Malak did what he could. He walked the streets and touched people, healing them and taking their sickness. It hurt him every time. There was always a price. He took pains to alter his appearance, his clothing, his hair, so that people would not know who he was. Some nights he wore the attire of a merchant, putting on a swagger and sneer and bright cloaks, while on others he appeared to be a beggar garbed in rags.

The dying residents of Florence, Malak included, did not understand what was happening to them. Most believed that God's judgement had come, and the end was nigh. People had varying reactions to this idea.

A good portion decided that if they were going to die anyway, then it was time to go out in a blaze of glory and gluttony. The rich hosted parties open to all, where the wine flowed and laughter and sex spilled out into the open with frantic urgency. Orgies abounded, men and women, women and women, men and men, twined together in rooms smelling of sweat and lust and fear.

Malak did not judge.

Others took the opposite approach, barring the windows and doors, praying, hoping, self-flagellating, finding a sudden piety they'd never known before. Shunning outside contact, they walled themselves away while the world kept dying. They couldn't have known that fleas spread the plague and ignored piety.

Many abandoned children, husbands, and wives. They fled the city in droves, carrying the plague with them and in them, cowards marching to destruction in a diaspora of death.

A brave few ventured into the streets with selflessness and empathy. Monks sat vigil with the diseased, mothers brought food to the wasted, strangers became friends with those on death's door. They ignored the howling and the fear, courageous and strong in the face of evil they could not understand. Malak was one of them. This endeavor took him to some strange places.

Rumors spread faster than the plague. Amidst the fear, there were voices of reason. Some of the clergy elected to view the scourge as a problem with a solution, rather than God's wrath. They knowingly risked their lives for the sake of healing and helping fellow humans, striding through the dying and the dead, offering prayers and comfort to those in dire need.

In the most notorious brothel in the city, a place spoken of with longing and disdain in the same breath,

Malak found an unlikely ally. For within those walls, rumors and information flowed wild and rabid, mostly false, but sometimes true. The wealthy merchants and ruling class frequented the establishment, and the whispers and grunts between the sheets could be more valuable than the Florin, given the right pressure and a certain moral flexibility.

The brothel was known simply as "*Dopo.*" The name of the establishment was "after dinner," or *Dopo cena.* The fact that the nickname meant simply "after" was not lost on Malak. And when the owner of that establishment reached out to him, he did not ignore her. She had her finger upon the thready pulse of Florence. The whispers found Malak, and one of her women found him. Malak discovered an envelope and an invitation stuffed inside his pocket.

"Men fear the world. They fear men because men and life are cruel. Men fear women, for without us, men have no reason to be. You and I, though, can help each other."

Intrigued, Malak accepted the invitation and met with Shellia Theissa. Before he walked through the stout wooden door, Malak regarded the three story building, hearing muffled laughter and music within. A woman giggled on a balcony above. He strode inside, and a beautiful raven-haired lady in an ornate dress smiled at him, meeting his eyes as she walked to greet him. She wore a floppy felt hat with tiny bells dangling from the edges, and her hands were concealed by white gloves.

Ornate tapestries and stunning oil paintings adorned the walls, and oversized couches in the foyer hugged the walls.

"Welcome, sir," the woman purred. "Would you like some wine?" She batted sultry eyes at Malak and touched his shoulder.

"No, thank you. I am not here to pluck a rose. I'm to

meet Shellia. Where might I find her?"

A minstrel played in another room, a tenor with a sweet voice, and candelabras cast friendly shadows. The establishment was not what Malak expected; it was as opulent as a castle.

The woman's smile fled, and Malak could see the disappointment on her face for a moment, but she recovered from one heartbeat to the next.

"You have found her," came a hearty voice from upstairs.

Shellia Thiessa stood proud and regal at the top of the stairs, pausing for a moment at the landing for dramatic effect, a flash of playful danger in her eyes. The madam wore a conservative black dress, highlighting alabaster skin, a finely sculpted face, and striking blue eyes, which missed nothing.

Her hair hung long and wild on her shoulders, and there was a mischief about her, a paradoxical flaunting of sexuality and denial promised in the tilt of her head, the flick of her tongue over her lips, and the thrust of her chin. Lust and self-restraint, and most intriguing, the possibility that she regretted subverting this, and that if the right man said the right things, and touched her soul in the right places, he would unleash the combined pleasures of heaven and hell in a long night of ecstasy and pain and release.

She was a work of art, and Malak appreciated her instantly. He saw through her in the same way she saw through him.

She looked him up and down, seeming to come to a conclusion, and cocked her head. "You're not what I thought you'd be," she said. "I thought you'd be taller."

"What can I do for you?"

"Come with me." She took Malak's hand and led him up the stairs.

She brought him to a corner room on the third floor, light and airy with sunshine pouring in through windows opened onto the streets. They sat on a sofa, and she grasped his hand. Her touch felt cool and warm at the same time. She leaned close, ample breasts inches from his body, and she stared into his eyes.

She pulled back abruptly and patted him on the leg. "The rumors may be true, then," she said with a faint smile.

"What do you mean?"

"I am a beautiful woman, and we are all alone. You aren't trying to fuck me. Maybe you could, and maybe you couldn't, but you have every reason to believe you could."

"And what does that tell you?"

"That you are different, at least. Not like other men. I know you help people. I wonder why you do?"

"Because people need help. Why does that require explanation?"

"People help others to help themselves, in my experience. *Especially* those who claim to be men of God."

"That's a cruel way of looking at the world."

"Do you deny it?"

"People are people."

"That's vague. All right. I want to help people, but I also want to help myself at the same time. I think we can work together to make Florence a better city."

"How?"

"You heal people, yes?"

Malak shifted on the couch. He didn't like where this was going, although he'd had a pretty good idea all along.

"I'm not sure what you've heard," Malak said. "I'm a simple man."

"Many of my patrons are rich and powerful. They are willing to pay for a variety of things to make them feel better."

Malak laughed. "You want me to heal people for money?" He rose to his feet. "I see I made a mistake."

"Think of the good we can do," she purred. "Your secret will be protected. We can take the money and give back to the city. Some of the families in power are not so bad. Take their gold and build an orphanage for the children who are begging on the streets because they lost their parents."

"And you will do this from the goodness of your heart, I suppose."

"I am already rich," she said. "I'll give you all the money and show you how to spend it properly. Yes, it will be good for business. But you can live here and continue the good work you do, rather than dwelling in squalor. Most importantly, you will be protected."

"What makes you think I need protection?"

"*Everyone* needs protection from the Inquisitors. Everyone. Especially you."

"Let me think about it."

"Do what you must," she said. "My offer stands as long as you do."

———

A week later, Malak walked through her door again, and this time, he stayed. Over the next two years, he healed many, rich and poor alike. Shellia kept her word and gave to the community, purchasing a building next to her brothel, and employing a staff of former whores to watch over and feed children living on the streets.

He had no way of knowing that the young, nondescript Medici man suffering from syphilis that he casually healed one night would give birth to a dynasty and inadvertently usher in a renaissance that would spread like wildfire.

When the Inquisition found *Dopo*, Malak was unprepared. Even he could not have imagined the horror that waited. When mankind's creativity and ingenuity are directed toward depravity, evil thrives.

CHAPTER THIRTY-SIX
TRUE BELIEVERS

Now

Jets took off and landed with regular, sky-tearing regularity. Malak could feel the power in his chest, a rumbling kind of exhilaration along with it. The base swarmed with activity, and he watched fighters and bombers lift into the air, bristling with missiles and bombs.

"This is some crazy shit," Hawk shouted over the roar of a departing F-35. "And those," he went on, pointing at the aircraft, "are pieces of shit."

"What are your orders?" Malak asked.

"We're flying map-of-the-earth to put you onto a Trident sub. You get to fly on a Blackhawk, but not your average bird. It's one of our more extravagant models." He chuckled. "You must have a whole lot of juice."

Malak decided he liked Hawk. "Where did your orders come from?"

"No disrespect, but I'm not at liberty to say. Why?"

"Just curious," Malak said. "How much longer?"

"Our bird is fueling now. Wheels-up in thirty. Eighteen-hundred. I've got to perform my pre-flight."

"I'm going to talk with my team. You'll send someone for us?"

"Sure. No problem. Just don't leave this area, all right?"

"Copy that."

Hawk jogged away, his baggy flight suit ruffling with his movements and the gentle breeze and cold German air.

Malak turned to face his men. Their eyes were steady, faces relaxed. Malak was grateful for each one of them and of the fact that he could trust them implicitly.

"What's up, boss?" Tiny Tim said. "I know that look."

"Can we reach Zhang or Kelli? On an absolutely secure line?"

"No guarantees," Syed replied. "Why?"

"I need information fast. I want to know more about our new President."

"Can do," Ben Cohen interjected. "I've got an encrypted connection on my tablet. The problem is on the other end. Either Zhang or Kelli are bound to be compromised."

"Do your best," Malak said. "I want to know *everything*. The first girl he kissed, the names of his parents, what he liked doing for fun when he was a kid in Texas."

"I learned a little bit from my people," Ben said, whipping out a black tablet from his rucksack. "That's why you love me. I've got access to Mossad's database, and no one will even know I'm there."

"Be quick," Malak replied.

"You're asking for a lot. This isn't the movies." He sat down on the tarmac cross-legged. His fingers flew over the keyboard. "Give me twenty minutes."

"Boss," Tiny Tim said, "talk to us."

"I'm missing something," Malak said.

"What do you mean?"

"I don't think this is how things work. Lucifer's been absent on earth for thousands of years, from what I understand, anyway. Now he's waltzing around making threats. Taunting us? That seems a bit inconsistent."

"Well, Armageddon and all," Tiny Tim said. "I was raised in the Baptist Church, and I'll tell 'ya that it makes sense to me. This is it. We've been in the End Times and, well, this is the end."

"Maybe you are right," Malak said. "But then, what's the point?"

"We fight until we can't fight anymore. Maybe that's *always* been the point," Ben Cohen replied while his fingers flew over the keyboard.

"You make me smile," Vladimir said. "You always have, because you are full of hope. But often there is no hope. That's the truth. You like to think there is. You've lived longer than anyone. You should know there is no hope. Not really. Things are the way they are. We try to change that, we fight, yes, because that is what we do. Because people like us don't have a choice. We don't surrender even when we know..." Vladimir stopped speaking and looked up at the sky, and Malak, with the others, followed his gaze.

Warplanes rocketed across the runways, joining others already in the air. Night was sound and fury, and Malak couldn't see the stars because the harsh lights on the base shrunk the universe to a tiny bubble. Doom, straining for release in the way of a volcano too long at rest. Pent-up destruction longing to fulfill its destiny.

Malak pondered. *The sword longs to taste blood, the round desires a target, and the bomb craves to explode. Men who wield weapons have always known this. They will kill us if we let them.*

Those who kill with a shrill laugh and childish giggle are as culpable as the stoic general or politician. Perhaps both should be put down like rabid dogs. While one man may commit murder, that is nothing compared to genocide. Men know this, too, on a primal level. It's not always clear who should be killed.

"Good news, boss," Ben Cohen said. "It looks like there might be hope after all. Our new President has formed an international coalition. Both Russia and China agreed to a ceasefire. Negotiations are underway now. The President is calling for a United Nations summit in two days. In Geneva."

"I see," Malak said. "What about the rebels?"

"Our Russian friends say they are under control. You're not elated?" Ben said, looking up at Malak from his keyboard. "I found what you wanted, but there's not much to see."

"Paul Shaker was born in Waco, Texas. His parents were killed in a car accident when he was an infant, and he was adopted by a wealthy uncle in England. He attended Cambridge and then moved to the United States to attend Law School. He graduated from Harvard as Editor-in-Chief of Law Review, then married Kate Drecker the next day. She was an undergraduate student at Harvard. The youngest daughter of a high-profile political family from Texas. As close to royalty as it gets in the U.S. There are some allegations and some disgusting pictures. That's as salacious as it gets." Ben laughed. "Her nickname was *Drecker, the dick-wrecker*. But really, this is just like anyone else in politics."

Malak gave him a hard look.

"Sorry, boss."

"And then?"

"Shaker won a landslide election against that Republican House of Representatives guy who was caught on video soliciting young boys. You remember the news."

"Not really."

"It was a meteoric rise from there. He was elected to the Senate and then landed the nomination for Vice President before his first term was up. He delivered Texas."

"And his parents? Who were they?"

"Middle-class working Americans. Scotch-Irish, with roots in the States dating back to the late eighteen-hundreds."

"And the birth certificate? Early records? Can you verify that?"

Ben gave Malak an odd look. "The certificate appears

to be valid." Ben paused, still seated on the tarmac with the planes taking off and landing, and the air sharp in Malak's lungs.

"Nothing off there?"

"Hmm. It's more about what *isn't* here than what *is*. His early school records have been deleted or don't exist. No class pictures, nothing like that. Blurry stuff with birthdays and football. Nothing up-close. I tried running facial recognition on some of those and came away empty. There should be more than there is. Maybe. This was before cell phones everywhere. Maybe they were extremely private people. This doesn't prove anything."

"Right," Malak said. "We need to go dark again, and we aren't getting on a damn submarine."

He wanted to tell his friends that he was relieved, but he could not.

Stripped of the freedom to move and choose, Malak knew he would cease to be. He knew that feeling of being boxed in and rendered useless, and he decided that he would not feel that way again. Not if he could help it. He wondered how much free will really belonged to him, and how much of it, if not all, was an elaborate illusion. There was that feeling of being a rat in a maze. His throat was dry.

"Why are you so worried about the President?" Tiny Tim said.

"True believers tend to scare me."

CHAPTER THIRTY-SEVEN
HERETIC

Florence, 1350

Men with swords burst through the doors of the *Dopo* on a sunny Friday morning while Malak slept. He woke to the sound of women screaming and bounded down the stairs, ready for a fight.

Shellia, a dagger at her throat, offered Malak a wan smile, and he slowed his assault. He could fight these men, but he knew that they would murder innocents first.

"What is this?" Malak said, grinding his teeth.

"We are here because Friar Michele di Lapo requires your presence," a surly man with a thin beard and dark, close-set eyes said.

Friar Michele di Lapo was the Florentine Inquisitor, a Dominican monk who used his unfettered authority to line his pockets through extortion. He was rumored to become the next Bishop.

"You are charged with heresy," the man went on, a sadistic smile tugging at his scraggly beard.

Malak considered how long it would take him to reach Shellia; her throat would be cut before he crossed the room.

The man pulled out a scroll and read legal nonsense, stating that the property now belonged to the church pending a finding of innocence or guilt.

"You can come with us peacefully, or we can cut you down here. It does not matter to me one way or the other. You are heretics and sinners, and though God will judge you, I'll be glad to send you on your way to meet him."

"Your friar is making a big mistake," Shellia said. "We've already met his demands for gold. You will pay for this."

"I don't think so," the man said. "Either way, it is not up to me."

"All right," Malak said. "Let's get this over with."

"Good."

The group of six armed men escorted Malak and Shellia from the *Dopo* and marched them through the streets of Florence. They walked to a small, drab church of stone, where two more armed men lounged outside a heavy wooden door.

"It's going to be okay," Shellia said. "We have friends who will pay for our release."

One of the guards opened the door, and a man behind Malak prodded him forward with the tip of a dagger. They walked into a gloomy room without furniture. A life-sized wooden Jesus, nailed to the cross, wearing a crown of thorns, looked down upon them with compassion.

"Move!" the cruel familiar said, cuffing Malak on the back of the head.

They crossed the church and descended a narrow winding staircase. The stone walls were wet, and torches mounted into recesses flickered with ominous urgency. The temperature dropped, and the sound of footsteps on the stairs reverberated with hollow echoes. There was the smell of rock and fear on the damp, close air.

The stairs ended in a room half the size of the church above. At a table on the far end, Friar di Lapo sat with elbows perched on the table between two men Malak did not recognize. The Inquisitor stood. Chains and manacles waited, mounted into the walls. The familiars placed shackles on Malak's wrists and ankles, one of them still holding a dagger to Shellia's back.

"The trial will begin now. The charge is heresy. Do you deny this?"

The Inquisitor was a small man wearing a black robe and a long beard. His skin possessed the pasty sheen of one who fears the sun.

The goons retreated to the walls, eight of them now, leaving Malak and Shellia standing alone before the Inquisitor and the silent monks seated at the table.

"Yes. We deny the charges. Tell me, monk, what do you think hell will be like? Do you think you will feel at home there?"

The Inquisitor looked pleased and amused. He sat down and folded his hands, nonplussed.

"You are witches. We have the evidence, sworn statements from citizens, that you are in league with the devil. Confess."

"We have nothing to confess," Shellia said. "We have done nothing but help people."

"So you do not deny that you use witchcraft?"

"We are not witches," Malak said. "But *you* are evil."

"You are of the devil. You *will* confess your sin before you die."

"So you are going to execute us?" Shellia trembled beside Malak, incredulous, enraged, and terrified.

"If you confess, your death will be swift. If you do not, you will be compelled to admit your association with Lucifer."

"An Indulgence, then," Shellia stammered. "I have more gold. I will give it to you."

"We have already taken your gold, child. No Indulgence will be granted. Only mercy, should you choose the correct path."

Malak knew Shellia to be an extraordinarily strong

woman. She wept, unprepared for a sudden end to her young life.

He remembered standing before the demon Caliph, watching his friends being slaughtered. He felt the same way now, staring into the face of evil. Only this Inquisitor was not a demon. He was a despicable human being who wore his piety like a cloak to conceal the rotted soul beneath. Di Lapo represented everything wrong with religion. A man twisting God's love for his own sick ends. A man certain in his belief and righteousness and willing to kill for it, even when that contradicted central tenets of his own professed faith.

"*Though I walk through the valley of the shadow of death, I will fear no evil,*" Malak said.

The Inquisitor grinned. "Yes. Even the demons believe and tremble. Confess."

"I confess," Shellia cried. "Mercy."

"Very well, child. Mercy shall be yours."

The soldiers led her away from Malak, who remained chained before the Inquisitors. They took her to the wall and restrained her there, each arm extended above her head, legs splayed.

Malak lunged, straining at his bonds, the cords in his neck and legs standing out.

Someone behind him clubbed him twice, sending him to his knees. The third blow knocked him unconscious.

He woke an undetermined time later to an oily darkness deeper than death itself, blacker than the deepest cave, unable to move, and only his hot breath drifting across his face gave him any reason to believe he was still alive.

He tried to move his fingers and toes, and found that they wiggled. He wrinkled his nose and discovered that it still worked. His limbs and torso were completely immobile.

He smelled metal, and as the panic in his chest receded, he felt the pressure and chaffing on his neck. The only sound he heard was that of his own breathing.

"Shellia? Are you there?"

His voice was distorted to his own ears. Louder than it should have been. There was no reply.

Closing his eyes, although that felt redundant, Malak prayed. He asked for help, for power. He did this for a long time, perhaps days, for there was no real way to tell time. He decided he was entombed in some sort of metal case. He grew hungry and thirsty, and spent time walking in the past to escape the present.

Finally, he heard a voice. Not God's. The Inquisitor's.

"Are you ready to confess?" it said.

"I've done nothing."

"You will now receive your punishment, then. If you elect to confess, the pain will cease."

Malak tensed, waiting for the inevitable.

He heard a woman screaming, the kind of scream that comes with agony more terrible than any human can bear. The screams cut off.

"Your woman is on a device that stretches her limbs," The Inquisitor said with a gentle voice. "She doesn't have much time left. But the last part is always the worst. She passed out from the pain. Confess."

"You are the devil," Malak screamed. "I'm going to kill you slowly."

The Inquisitor chuckled. "I think you've got that backwards. But first, your harlot. Her joints are about to crack. You will hear the sound, and know it. I want you to listen carefully over her screaming. It's a popping sound, like wood snapping over your knee."

"All right, then, I confess," Malak said. He figured it

didn't matter anymore.

"Excellent. You will be purified now. Your sentence is, of course, death. My familiar is going to pour molten metal into your left ear. But first, I want you to hear the sound. Your woman is coming awake."

There was screaming and the sound of tearing. Some of the screams belonged to her, and some of them were his. The red-hot agony penetrated his head and consumed everything until there was nothing but the pain itself, eternal and relentless. He could not form thoughts, for his entire universe was anguish.

CHAPTER THIRTY-EIGHT
THE SIXTH SEAL

Now

Malak was torn. He sensed he stood at a crossroads where all paths led to doom. By following President Shaker's orders and heading to Jerusalem to confront Lucifer, Malak feared he would be falling directly into the Devil's trap. He didn't know how or why, but that was his gut feeling.

He knew that Lucifer was far more powerful than he and was doing little to conceal his whereabouts. How could Malak possibly defeat him? According to prophecy, Malak would have nothing to do with the ultimate battle, for that was up to God.

The prophecy said many things, though.

He struggled to understand his role, knowing that his actions would have potentially catastrophic consequences. He did not trust Shaker's motives.

The timeline laid out in Revelation was convoluted and cryptic, with specific events interlaid with post-apocalyptic imagery. He didn't know where he was in the story, and never had.

The ground shuddered beneath his feet. It was a vibration at first, a sensation Malak ignored. When the tarmac bucked and sent him lurching sideways to the pavement, he rolled back to his feet, alarmed. His team members sprawled awkwardly around him.

A deep rumble came from everywhere, cracks erupted, and the tarmac buckled. A half mile away, something big exploded, sending plumes of orange billowing into the night. The floodlights mounted atop hangers and poles flickered and went dark, falling to the ground. Buildings shifted and some crashed and groaning and creaking.

A cargo craft hurtled onto the runway for a landing on an adjacent runway, engines roaring, straight at first and then sparking and spinning, landing gear torn off by the wrecked strip, groaning and spinning out of control. The jet spun sideways into another hulking aircraft, a C-130, and both planes exploded, sending metal and fire into the sky.

Hawk sprinted toward Malak and his team.

"Let's go!"

Malak did not wait for further instructions. He and his team followed Hawk, jumping over crevices while the ground continued to shift below them. It was like running on the deck of a ship in rough seas.

Malak followed Hawk to the waiting bird, head low beneath the whirling rotors, and climbed through the side door, strapping himself in while his team did the same. The flight crew was already aboard, flipping switches and pulling levers. Hawk scrambled into the pilot's seat. Malak pulled on a helmet equipped with a headset.

"Chief, what's happening?" Malak said.

"Earthquake. Let me fly this thing."

Malak shut up. The helicopter lifted, unsteady at first, and then smooth, rising thirty feet and forward at the same time, gaining altitude quickly.

Wind whipped through the open door, and Ramstein Air Force Base, dotted with flames and mostly dark, receded. Beyond the base, where the town of Ramstein should have been vibrant and bright against the surrounding fields and farms, only flames stood out against the darkness.

"Okay," Hawk squawked in Malak's ear. "That was

bad."

"What's the situation?"

"That was a massive earthquake. Not just here, either."

"What—"

"Hang on. Let our communications officer do her job."

The rotors churned, and the air was cool on Malak's face. His hands clenched the sides of his metal seat. Far to the west, the sky glowed orange and pink as if to herald the rising sun. His seat vibrated under him, and his throat was raw.

"Gentlemen, this is Warrant Officer Warren," a woman's voice said. "I'm juggling communications from all over the place, so I need to keep this brief. The situation is fluid."

"Copy that," Malak said.

"Multiple fault lines shifted. The Pacific plate, all along the so-called "ring of fire," moved. From the Philippines, through the Aleutian Islands, down through the Cascades, and into South America, earthquakes of 7-10 on the Richter scale occurred. Tsunamis are expected to strike the Western seaboard, while the far east is bracing for them as well. Japan is chaos…It's too much at once."

Malak choked down bile, his guts tight and angry.

"The west coast is bracing for tsunamis and the—" her voice cracked, and although he couldn't see her face, Malak felt the ache in her words. "I'm sorry," she continued, clearing her throat. "The San Andreas went." Her tone was professional and calm. "I'm getting updates. Stand by."

The Blackhawk cut the night, blades thumping, oblivious to the aching world below. Malak bowed his head and crunched his eyes shut. No one else in the aircraft spoke. No cries for the dead and those who would perish in the coming days and years. It was a moment of silent reverie and an anguish which could never be healed with words, for there were no words for such deep, jagged pain. In the last half hour, millions of people around the world died. In the coming days, another three billion would be dead.

The tsunamis hurtled toward coasts, towering waves hundreds of feet high. They would smash humanity. Saltwater would contaminate aquifers and kill crops. Starvation and disease stalked the earth, the rider on a pale horse among us, death his name.

God help us. Worse was yet to come. While the earth had teetered on a dagger's edge for thousands of years, the time was now.

The veil was torn, the sixth seal broken. The great tribulation was now, not something to fear in a distant tomorrow. There would be nowhere to hide, no safe place, only the temporary illusion of security.

When men become objects of God's wrath, there is no escape.

Science would explain it in ways that made sense to scientists, and they'd be right. But that wouldn't be the whole truth, or even most of it. Even plate tectonics was subject to the laws of the universe, and when the Creator decides it's time, there is no arguing.

Despite the fact that he'd had two thousand years to prepare for it, the reality crushed his chest like a massive Pict battle-hammer, knocking the breath from his soul. He was tiny. Irrelevant. A failure, and worse, a Judas to mankind. He'd attempted to serve God, and in doing so, save mankind from itself. He believed he could make a difference through fighting, healing, learning, and praying.

What he'd known to be true was stripped away in a moment.

The good he strived to do over the last two thousand years was dwarfed by the death of the world. The children saved, wars averted, and victories achieved felt pointless, for the end of the story had already been written, no matter how much he raged against it and fought to change the ending. He thought he could give men a chance at a future, but the story wasn't his and never was.

He was not the hero of his own life, and perhaps it was pure hubris to believe he ever could have been, but heroes don't quit until they are dead. Malak had died many times, yet he was not dead.

"Chief."

"Yessir."

"Where are we going?"

"Refueling in Spain. Landing in Jerusalem. Apparently, your orders haven't changed."

"I guess not."

CHAPTER THIRTY-NINE
WINTER OF THE SOUL

Valley Forge, 1777

The Continental Army died in pieces. Frostbite took fingers, noses, and toes. Starvation reduced men to shambling skeletons. Sickness claimed many. Smallpox, pneumonia, and hypothermia proved more devastating than musket balls and cannons. When Malak staggered through snowy rows of tents in the pale morning light, the sound of coughs and moans mingled with the scent of wood smoke and despair in the sharp air.

The cold killed hope and men, and with it the dream of America.

When hope is torn from men and armies, the war is ended. That moment a man looks at the future and wishes for the past because tomorrow stretches eternal and gray as far as he can see, when his belly is full of empty and his chest is tight with ache, then he is already dead. It is too late. He is defeated. He knows this in his soul, and the fact that he keeps breathing doesn't mean he is alive, only that his body refuses to surrender, fighting because it has no choice, while his spirit has fled the battle.

Malak, however, remained undefeated. He walked among his fellow soldiers, speaking, healing, fighting, to bring them hope where he could. He knew the scent of death, and it hung heavy in the valley.

He was a scout, and this afforded him a certain freedom to move about. Discipline among the men was as lax as self-pity was rampant.

He drank gruel and soup while his body ate itself and healed at the same time. He had far more meat on his bones than most of his companions, although he ate less. Eventually, in a kind of experiment, he quit eating completely. Still, he managed to survive, although he was weak and sometimes delirious.

He caught glimpses of General Washington only from afar. Most of the men seemed to adore Washington, at least in the early parts of the winter, before the deep cold and hunger set in with a vengeance.

By February, the mood turned from loyalty to a resentment that bordered on treason, at least among some of the soldiers.

"I say we cut his throat and eat his pretty horse," Angus Macdonald said one night in front of a quiet fire by Malak's tent. "He's fat and cares not ere we live or die. As long as he has his land and his horse. If we eat the horse, maybe we can go home."

Malak eyed the big man over the fire while Angus whetted a wicked blade on a stone, scraping it back and forth in perfect rhythm like a deadly, gleaming metronome, his eyes flickering with the hunger to commit murder and shaking his head with regret because he knew he would never do it.

"Go ahead," Malak said.

"I will." He looked up at Malak, eyes bright with fury and starvation.

"I am sure you are right. You will eat well and go home."

"I could do it."

"Yes."

"No one would know. Just you."

"Right. And *you*, of course. Just the two of us, though."

"What's that supposed to mean? Who would I tell?"

"No one."

"Then shut your mouth."

"All right. You brought it up."

"Do you think I'd care? Do you think I'd feel sorrow? I wouldn't. I'd roast that beast, and the taste would be enough."

"I think you are right. The horse would be savory. Better than bark soup."

"It would be heaven. Grease streaming down my arm, each mouthful better than the one before it. Damn, I am hungry. All I think about is food. And that fat general and his fat horse. And when I'm not thinking about meat, I think about the cold. When was I warm? I don't know. In the summer, I was hot. I can't remember what it felt like."

"The heat was unbearable, you said. You complained then that you wished for winter and you hated your uniform," Malak said. "You called it confining."

"Well, it was hot, though I can't recall the feeling of the sun on my face. The sun does not descend into this valley, not with the warmth it should. All is frozen forever. There is no power left in the light."

"It will pass."

"It will pass. And we will not live to see it." He spat on the frozen ground. "It won't matter. You talk too much, Malak. I like you. But you talk too much."

"Yes," Malak said. "I hear that sometimes."

"I received a letter from home. She sent it in September. Sick with fever." His voice grew thick. "And my son..."

"I know," Malak replied. "I'm sorry."

Malak respected Angus. Despite the man's constant complaining, he was brave and kind, and that was part of his problem now. Angus cared for others. Malak was convinced that if Angus went forward with his hair-brained plot to cook

Washington's horse, he would end up giving all of the meat to other soldiers, watching them feast with a self-satisfied grin on his face, not taking a juicy bite.

"It's not fair," Angus said, stabbing the blade into the frigid ground.

"No."

"He was a good boy. Better than his daddy." Angus stared off into the night like he could see the past and the future at the same time, breaking with the knowing. Malak saw the regret and defeat, the cracks in a man Malak knew to be stout. There was talk, and then there was this. A man doesn't look like that unless he is *done*. Smashed.

"You are brave and good, Angus. Remember that. You are hungry and sad now. You won't always be so."

"And you, my friend, are a terrible liar."

"I am not a good liar. True. But I am not lying. You are stronger and better than you think. You cannot help Emily now. Either she passed, or she lived. You could not help your son, whether you were there or not, and you *know* this. You do not like it, but somewhere you see the truth of it."

"Maybe I know I could not have helped. But I could have *been there*. That's the thing. Fathers do that. Tread lightly, my friend. I've a thirst for blood this night, and I would rather it not be yours. What do you know of wives and sons?"

"I watched my wife and son die. I know little, but that pain I know."

The fire cracked and popped in the night, filling what might have been an uncomfortable silence, while Malak and Angus decided fire was the best place to look, contemplating the ashes and the flames and the seemingly random way the light and energy leaped from one moment to the next.

Malak drifted back in time to Ariel and Isaac. Laughter and firelight stolen, the future ripped from his dying hands.

Men with good intentions build walls to protect the innocent. Evil men claw the rock until their fingernails are ripped and torn, seeking the crack, probing for weakness with the lie, the battering ram, the poison, the missile, until shadow slinks over the battlement.

But evil has already won by the time men build walls against it. It is within, constricting, seducing, whispering.

Evil makes walls, for without it, walls would never exist. But evil also lurks within the gates, grinning and growing strong. Walls may work for a time, but they always fail; Rome fell, Jerusalem burned, and the Berlin wall crumbled under the weight of darkness.

If his village had a strong wall, though, perhaps Ariel would not have been slaughtered, and his son would not have been taken, at least not on that day.

"I am sorry, my friend," Angus sighed. The night was clear and frigid, and when his friend spoke, plumes of smoke curled around his beard. "My mouth gets ahead of my heart more often than not. I did not know you knew…about that loss. That feeling of bottomless despair. I am hungry and wretched and freezing to death, and that's why I say the things I do. It would be better for me if I didn't care anymore."

"It's all right. I know."

"I've tried to be strong. You saw me. You remember. You know."

"Yes."

A man can build a wall around his soul to protect himself, but that doesn't work in the end, as any man who has done so can attest. Memories and pain fester behind bricks erected to make us impervious to attack, until we betray ourselves, either overwhelmed by the pressure from within, or dying the slow death of isolation, numbness, and fear.

"I was once a better man," Angus said, his voice gravel and grating with wistful regret; the sound of a man who has resigned himself to his fate, rather than raging against circumstance. He touched his left arm as if still feeling the pain of the old wound.

"You are the same man," Malak said. "You must remember. I do. You are strong."

Sometimes a wall which stands only a day is enough to change the world, a barrier of light thwarting shadow. The defenses that work in the end are goodness, strength, and fierce love, willing to kill and die when evil shatters the gates.

"I remember," Angus sighed. "And I am not the same man anymore."

———

Before Valley Forge, there was Fort Ticonderoga in northern New York. The only way to get through British lines and relay crucial intelligence to the rest of the Continental army was through stealth and cunning.

The English made a mistake, and the only way to capitalize on it was by mobilizing the rest of the army. There were many British scouts in the woods along with infantry.

"You!" shouted an officer in a creased blue uniform. "Come with me."

"Yes, sir," said Malak. The man led Malak to an office with a dirt floor built into the far wall of the fort, while soldiers cursed and shouted in the main yard beyond a single window.

"From what I understand, you are fluent in some of the local languages, right?"

"Yes."

"You're a half-breed, or something. Good. We need you to bring a message. It is imperative that you evade detection. You *must* not get captured."

"*Really?*" Malak said in his mind, but did not say out loud. "*Because I want to get captured and tortured. That's what I wake up each day to do. Thank you, Captain.*"

What he actually said to the officer was "Yes sir."

Malak and Angus dropped over the rear wall of the fortress in the middle of the night by ropes and slipped into the darkness.

The meadow gave way to forest, and Malak stayed low to the ground, his feet light and quiet, aware of every cracking twig beneath his moccasins, each breath, the rustle of leaves, and the whisper of wind and music of crickets.

Redcoats were everywhere. The main army rested in tents circling the fort, while Indian scouts and British troops lurked within the shadows to prevent an expedition exactly like the one Malak and Angus embarked upon.

It took most of the night to go less than two miles, finding shelter in the shadows, crawling, darting from one tree to the next, keeping away from the fires, and listening. Always listening for the sound of footsteps and breathing, coiled and waiting to strike. They slipped past patrols and sentries and took a wide berth of the area where English scouts slept.

In the gray morning, with fog clinging to the high grass of pastures and snaking through the fields and trees, they paused behind a log farmhouse while a Redcoat stepped outside to relieve himself, slurring a bawdy song.

"These Yankee-Doodle girls
Are the tightest in the world
And there's nothing swee-ter
Than a bitch fighting back
Who won't pay her tax
Here's my cock and here's your free-dom."

From inside the cabin, screams and laughter spilled into the dawn, and they were bad screams and laughs, with only pain in them.

"Let's kill them," Angus whispered. "Quietly."

"Yes."

It was not a simple proposition. This was the thing in front of him, an evil to be destroyed. He believed in the revolution, but he also believed that single deeds mattered. He was not willing to pass by this atrocity, no matter what his orders were. Perhaps the fate of the rebellion hung in the balance, while the woman inside that cabin died again and again. He had to make a choice between saving a life in that moment or walking away in the name of orders and greater good.

"I'll take the front door. You go through the rear," Malak said. "No shots."

Malak did not wait to discuss it. He ran ahead, feeling the weight of the tomahawk in his right hand, observing angles, sensing the snow beneath his feet and the way it crunched with every stride, visualizing the trajectory while he raised the weapon to his shoulder, bounding forward. The Redcoat stuffed his shriveled piece back into his white trousers and turned to the door.

The weapon whistled through the air, flying end-over-end, and Malak sprinted behind it. The wet *thunk* of steel splitting bone and brain was lost in the wind, and before the man could topple to the ground, Malak caught him and laid him down on the porch, wrenching the weapon from the base of his skull. His eyes fluttered, and his mouth opened and closed like a minnow stranded by the tide, gasping and dying and surprised.

Malak crouched over the British officer and crushed his throat with one terrible blow, offering the pasty man one last view of the world, but with a bearded Jew dressed like an Indian being the last thing he saw. That had to hurt.

He opened the front door and slipped inside the farmhouse. Directly across from him, another British soldier lay face down in a pool of blood.

From the shadows, Malak watched Angus move toward the bedroom, and Malak leapt forward. The two of them burst into the room.

"No! Stop. Please, Jesus. Stop. Why? Oh, God." A woman wailed from the only bedroom in the house. Creaking and the sound of bedposts banging against the walls, and men grunting and laughing.

One of them was standing in the corner of the room, watching, while the other man pounded at her from behind, pulling her long hair. Another man, eyes white and mouth open with dried blood on his face and chest, lay bound and stiff on the ground at the foot of the wooden bed. The woman's husband, Malak guessed.

Malak hurled his blade while he stepped forward, and it found the watcher's throat and pinned the man to the log wall with a solid sound, buried to the hilt, a fountain of blood spilling from his mouth while he choked and died.

Angus rounded the bed, dagger in his right hand, while the rapist stepped back from the woman and reached to the table beside the bed. The woman screamed, and the soldier drew a sabre, a mocking arrogance on his blond face and in his blue eyes and rapidly shrinking member, and rather than fight Angus, the man raised his sword to strike the woman.

Angus stretched his left hand out to take the blow, while he blurred his own blade into the officer's neck.

The officer died, Angus almost lost his arm, and the woman lived.

Angus nearly died from that wound, but he remembered what he'd done, and perhaps that's what saved him later, in the valley where it was cold and dark.

———

In the spring after Valley Forge, the fighting resumed

in earnest, and Malak fought alongside Angus until the war officially ended. They parted ways in Virginia, and Angus went home to his wife, while Malak went to the sea.

CHAPTER FORTY
KUM-BY-YA

Now

"When we land, move your asses," Hawk said. The helicopter thudded over Jerusalem, and through the open door, Malak caught a glimpse of the Dome of the Rock, the sun reflecting from the golden dome. The skyline in the distance, apartment buildings and office towers interspersed with cranes, was partly obscured by smoke coiling into the sky from multiple locations.

Malak felt the tingle of electricity, a thrum in the air itself like nowhere else on the planet. There was power here, as if the rocks themselves absorbed blood and tears and energy from the universe and reflected a fraction of it back, storing the rest in the land where it strained for release.

"Where, exactly, are we going?" Malak asked.

"We're dropping you off in the courtyard of a CIA black site in the suburbs. The area is taking mortar and small arms fire from Hamas. I'm not thrilled about this."

"Boss," Tim said, "what the hell are we doing here?" Tim was kitted up for battle, an array of weapons laid out on the deck of the helicopter.

"We're going to stick to the plan. I don't know what else to do."

"It's going to be a trap."

"Yes."

"Help us understand," Vladimir said. "Why would you comply? What good can we do here, now? Why don't we regroup somewhere else, even if it's here in Jerusalem? What good will dying do?"

"We won't die. Probably not, anyway. We need to know where we stand. I want to find out exactly what he wants. I believe he'll tell me."

"I think we already know that much," Syed said. "He wants to kill the world."

"It's not quite that simple," Malak said. "At least not in his own mind."

"I'd like to take some precautions," Ben Cohen said. "I can have an IDF team on standby, I think. If things go sideways, they could be helpful."

"All right. I'm guessing they've got their hands full at the moment, though."

Ben relayed coordinates to his contact within the Israeli Defense Forces. Malak was fairly certain that Ben never really left Shin Bet. It didn't matter anymore.

"If God wills it, we will live," Syed said.

Malak smiled at his Muslim friend and slipped a Sig Sauer into his thigh holster.

"Two minutes," Hawk said. "Stay frosty."

The bird banked and dropped rapidly, and Malak's stomach lurched. Five or six miles away, a pair of F-15 fighter jets tore through the sky.

The helicopter lurched as it descended into the courtyard, the tail spinning.

Hawk cursed from the cockpit.

A squat concrete building the size of a small church sat in the center of a walled, open area. Malak spotted sandbags on the flat rooftop and noted the armed guards on either side of the gated entrance to the compound.

Three bearded soldiers sauntered from the building, assault rifles slung over their shoulders, shielding their eyes from the swirling sand kicked up by the rotors. Malak and his team jumped from the helicopter and walked to meet the men.

The Blackhawk lifted as soon as they were clear, lumbering unsteadily at first, gaining speed and altitude, before churning off into the distance.

One of the soldiers stuck his hand out. "Hullo. I'm Pete. That's Cliff, and Andy." He nodded at the other two men. "Y'all picked a hell of a time to come here. What a shit-show."

"Sorry," Malak said. "Not my call."

"Copy that. Let's get inside. The locals ain't too happy today."

The interior of the building was Spartan and neat. A weapons locker dominated the wall beside the door, and beyond that were two rows of desks with computers on them. Three large flat screen monitors on the far wall displayed images of destruction from around the world, while the fourth gave an aerial shot from above Jerusalem, a live stream, Malak guessed, from a drone.

"The station chief will be back shortly," Pete said. "Meantime, you all look like you could use a shower. There's grub in the fridge. If you want, you can hit the rack."

Malak wolfed down a few bites of hummus and pita while he watched the news on Al Jazeera. He lost his appetite.

The screens depicted suffering around the globe on a scale unprecedented in human history. Coastal cities were smashed, with bodies floating on city streets like log jams. Lines of refugees overwhelmed relief staging areas and temporary refugee camps. Civilians clashed with police and soldiers in riot gear from South America to Africa. Scientists warned that many nuclear plants were in imminent danger of meltdown. Fires burned out of control along the U.S. West

Coast and along vast swaths of coastline around the world.

Global commerce was halted in its tracks. The flow of goods and services was halted, as shipping ceased, markets froze, and the global banks shut down.

Malak watched an aerial shot of Pearl Harbor, where warships lay capsized and broken like children's toys, some tossed upon the beach with reckless abandon.

"I fear your God has forsaken the world, or worse," Vladimir said.

"God?" Pete exhaled and stroked his beard with his left hand and touched his sidearm with his right, a reflex.

"I used to believe in God. Then I went to Afghanistan."

"Yeah, we've all been there," Tiny Tim said. "Funny thing is, I didn't believe in God until I *got* there." Tim pushed away from the table, rose, and walked toward the open door, hands on his hips.

"Well, you can believe whatever you want," Pete drawled. "I've got no beef with anyone, long as they aren't trying to kill me or my men. Or I've been ordered to kill them. Or if they're bat-shit crazy zealots with bombs strapped to their nuts, blowing up kids. Also, if you're that loudmouth in the bar who won't shut the fuck up and keeps staring holes in the woman I'm with."

Malak chuckled.

"Hell," Pete went on, "I grew up Baptist as you can, southern Alabama, baby. Kum-by-ya, motherfuckers. And then all that *God is love* shit went right out the door when I got to see the real world. The one they don't tell you about in Sunday School. Ain't no God. We're just a bunch of fleas the planet is shaking off."

"Where's the rest of your team?" Tim said, turning back to the table.

"Huh?" Pete said. "Perimeter patrol. On the roof. Two in the rack. We know what we're doing. We're professionals."

Tim reached around Pete from behind, a blade in his hand appearing as if by magic, and stabbed Pete in the gut, pinning his arms to the chair. Pete kicked and screamed. "What the fuck!"

Tim stared at Malak and nodded his head, intense and urgent. "We don't have time. Show him."

Malak gripped Pete's arm. "I'm sorry, my friend." A river of agony flowed into Malak, and his vision blurred. Images and emotions assailed him, memories which did not belong to him but now would.

A little boy on a purple Mongoose bicycle racing downhill on a red dirt road...Blowing out candles, while Nanny and Papa smiled from a screened in porch in a yard full of live oak trees with Spanish moss hanging down and fireflies sparking across the pasture...a beautiful brunette in that same field, looking at him like he was the most important thing in the world, whispering promises in his ear, breath wet and warm... blue lights and pain and fire and the taste of blood and gasoline and her blue eyes vacant and cold... a screaming drill sergeant... jumping from a plane with the wind and the feeling of flying... explosions from near and far...Arlington Cemetery... shooting, shooting, screaming, adrenaline, and fear.

"What the fuck?" Pete said.

The guys who were sleeping in the back rushed into the room, weapons drawn.

"Stand down," Pete ordered. "And you," boring into Malak, "tell me what the hell is going on." Andy and Cliff lowered their weapons, tense and bewildered, looking from Malak to Pete, twitchy.

"I'm sorry, Pete," Tim said. "Seriously. I hope you won't hold it against me. I didn't see another way."

"Uh-huh. You made your point. Now make your *real* point."

"What if I told you that the things you learned in Sunday School were mostly true? Especially the last part," Malak said.

"There's a lot in the last part, I guess. You talking about the New Testament or Revelation or what? So are you trying to tell me you're Jesus or something?"

"No. God forbid."

"Then what?"

"God is real. He exists. So does the devil."

"And Angels and demons, too, I'm guessing, this being Armageddon. The rapture and the end days. Which makes you...what?"

"He's an angel," Tim said. "He won't say it. But that's the truth."

"That so?" Pete lifted his bloody shirt and probed at the place where moments before a knife had pierced his skin. "I've seen some shit. This is new."

"I'm no angel," Malak said. "I'm the worst thing you've ever seen. But there are worse things than me. And they are here, now, working to destroy us. God will do what He will do. I've spent a long time trying to figure it out, and I'm not closer now, really, than I was when I started. There is a war, though, between light and darkness. You know this to be true, deep down. It's why you became a Ranger and why you joined the Unit. Right here, right now, this is the fight. The one that matters more than anything."

"That's bullshit."

"Why is that?"

"Because if what you're saying is true, then God just killed one-third of the entire planet. And that's pretty damn dark. So maybe you're on the wrong side."

An explosion rocked the building, and alarms blared. A machine gun chugged from the roof, and the radio squawked. "We've got hostiles inbound."

CHAPTER FORTY-ONE
TO THE SEA

The South Pacific 1820

The endless fighting and killing took its toll on Malak, and after the end of the American Revolution, he made his way north to Nantucket, where he boarded a whaling vessel as an inexperienced seaman.

Over the course of many years, he learned the way of the sea, and his hands were calloused and as hard as stone from gripping the ropes and oars, and his legs were steadier at sea than on land.

On his first voyages, he was at the bottom rung of sailors, a simple greenhand doing whatever he was asked. He swabbed decks, watched the deck in the middle of the night, and did his best to keep to himself. When asked about where he was from, he was vague. He sailed to ports in South America, the Galapagos Islands, and Greenland.

As time went on, he grew adept at his job, and he was a crewman, a mechanic, a harpooner, and a mate. By 1820, his reputation as a hardworking, quiet sailor earned him a spot on the Essex as second mate. She was an older ship, proven and true, with a new young captain.

Life at sea made sense to Malak, as it was simple and mostly peaceful. He ignored the constant bickering and fistfights around him in the way a rocky island ignores a hurricane, impervious to the bluster. He grew adept at carving whale bone and read poetry to avoid boredom. He never grew tired of watching the sun rise over the open ocean or the view of the stars at night while the ship slapped the waves. The storms did not trouble him, and he would grin in his bunk or on deck while other men wailed and cried out to God. Some of the men found his demeanor vaguely unsettling.

In January, when the ship rounded the Great Horn, crossing into the South Pacific during a ferocious storm, Captain Pollard remarked to Malak, "You are an odd bird, aren't you?" At the time, Malak was on the deck grinning into the gale with the cold wind and water whipping his beard.

"Storms don't worry me much," Malak said. "It's people I worry about."

The Essex managed to successfully kill 10 whales over the next two months, and Malak watched the slaughter as if from a distance. He did his job. He knew that humans would benefit from the oil and meat and was untroubled.

They were just south of the equator and off the coast of South America when disaster struck.

When the 85-foot-long sperm whale smashed into the ship, Malak was thrown off his feet, smashing his head onto a mast. Men screamed and swore all around him. The deck swam beneath him, and his vision blurred. The sky was grey and mean that day, and the wind had wolf's teeth, the sort of wind that bites into the bone and takes a piece of soul with it. The ship listed hard to port, and Malak fought to regain his footing and his sense of balance.

"She's coming round again!" someone howled.

Malak watched through a heavy mental fog, feeling stupid and slow and uncomprehending as the whale breached the surface less than a hundred yards away, a visible frothy wake around it as it hurtled toward the boat, purposeful and cruel.

The whale crashed into the starboard bow of the boat, and the world went sideways. Malak thrashed in the warm water, fighting to breathe and stay afloat, grasping at pieces of splintered wood, looking at the wreckage of the ship that had been upright moments before. The *Essex* now listed to port, taking on water.

One of the returning whaleboats picked him up, and he and the crew attempted to salvage food, water, and wood from the ship. The situation was grim. The Essex herself was not salvageable.

More than a thousand miles from land, with scant supplies and makeshift sails, they were all stranded and adrift in the Pacific. The men retrofitted the three twenty-foot whale boats with masts and sails, and ascertained that they had perhaps thirty days' worth of hard tack and water.

After several weeks, the men aboard Malak's boat were already malnourished.

When the storm hit a month into the journey, they were all starving.

Whale boats are designed to be rowed over short distances, not sail through twenty-foot seas. The wind roared, the waves frothed, and the boats were tossed like a child's toy on rapids. Malak put all of his being into the oars, struggling against an insurmountable power which there was no way to defeat. He did his best to keep the bow headed into the waves, and the boat would climb up a wave, feeling like it would flip, and then sled down the backside of the wave, bow often plunging into the ocean. The sky crackled with lightning, and thunder boomed with a ferocity so hard that it reverberated through his bones, and to Malak it felt like the end of the world.

The men, already suffering, were all but helpless in the face of the wind and the waves.

The storm passed during the night, but in the morning the boats were separated, and Malak was alone with his six men.

He tried to cheer them up with a half-hearted speech that he didn't really believe and ended up making things worse. The storm had contaminated much of their food and water.

As the days wore on, the sun blistered his skin, unrelenting and mean. He was strict about rationing the scant supplies they had left, and more than once had to physically restrain a man from drinking ocean water. They needed another storm so that they could collect drinking water, but a storm never came.

The first man died shortly after that storm. They debated on what to do with his body, and Malak let the men argue, knowing where it would end up. Three of the men argued that a burial at sea was appropriate, while the other three said that it only made sense to make use of their friend's body and consume it.

"He'd a wanted us to live," said Thomas. "No sense in giving him to the fish. We need it more than them."

"No!" said Miguel, a young man from Portugal. "That is against God. The very reason we did not try to go to the Marquesas was because you were afraid of the cannibals. Now you want to be one?" He spat, or made the impression of it, since there was no moisture in his mouth to give to the insult.

"What do we do, Malak?" said Herman, a kid from Cape Cod. It was his first voyage, and he was terrified, starving, and dying of thirst.

"Do what you must," Malak said. "Charles doesn't care anymore, I can tell you that much. I'm not going to partake, but if you men need to eat, then here is food."

The butchering was not the worst thing Malak had ever seen, but it was unsettling.

They cut thin strips of flesh and dried and salted them, and this sustained the men for a week. Even those who had been against it ended up consuming the flesh, although Malak was not among them. He tried to catch flying fish, which were constantly jumping around the boat, almost mocking the men with their presence. He managed to catch only two.

The next week, as hunger pain became all consuming and conversation revolved entirely around the next real meal, the conversation took a somewhat malevolent turn. Thomas proposed a lottery, a drawing of lots, for the next man to die. He would be shot in the head, mercifully, so that the others might have a chance to survive.

Malak considered volunteering, especially since he figured it would not be his last death.

After a day of bickering and debate, the men did agree to draw straws. Malak drew his in turn.

To his dismay, it was the fifteen-year-old cabin boy who drew the short straw. His older cousin immediately offered to take his place. Malak was moved.

The boy, from a good Nantucket family, said that he would accept his lot because that is what he was dealt. He gracefully accepted a bullet to the back of his head delivered by his weeping cousin.

That was the death that Malak regretted the most. The sacrifice that he should have made, but did not.

The next day, they were rescued by an American whaling boat.

CHAPTER FORTY-TWO
INBOUND

Now

A mortar exploded in the courtyard of the compound, followed a fraction of a second later by the impact of another, while small arms fire rang out. Rounds smacked the exterior of the concrete building while Pete communicated with his team via headsets, giving orders to them and Malak's men at the same time, making it difficult to tell who he was talking to.

"I need eyes on the perimeter. Suppressing fire on that main gate. Get a Reaper dialed in. On me, up to the rooftop."

"I'll stay down here, I think," Malak said. "That's the best way to use me, if they get inside the wire."

"Copy that," Pete said, turning away. Keep outta my lines of fire, and don't fucking shoot my men in the back.

Malak accepted the M4-A1 rifle Tiny Tim offered him and dropped to one knee beside the solid door frame. Another mortar rocked the building, and dust showered the roof from the ceiling.

He recognized the heavy crack of a .50 caliber sniper rifle from somewhere on the rooftop over rapid bursts from a light machine gun.

Tim took the right side of the door, while Malak hunkered on the left. Syed, Vladimir, and Ben moved to the doors and windows at the rear of the compound.

Malak waited, sweeping the open space with his weapon, finger on the trigger guard, alert, tense, and patient.

At times, he couldn't see through the smoke and dust, and he expected to fire at any moment upon attackers running through the hellish landscape before him, emerging from the cloud of war.

The enemy did not come.

During a lull in the small-arms fire, Pete bounded down the stairs, boots jarringly loud in the sudden silence. He grabbed two hydration packs and canisters of ammunition for the M-249, and grinned at Malak over his shoulder.

"End of the world, and we're still killing each other, right? They're massing for a major assault, and we're all on our own. Eyes on a swivel. And if you're going to pull some angel-shit, this would be the time! He took to the stairs and vanished.

"Like old times, eh, boss?" Tim said in a crusty voice with sadness in it.

"Yeah," Malak replied. "Like old times."

"Am I going to heaven, do you think?"

"Sure, brother."

"You made me believe, man. You're the reason—"

The main gate exploded inward and upward thirty yards away, thundering and mean. The militants hit it with a car loaded down with explosives, and Malak caught a glimpse of a burning vehicle through black smoke. Men ran around the truck through the smoke, breaking left and right, seeking cover.

From the rooftop, one of the Americans fired an M-203 grenade launcher and added to the chaos. Torn bodies lifted sideways.

The attackers came in a three-pronged assault, with most of them hugging each wall, while those prone to martyrdom ran straight up the middle.

Malak fired short bursts, the weapon bucking against

his shoulder. He adjusted for recoil and continued to fire.

He snapped another magazine into his weapon, scanning the walls. Some of the attackers lay prone, firing on the doorway.

"Shit!" Tim swore across from him when a round snapped inches from his head, shredding the door frame.

Someone lobbed smoke grenades into the center of the courtyard. Malak could not see more than ten yards away.

The SAW on the rooftop chugged, and more M-203 rounds exploded in the swirling gray. Malak held his fire, and within less than a minute, the first cluster of militants came through. Malak and Tim cut them down at close range. One of the men, wounded in the torso, kept coming. Malak shot him twice more in the chest, and the man fell almost at his feet, hands still clutching an AK-47, face down in a spreading pool of blood.

The next onslaught brought more than ten men into close proximity with the building, and Malak was not fast enough to stop them.

He ran out of ammunition, and before he could replace the magazine, they were on him. Tim took a round to the face from only a few feet away, toppling sideways, his right eye gone.

Malak dropped his weapon and engaged the enemy with his fists, elbows, and feet. He felt the searing pain of a gunshot wound low in his back. He grunted and kept swinging. Hands clawed at him, and a rifle-butt came for his head, knocking him in the temple.

He bit a hand on his face, tearing with savage teeth and coming away with a bloody finger in his mouth. The weight of many men was on him, knees digging into his chest, pinning his arms and legs. Though his hearing was almost gone, the curses and exhortations in Arabic pierced the air. He was dimly aware that the gunfire from the roof had ceased. Before the final blow knocked him unconscious, he heard a familiar voice shout, "Enough! He is finished."

CHAPTER FORTY-THREE
DEVIL'S DEN

July 2, 1863

Malak wiped sweat from his forehead, and his hand came away wet and covered with soot. The rolling green hills and forest around Gettysburg swarmed with men killing each other. Heat and smoke clung to the land, and cannons boomed over the crack of rifles.

He gazed down from a craggy rock formation that stood out on the battlefield across the boulder-strewn pastures below. Behind him, a salvo of Potomac artillery belched smoke and death. Seconds later, the explosion on the field below bloomed orange. Malak's hearing was diminished by then, but he could feel the concussions in his chest, and the thunder of cannon and rifle loud enough that even the deaf could hear. Lead musket balls zipped over his head with a sound like angry bees and smacked into the rocks, fragments needling through the air seeking eyes and flesh.

Lying prone, elbows forming a bipod, he tracked a Confederate sniper for a few moments, Spencer rifle light and warm in his hands, the wooden stock pressed firmly into his shoulder, steel sights on the soldier's back, and the rock beneath his chest strangely cool. The gray soldier wormed his way across the ground, trying to get to a white boulder that would offer him meager cover. Behind him, rebel forces formed up for another assault. Malak decided the man was out of range. Maybe he was, and maybe he wasn't worth killing. At least not yet.

Thousands of men massed, bayonets catching the sun, a field of gray interspersed with the red of the rebel battle flag.

Josiah, a boy from Maine, crouched beside Malak and spat heavily on the rocks, taking a long pull from his canteen afterward. "I'm gonna kill me some Rebs today," he said. "Think they'll come soon?" He had that false smile on his face. The one boys make before they die, trying to be heroes. Fear and misplaced swagger at war on a young face.

"Yes. They will come."

"There's a lot of 'em. But we've got the high ground, right? We'll cut 'em down."

"We will. But there are many."

"You'll look out for me, right, Mal?"

"I'll do my best. You know where to go if we get overrun, right? You remember?"

"Yeah. I know. Head down toward the field behind us. I won't drop my rifle. I promise."

"Good boy. Keep your head down. Stay behind cover."

Josiah claimed to be seventeen, but the boy wasn't old enough to shave yet. He should have been climbing trees and stealing apples from his neighbor's orchard rather than sitting on this battlefield with a rifle in his hands.

"I ain't scared," Josiah said. He grinned up at Malak, hat slightly askew, new blue uniform hanging loose from his bony frame. Hands too small to properly hold the musket, but his finger was big enough to pull a trigger.

"Sure," Malak said. "It's okay to be afraid, though. I am."

"You? No. I don't believe you. I hear you're the coldest son-of-a-bitch on this hill. Killed a dozen Reb officers yesterday. I know you're fierce."

"I didn't, and I'm afraid."

What Malak could not tell this child was that he was

not afraid for himself. He felt confident that if he fell on this piece of rock, he would crop up again. Malak was afraid for this kid and the thousands of other kids who were about to die.

The Confederate barrage began in earnest. Cannons thumped in rapid succession and shells exploded in the air and on the ground, raining rock and debris onto Malak's head. Smoke drifted like fog across the battlefield, obscuring the enemy lines. The artillery fire lasted for about an eternity, though it was hard to tell time during any kind of battle, let alone an artillery barrage. Malak despised artillery.

There was no honor in artillery. Death came from above, random and removed, and the man on the other end would never see his target. He'd know he was killing, but he wouldn't get to look someone in the eye when he did it. There was a falseness to it, a distance that seemed to diminish what battle was about.

Malak knew he was old and wrong in his thinking, for war was never about honor, not for those who caused it in the first place. Not for those who gave the orders. There was an honor among brothers on the field, and that's what mattered, and that's why Malak hated artillery.

Because brothers cared. They cried and died and sometimes took it for another brother. They sacrificed themselves because they knew, and when death came down from above, no one knew why they'd really died. What they'd died for.

There was no chance for remorse, no changing of the mind, for there was no mind in a cannon shell, not like when you'd already won a fight and could decide to let a man live. Even if you didn't, there was the choice. Most men shot high.

The further away we get from the eyes of our enemies, the easier it is to kill them.

A shell didn't care that you'd gone to West Point and learned to fight from the time you could walk, and believed you could make a difference. Shrapnel did not consider whether or not you were a father, a husband, or a son who did not want to be on the field in the first place. Death came from above, and it didn't give a damn.

Shells exploded, sending shrapnel and hot metal through flesh, taking limbs and fathers and sons.

Union artillery answered from positions atop Little Round Top just to the east of Devil's Den. Malak hated it just the same. It didn't matter that it was Union artillery killing Confederate soldiers. They were all Americans, all humans. He wanted to throw up.

"Open fire!" came the order down the line.

Malak could not see what he was shooting at because of the thick smoke. He found this to be a waste of ammunition, but complied, nevertheless. That was the strategy. Shoot blind, reload, and shoot again. Unleash a storm of lead too fierce to walk through.

The Spencer rifle was new to him; he'd lifted it from the body of a Michigan man who didn't need it anymore, along with a bag full of cartridges. This weapon was a repeater, so Malak didn't have to spend precious time reloading between each shot. The barrel was considerably shorter than the muskets carried by most infantrymen, and the .50 caliber rounds did terrible damage to flesh. He found that he could fire more than 20 shots in a minute with this weapon, while with his old musket, he was lucky to get off 3 shots between frantic reloads, stuffing paper and linen ammunition into the muzzle.

He fired downhill into the smoke, wondering if the charge had begun. Beside him, Josiah fired and cussed and reloaded.

There was only a slight breeze that day, so the smoke grew thick. Every now and then, it would part enough so that Malak caught glimpses of gray upon gray and flashes and sparks. The rebels were charging.

Shouts and screams drifted over the field, and the next time the wind shifted, Malak saw the men coming on like a ragged, unstoppable wave.

He took aim, steady and cold. He squeezed the trigger, and an officer toppled backwards, the .50 caliber round tearing a hole through his chest. Malak was already seeking the next target. His breathing was controlled and calm, his weapon an extension of himself. The rebels came, some running, others crouched low to the ground, bayonets fixed. Chaos and smoke.

Malak kept firing until his magazine was empty, and he snapped another into place. He could see there was no way the Union would hold this hill on this day. He kept on shooting, while cannons boomed and muskets bucked and the bayonets flashed.

They were close.

He saw beards and fury, and he kept shooting. Men fell among the boulders and the swirling smoke and the screams and constant cannon fire. Boys died with a rebel yell on their lips when Malak shot them in the face. Malak was terrible. Good at killing, though.

"Retreat!" He screamed at young Josiah.

Josiah kept reloading.

"Kid, fall back."

"No!" Reloading his rifle. Resolute. Kneeling and foolish and brave, stuffing his weapon when he was shot in the throat. Sagging back and dropping his weapon and putting both of his hands on his neck, blood flowing around his fingers. That desperate look in his eyes of betrayal, choking and dying.

Malak was angry. He knew this war was bloody. He'd been a citizen of many countries, but he *believed* in America. This was another war about money and power, but there was also right and wrong. Malak believed that evil existed, and he'd fought it face to face before. The idea that people should be able to own other people was an awful idea, in Malak's mind. He'd been a slave himself long ago, and he sided with the Union because the war was about halting the spread of slavery, no matter what the South argued about states' rights. The war was about the right to own human beings and whether or not that idea should keep spreading to new states and territories. He was willing to kill and die to stop that.

He couldn't save the kid, though. Josiah was gone. Brave and young and dead.

Malak charged the rebel army, screaming and angry, and at that moment, he knew and didn't care that he was about to die again.

Even wise men have breaking points. Malak broke that day on that hill, after enduring centuries of war and hate and the seeming futility of all of it.

He dropped his rifle and launched himself into the smoke. With a long knife in his right hand, he danced and slashed and cut and broke necks and stabbed. The rebels were bunched together and unprepared for Malak. There was no way they could have been ready for his insane assault. The smoke swallowed him, and he was among them.

He cut a man from balls to sternum, while crushing another man's throat. He stabbed a bearded, pleading man in the stomach, and this took longer than it should have because someone stabbed Malak in the back, so his strike was not as efficient as he intended it to be. Not the thrust up into the heart, which was quick, but a blundering straight forward jab to the guts, where he wound up falling on top of the man.

"Please, no," the man said. Malak's weight on the man, straddling him. Long blade twisting in his insides. Blood leaking from his mouth.

"You don't have to—"

Malak wrenched the blade out and cut the man's throat with a savage slice, his weight on the steel, and felt spine grate against blade and the splash of hot blood on his face.

Pushing himself to his feet, Malak took a lungful of sin and ripped the musket from a man's hands who emerged from the fog. He looked astounded when Malak spun the weapon around and used his own bayonet to skewer him through the heart. Eyes wide, mouth hanging open, gasping there at the end, shocked.

Malak killed two more men before a round entered his forehead and exited through the base of his brain.

Many years later, when he researched the battle, Malak learned that the battle of Gettysburg was perhaps the turning point of the Civil War, and that his actions might have played a part. Union soldiers retreated and were able to provide cover fire, and while Little Round Top is remembered, the battle around Devil's Den was part of that ultimate Union victory. Malak died, though, like he knew he would when he started his charge.

When he opened his eyes again, men were still trying to kill each other. He hated war and wondered why he was so good at it, and worse, why God would allow it.

If man is created in God's image, then why are men killers?

CHAPTER FORTY-FOUR
MT. MEGIDDO

Now

Malak hurt all over. His bones ached, and the gunshot wound in his back throbbed. He felt warm, sticky blood trickle down his leg and across his stomach. He lay face down, with his face sideways on rocks, the pebbles cratering his flesh.

Across the valley floor, lines of armor churned up clouds of dust, and helicopters dotted the sky. In the distance, Malak recognized the roar of jets ripping through the sky.

He pushed himself to his feet, staring at the armies below.

"It's beautiful, isn't it?" said that cursed voice from behind him. Malak turned to face the devil.

Lucifer beamed at him. "What? Not what you expected, I suppose."

"Go to hell."

"Oh, I've never heard that one. Behold."

"What would that be?"

"Armageddon, now, where you sit. Are you prepared? Are you ready to sacrifice billions of lives before a slumbering God? Do you really think that Jesus will descend now with a sword and toss me into a lake of fire? Is that how this actually ends? Or do I win either way? Because, you see, the world dies. Isn't that prophecy?"

"That's not the whole story."

"Your faith amuses me. Because you lack both faith and facts, my simpleton brother. You know not your own history or the truth, so how can you possibly be so arrogant as to believe you understand anything? You hold no power here. I love moments like this. Moments of revelation and truth.

"I have no power here. You're right about that. That's the first true thing you've said. But you know where the real power is. You do. You deceive even yourself because you are so skilled at lying. You believe your own bullshit."

"I know far more than you do. I'm surprised you haven't figured that out yet."

Malak groaned, forcing himself into a standing position, refusing to sit at the devil's feet. His body howled in protest while he looked Lucifer in the eye.

"Your arrogance is astounding," Malak said. "Tell me why you care about any of this. What's your goal?"

Lucifer smiled a secret smile, his blond hair and fine features radiant in the pale light of the afternoon. "I'm glad you ask."

"So?"

"I am what I am," Lucifer said. It pleases me, and that's why I care about this fight and the affairs of men. *I am the ultimate creator.*"

"Is that what you believe?" Malak said.

"It is one thing to make mud, but quite another to sculpt mankind," Lucifer said. "The excrement was there, lacking in form and purpose, while I gave it shape. From the club to the sword to the ICBM, I have unleashed man's potential, molding, shaping, reducing, sometimes destroying. This is my domain. My canvas is eternity, and I paint with souls."

"Why didn't you make something beautiful, then?"

"I did. I made men."

"No."

"I made men what they are from a pile of stinking shit. I formed them from filth."

"Into what? Do you hear yourself? What is it you claim you made?"

"Beauty. Is not man beautiful? Man scratches at the outskirts of this solar system, in the reality of a universe more vast than the best of their simple brains can begin to conceive. I propelled men from the mud to the stars. That is beautiful. I am beautiful."

"No. You are insane."

"Oh, that's rich," Lucifer chuckled, a musical sound. "You amuse me. You have lived like them for so long, you think like humans. I am not constrained by petty concepts like sanity. I am a force of nature like hurricanes or earthquakes, or the solar wind. Like gravity, Malak. Can gravity be sane or not? No. It simply *is*."

"Nature lacks intent. You are evil."

"Again, you are falling into human thought processes. You have not figured out that there is no right or wrong, no good and bad. Evil is entirely a human construct."

"You are wrong," Malak grated, feeling weak and depleted.

"I am right. And now I make a case against God before the sanity police." He laughed, a melody without soul, music without heart. "Oh, but wait, I already did that, didn't I? Made that case, and Jesus lost that one. Deemed a threat, crucified on a cross, and treated like an animal. I think you were even there. At least for the last bit. Hammer and nails, oh my. I do love me some Judas."

Malak spat on the ground.

Lucifer's eyes bored into Malak with abrupt intensity, power burning and shifting below the surface, the affable mask dropped and replaced by naked hate, a mocking evil, and twitching energy straining for release, like he wanted Malak to see the transformation, to feel the power of darkness, to see the beast beneath.

"If it was that easy," Malak said, "then you wouldn't be here, I think. You wouldn't bother. What is it you really want?"

"I want to watch you squirm, to agonize like a fish on a hook." He smirked. "Or a dying man on a cross. Like that."

"You continue to delude yourself that you have the real power, or that I can influence anything."

"And you, brother," Lucifer said, "keep denying the truth. Here's a taste of reality. Below us, the armies of the world are assembled. Syria, Iran, Saudi Arabia, Jordan, Egypt, Israel, the United States, and Russia are poised to unleash hell on earth on this field. All it will take is a single word from me. A single tactical nuke detonated here ends the world. You know it, for men excel at escalating when it comes to violence."

"So do it, then. I can't stop you."

"Correct. You cannot."

"Well, get it over then, devil. It won't end well for you. There is no winning."

"Wrong. This is my time. And that's what I need for you to finally understand. I want to watch you break inside, to witness the truth shatter your simple soul. You have been led to believe that God cares about men. He does not. He is gone, eyes turned elsewhere in the universe as they have been for thousands of years. He has abandoned this place, as men have abandoned Him. You should know this by now, Malak."

"And I'm supposed to be broken by that statement? I'm to be shattered?" Malak laughed. "Keep lying."

Lucifer smirked. "Hubris makes men believe that God cares about them in a universe of billions of stars, here on this tiny ball of rock on the outskirts of an insignificant galaxy among billions of other galaxies. Here is the truth, Malak: *I am God here."*

"Do you really believe that?"

"I don't believe it, I *know* it. And I want you to feel and understand the truth of it. I want you to remember this little talk when you curl into a pathetic ball and cry out to your uncaring God. Because I love my creation. I love mankind. I want to watch humanity fulfill its potential. God has always stifled it, suppressed what I strived to unleash from the beginning."

"So, you're the good shepherd."

"I've been God on Earth all along. You have not acknowledged it. You have raged against it, even though somewhere deep down you knew, Malak. You have seen the evil in men, tasted the blood and agony. Even now, in the dark corners of your soul, that knowledge is gnawing at you, and I'm sure it hurts. Where is your God now? When did you last feel him?"

"Here. He never left."

"You will find," Lucifer said, "that he was never here in the first place." He snapped his fingers, and the world flashed and went dark.

Images flashed before Malak's, boring into his mind, invasive and cruel, like a swirling swarm of wasps which lay eggs inside hosts, every sting a vision, each memory an unspeakable horror.

He watched the nuclear war as though he looked down, disembodied from space, cities blooming, the missiles arcing through the sky like shooting stars falling to the earth. He saw children dying by the million as famine swept the globe, disease ravaging the survivors. The sound of anguished wails filled his ears. Darkness consumed the bleeding earth.

CHAPTER FORTY-FIVE
MOUNTAIN MAN

The West, 1865

Soaring peaks thrust from the Wyoming plateau, evergreens dotting the land in stark contrast with the pristine, shining snow and gray rock. The sharp air tasted like sweet sunlight and the promise of spring. Low silver clouds shrouded the distant slopes, shifting with the wind, and the lofty mountain peaks held the sun and seemed to shine with a golden light all their own.

It was the kind of vista that sucks the oxygen from a man's lungs and makes him believe in a creator, the master artist who took particular care here, painting beauty, sculpting hope, until the land sang a song of joy and awesome wonder only a fool could not feel in his soul. This place cried out to the universe that God existed, and though He might appear distant and uncaring, His love was infused into the stone and sky, for such majesty could not possibly be random.

Malak inhaled the scenery for a few quiet minutes before setting out again. He crossed a meadow, oiled boots making crunching sounds in the light snow over the occasional bird call, while sunlight streamed through a cathedral of pine and birch trees.

He traversed the plateau throughout the morning, the temperature well above freezing now. He shed a few layers of clothing and rolled them into his pack, an unwieldly thing that weighed a hundred pounds. Up ahead, the music of rushing water beckoned.

Pushing through willows, he emerged on the rocky banks of a river. The water flowed swift and cold, snow melt from the peaks providing force and volume, and the rapids swirled around rocks jutting up from the water, creating eddies. Malak plunked down on a boulder and took out some dried bison and munched with the sun on his face.

He hadn't seen another human being for more than three weeks, not since he'd sheltered in a tiny Shoshone village while the last blizzard of the year blew itself out. They told him about this place, and now he understood why they revered it.

Since the fur trade dried up and the Civil War took able-bodied men into battle, this land was gloriously empty and vast.

Beyond the river, a few bison plodded through the snow, and Malak spotted an elk silhouetted on a ridge against the blue sky.

Despite good intentions, Malak believed he'd spent most of his life running away from God; even when he thought he was seeking Him, Malak could never get close, and the harder he fought to close the distance, the further God seemed.

It was not as though he'd lost his faith, but rather longed for something deeper and more substantial. He envied men who carried that with them, that deep serenity and peace. He'd known men who felt that connection with God, and found it to be elusive and fleeting in his own life, like trying to catch a whisper of smoke or hold the wind.

After Gettysburg, he found himself wearing heavy mountain clothes at a railway yard in Kansas. He hopped on the train and headed west, shunning fellow travelers and embracing solitude. When the rails ran out, he worked in a shabby saloon, where he earned enough money to purchase another Spencer rifle and ammunition boxes before embarking on the long trek to the mountains.

Now, on the bank with the sun dancing on the river and the cool wind on his face, Malak knew that it was worth it. His stained soul needed restoration, healing, and solace.

Over the next weeks, he scouted for a place to build a cabin, ultimately settling on a clearing beside a perfect blue lake with water clear as glass. He used pine and rock to construct a one room shack, sturdy enough to withstand the wind and snow of the coming winter while the forest came alive.

Wolves scampered along the shoreline and sang mournful songs into the night when the moon rose high. Sometimes he howled with them, and others he sang songs he remembered from his time in the monastery on the other side of the world.

During the short summer, he encountered a mother grizzly bear with two cubs ambling along behind her. He made the mistake of venturing into a berry patch where he knew the bear liked to forage.

The bear surprised him, and he surprised the bear. She reared up on her hind legs, not twenty feet away, her head popping up over the shrubs, towering over him. She looked curious at first, and then as angry as a bear can look, yellow fangs bared and growling a deep growl that vibrated in Malak's chest. She dropped down and her paws slapped the ground, and the branches crashed, and then she was in his face, on all fours, clawing at the earth and making that awful sound.

Malak took the rifle from his shoulder, moving in slow motion, and brought the butt of the weapon to his shoulder. He backed away, one careful step at a time.

Her cubs peered from behind her bulk, and she roared

again.

"All right," Malak said in a gentle voice. "Look here. I'm sorry I got in your way. I'll be leaving now."

She reared up again, and Malak admired her size and girth, every bit of 700 pounds of fang and fur.

He continued his retreat, and she gave him a final bellow before vanishing into the bush. Malak sighed with relief and decided to give that particular patch of berries a wide berth from then on.

Over the next two years, he spotted her frequently. The last time, she had a new set of cubs with her. She respected his space, and he made sure he stayed far away.

He hunted small game with a bow he fashioned by hand, and during that first cold winter, he almost starved to death, his body eating itself again the way it did a hundred years ago. He survived, though, and the following year he laid in enough dried meat to last through the long dark months.

He hoped to draw nearer to God, and in this regard, he was disappointed, for despite being surrounded by grandeur, he still felt separated from Him, as though a veil kept him from seeing the truth and feeling the love that was promised. He communed with nature, which is not quite the same thing, and left him vaguely unfulfilled. Nature and solitude were not enough to fill a God-shaped hole.

It was as though Malak could sense God's presence all around him, within tree, rock, and stream, and yet could never draw near enough.

He tried to empty his soul of the flotsam and detritus accumulated through the centuries of crying out for that overwhelming flood of validation, purpose, and redeeming love he'd known in the past, perplexed, alone, and thirsty like a nomad in the desert who sees the oasis, yet cannot drink, recalling that sweet taste of water over parched tongue, crawling on elbows and knees, salvation always close enough to touch, yet just beyond reach.

Malak was certain he sought truth rather than a mirage, and that yearning grew stronger in him as the years passed.

In 1871, a government survey expedition intruded upon his lake, and he answered questions in terse fashion, resenting the necessity to be civil. Later that year, more people came to the mountains, and he decided it was getting a little too crowded.

He pushed west to San Francisco, caught a boat, and steamed north to the end of the world. In the Klondike, he found solitude and a fortune. He lived the life of a monk in the shadow of the mountains, and when he sold his claim, he was astounded at the number of zeros written upon the check the mining firm delivered to him. He contacted an attorney in San Francisco and established a series of trust accounts, anticipating his demise or at least the need for the illusion of it.

When war erupted in Europe, Malak resisted the impulse to join either side. Ultimately, God and a grizzly made the choice for him. She got him in the springtime beside a river where the willows hung low and the water hushed over smooth rocks.

When he lifted his head again, he was soaked in mud, and boys screamed and cried in the trench beside him while shells pounded the ground and shredded men.

CHAPTER FORTY-SIX
BRINGER OF DAWN

Now

He dreamed he was dragged from the rubble of the CIA compound, screaming and deranged, and that he asked Tiny Tim for forgiveness, his friend's eye a ragged hole. Later, there was a plane and pain, and he couldn't move.

He came to his senses with clean white sheets, a plush bed, and Kelli hovering over him with worried blue eyes. The large room reminded him of his time in Florence, floor-to-ceiling windows open, and airy curtains billowing in a gentle breeze while paintings from the masters looked down. He felt out of place and time.

"Thank God," Kelli said. "They said there was no way you would live."

"I'm not entirely sure I did. Ugh. Where are we?"

"The Vatican. We are guests of the Pope, at the request of the President."

"I've missed something."

"More than you can imagine," she said. "We might just make it through this."

He felt wrong, not entirely himself, as though he'd been violated in his sleep, and while he couldn't identify anything specific, the sensation did not leave him the way a bad dream should, but lingered and slunk around the corners of his psyche.

"What happened?" What happened at Megiddo? How are you here? How did I get here?"

She smiled at him with empathy and hope and a trace of sadness, touched his hand, and sat on the edge of the bed with her legs on the floor.

"Slow down. Nothing happened at Megiddo; you kept talking about that while you were sedated. Our guys rescued you from the compound in Jerusalem. You were the only survivor. But there is good news. The ceasefire holds, and all of the nuclear-capable countries have agreed to it. The leaders of the world are meeting here, in the Vatican, to discuss the future. Everything has changed."

"Why am I here, then? Or you?"

"I flew here with the President. We're going to make a better world together now. Something you've dreamed about forever. Imams, Rabbis, Catholics, Protestants, Buddhists, and Hindus are gathering here to put away grievances."

"Forgive me, old friend, but I'm still missing something.

"The world almost ended, *but it didn't*. It's still dicey, but you wouldn't believe how quick things are coming together. People are helping each other. Pakistan and India are mounting joint flood-relief efforts. China is flying supplies into Japan. Israel withdrew from the West Bank. A massive Russian convoy is underway now, bringing food, water, and engineers to the United States. A new day dawns for humanity. A fresh start."

He arched his eyebrow. "Interesting."

"How is this not good? This is why you recruited me. To do good in the world. It's what we've been fighting for since I've known you. Unity. Peace. Tell me how I'm wrong."

"You're right."

"Except, somehow I'm not, you think."

"We have worked for peace, yes. That's what we did. What's coming is different, I fear. Insidious. Toxic. Venom to the soul. A peace that isn't really peace."

"What are you talking about?"

"The end of faith. The beginning of the reign of lies. Where men cannot see the truth because it is cloaked in a comfortable reality defined by disbelief. I fear the world enters a new age where man's inherent straining of the soul to understand the deeper truth is crushed by the weight of an arrogant darkness masquerading as light."

"Coming from someone who has raged against religion, that's a strange comment."

"Religion and truth aren't the same things. In fact, they're often opposed. Religion claims to strive for truth, yet obscures it, sometimes with smiles, others with swords, and always with certainty. Faith in a lie is worse than no faith at all."

"Still," she said, an earnest glow about her, " Put religion aside, and you've got to see the potential here. Where is your faith in humanity? Haven't you always believed we deserved better? That we could do better than we have?"

"Do you know what the name Lucifer means?"

"Not off hand."

"Lucifer is translated from the Hebrew word meaning *'shining one*, or *morning star.'* In Greek, the translation means *'bringer of dawn.'*"

"Forgive me, Malak, but I think you're still heavily indoctrinated, and you don't know it. You are so entrenched in your distorted beliefs that you can't see the truth."

"The word appears in the Old Testament, referring to a fallen king of Babylon; Satan liked the sound of it, I suppose. It fits nicely with his pride."

"So, what are you trying to say, Malak? That Lucifer is behind this newfound unity?"

"Yes, something like that. It's what he wants."

"Isn't that better than killing the entire planet? What's

the alternative?"

"I struggle with that," Malak admitted. "Then again, the Bible is full of destruction. The books of prophecy are the hardest of all. In the book of Revelation, the world is smashed, but the devil walks the earth first. I fear that's where we are. He doesn't think he will lose, though. He believes he knows something we don't."

"Have you ever considered that maybe it's best for mankind if he is *right*? That it's better for us all?"

"Yes. That's not the end of the story, though."

"So what can you do, then? You know I'm not religious. You healed me, yes. But that doesn't mean that I believe what you do. Christianity is rife with contradictions, and I refuse to believe in a God that is so willing to kill what he created. To me, the Judeo-Christian concept of God is awful. He's a kid with an ant farm; then he gets bored and decides to pour acid onto his little experiment and watches the ants die. That's not a god I can believe in. There is a scientific explanation for you. We just haven't figured it out yet."

"Sure. And one for God, as well. They are not necessarily opposed. Each strives to explain underlying truths, and neither has all the answers. Scientists and theologians have more in common than they think. Those who claim to know everything don't."

"You're driving me crazy. What are you going to do?"

"I don't know. Hopefully something will present itself."

A man in a dark suit entered the room, his face stoic. "If you are able to walk, the President would like to see you now," the man said.

CHAPTER FORTY-SEVEN
THE FOG OF WAR

Ypres, France, April 23, 1915

German artillery shells smashed the unlucky mud and hills and men beneath a mindless rain of death. The concussions and shockwaves tore the air from Malak's lungs. His ears hurt and rang with a high-pitched keening pain, and he could not hear the screaming men hunkered down in the wet dirt beside him. Some of them cried, but Malak could not hear.

Machine guns hammered at enemy positions through tangles of barbed wire. The sun was bright and warm that day, yet there was no hope in it. Within minutes, its rays were meager and muted by smoke, still shining, but essentially absent from the swirling chaos below.

The middle-aged man next to him, a carbine clutched to his chest like a True Relic of the Cross, shouted something at Malak, eyes rolling white and wide like a snake-bit horse, and although his mouth moved, Malak heard nothing he tried to say.

His name is Jean, and his wife is a pale skinned, wholesome brunette with green eyes. He has three young children and a mistress in Paris, and I smiled at the pictures of all of them when he showed me, back when it was quiet.

Maybe they'd both lost it. Lost that part of themselves that cared and wanted to care because there is a silence of the soul, a numbness of spirit which descends upon men when hope is as dangerous as bullets and bombs, and the only defense is not giving a damn anymore.

A young officer huffed his way through the narrow trench, slapping men on the head, screaming at them to return fire. The man was impassioned and brave, and *he* still gave a damn.

He died, twitching and spurting blood from his torn helmet after a round punched through the top of his skull, tearing through his brain and future with hardened, lethal purpose.

Hope could kill a man quicker than mustard gas.

The *lack* of hope destroyed men, too, only it took longer and was more painful. Malak remembered this essential truth, gripping his weapon and firing into the abyss.

When the gas attack came, no one knew what was happening, for this was the first time in the war that gas had been used as a weapon.

Tendrils of sickly yellow smoke wove together with the gray smog on the field, that fog of war heavy like a lead cloak upon the field that day. Jean's eyes rolled up into his head, and he frothed at the mouth, hands clawing and clenched at his throat, his face a rictus of pain.

Malak burned inside and out, his lungs eaten from within, his skin feeling like it was on fire. His vision blurred, and he felt he was falling; when his face hit the dirt sideways, he realized he was dying.

A mortal man would have succumbed then, but Malak lay in agony for what felt like years. The shells fell with distant thumps, and machine guns continued to fire until an eerie silence descended upon the trenches, as if that place was no longer part of the rest of the world, but existed in a kind of purgatory, a separate plane of existence where weapons of mass destruction and dying for years, bereft hope made sense.

Jean stared at Malak with lifeless blue eyes, his face

only inches away and caked in mud, while a single drop of water snaked its way across his frozen face from his forehead to the tip of his crooked nose, a ponderous, aching journey which was the only thing that made Malak certain time still existed.

The German soldiers wormed through the wire and climbed down into the trench. Wearing gray uniforms and gas masks, they prodded the still bodies of the French soldiers. While they set up defensive positions and rifled through the dead for cigarettes, shoes, and souvenirs, a gentle breeze whispered through the valley, carrying away the last vestiges of gas. Malak healed while the soldiers threaded through the trench in his direction.

He kept his eyes open while a man in a gray uniform streaked with mud and blood rammed a muzzle into his genitals.

"They're all dead," said the man through his mask, voice far away and muffled. "I pity them."

"Better them than us," the soldier behind the first man said. "I don't give a shit. Helmut, you are a woman at heart."

"Philipp," Helmut replied, "you have no honor. At least you know it. These men died like rats."

"Humph. They're not men. They're French. Oh, that's nice."

"What?"

"What a pretty girl. When we get to Paris, I'm going to fuck her."

Philipp rifled through Jean's coat and found his wallet, along with pictures of his family; he held it up for his comrade to see, giggling.

"You're vile."

"Shut up. You love me. I've saved your ass more times than you can count."

"I don't want to be here. You do. You *like* it."

"Which is why you and I are both still alive. Stop whining. If you start to cry again, I'll gut you right here, and no one will know."

"Fuck you, Philipp."

"Fuck you, Helmut. You are weak. You didn't have to shoot your rifle today, did you? You got off easy. Nothing on your perfect hands. No blood. If we charged without the gas, how many would have died? You think too much and not enough."

Their voices receded as they moved along. Malak's lungs burned, and his muscles ached. He became whole again as the German soldiers walked away. In the other direction, men in gray set up machine gun emplacements, turning the weapons in the opposite direction to face unsuspecting French lines further in.

Malak took a deep breath, inhaling the smoke and death and bracing himself for what had to come next. His ears recovered, along with the rest of him, while he considered his options.

"You don't think at all," Helmut said through his gas mask.

A weapon cracked.

"See," Philipp said, "that one was still alive. Would you have done what I did? No. And maybe when your back was turned, he might have cut your throat. If you were not my little brother, I think I would have killed you myself by now." He chuckled. "Then again, I still might."

Malak rolled onto his stomach, pulling his serrated blade from the sheath at his side, aware of the scraping sound it made, willing it to be silent, commanding the Germans to keep walking with sheer hope. He glanced over his shoulder, where the forces embedded in the trench under a heavy fog of smoke, and more soldiers came through the wire, muttering and laughing with secret voices.

When he pushed himself into a crouch, the mud made a sucking sound, and he tasted stale water and polluted air and a gravelly thirst for violence.

He bounded forward, feet slapping the water and sinking into the mud, and the men he used to know.

Helmut, the philosopher-soldier, turned his head at the splash of Malak's attack. The soldier crumpled when Malak struck him with four fingers in the lower back, at a place where nerves congregate and refuse to obey when smashed, hitting his knees, while Malak jumped from the wall to his right, kicked hard, and launched himself into the air, slicing Philipp's neck.

His blade found Philipp's carotid artery, while his left hand gripped Philipp's mouth and wrenched. Malak landed in one fluid motion, feet slapping the water while blood fountained from the German's neck, his hand a vise grip on the dying soldier's mouth. Philipp's eyes went wide and terrified. Malak buried his blade in Philipp's sternum, angled up, and he twisted once with ferocity and violent precision before ripping it out. Philipp died before he slipped back into the mud.

The sound of whistles pierced the air while Malak attacked the Germans in that trench, machine guns chugging and mortars falling, an angel of death among men, churning through them like a propeller, whirling, spinning, stabbing, slashing, and killing for almost a quarter of a mile. The blood and the mud and the crud were one song, and Malak sang it with everything in him, dancing death and the thump of artillery in his chest and the rhythm of mayhem in his soul.

It was a fellow French soldier who killed him, shot him in the back of the head from ten feet away, and Malak didn't have any time to reflect on that then. Later, he decided his exit from World War I was proper and good, and that he wouldn't have changed a damn thing.

CHAPTER FORTY-EIGHT
ANTICHRIST

Now

Two members of the Swiss Guards escorted Malak to the Casa
Santa Marta. One of the guards, dressed in an anachronistic,
tri-colored uniform of yellow, red, and blue stripes with a
black beret cocked jauntily on his head, explained that the
building was the Papal residence, as well as a guest house.
Along the way, they strode through polished marble corridors
with arched ceilings painted with ornate depictions of angels,
God, and men.

The President of the United States of America stood
from his seat at a simple oak table when Malak walked into
the sunlit room. Wearing an impeccable black suit and a
somber expression, President Shaker extended his hand.
Malak shook it, the man's grip firm but not overbearing. He
grinned at Malak with his mouth but not his eyes.

"Welcome back," said the President. Two Secret
Service men retreated to opposite corners of the room, while
another shut the door from the outside. "We have much to
discuss. Please, sit."

"Thank you," Malak said, glancing around the room.

A wooden crucifix hung on one wall, Jesus gazing
down with mercy and nails in his hands and feet. Several
medieval paintings adorned white walls, with baroque gold
frames and color faded by the ages. The room smelled of old
books and flowers.

They sat in wooden chairs with white padded seats

and backs, facing one another and not speaking for a few heartbeats.

"So." The President said. "The world is a very different place than it was the last time we spoke. I understand that you did not find what we were looking for. Or *who* we were looking for, to be more specific."

Malak nodded without speaking, considering what he should reveal.

"The world is evolving," the President said. "There is a lot you don't know."

"I see."

The President reached behind him and laid an ancient, weathered artifact on the table. It was the tip of a spear, the metal worn and corrupted and dull.

"Do you know what this is?"

"I can guess."

"It is the Spear of Destiny. The tip of the spear that pierced Christ. What you don't know is that U.S. forces captured this from Hitler's bunker in 1945 and delivered it to the Vatican in the late 1960s. Our top scientists have vetted this thing. It's the real deal." The President closed his eyes and ran his fingers across the shaft. "This gives mankind another chance, with your help."

"So, let me guess. You want me to do battle with the devil and kill him with this thing. Because you think it has power since it's really old, and also Hitler had it. That's not how things work. Not in my experience. And I've had some of that."

"Hold that thought for a moment. You have come face to face with the devil?"

"Yes."

"And every time he was stronger than you, right? At each crossroads, you were not enough. This could tip the balance. The last time, did you find him? In Jerusalem?"

"He found me. It didn't end well, as far as I can tell. He let me go."

"That's a good thing," the President said. "Because what we have now is an opportunity unparalleled in human history. The nations of the world can come together as one. Sometimes the old must be destroyed to make way for the new. It's time to embrace a new world, one of order and peace."

"All right," Malak said. "And who will lead us into this new era of rainbows and tranquility? How will we decide?"

The President smiled again and put his hands up in a dramatic *you caught me* pose. "Hold on. You're jumping to conclusions and missing the point. Everything has changed, almost overnight. The earth is reeling now, wounded and bleeding. We need to heal. We need to believe."

"I don't disagree with that," Malak replied.

"Do you know what has truly changed? What's different now than any time before this? Sure, we can do wonders with technology. We've got computers and cell phones, and soon we will travel among the planets. But there is something unique we have now, a gift to humanity that we have received from the heavens."

"What might that be?" Malak said.

"We have *you*."

"I don't understand."

"We have proof, in you, of the existence of God. You are an angel. You don't die. You perform miracles. Can't you see that you will unify this planet in a way that was previously unthinkable, impossible, until now? Already, the word of your deeds is spreading like wildfire around the globe. There is a crowd gathered beyond the gates waiting to see you, cheering your name."

The room seemed to tilt. Down was up and up was down, the earth wrong on its axis. He found it hard to breathe. He understood.

"There is evidence of some of what you have done. In Jerusalem, in living color, a feed of you bringing a man back to life without a scratch on him. Cell phone and surveillance footage of you glowing white in the middle of battle. Photographs of you throughout the last hundred years. We have documented proof. A woman who could not walk who can now run. You, a man who is not a man, coming back from a bullet to the spine, healed within days. It's all over the internet, all over the planet. We need hope. And our hope is in you. You will save us."

"No," Malak whispered. "This cannot be."

The truth assailed Malak. Clarity wounded him.

I am the antichrist.

Now, he understood the cryptic remarks from Lucifer and Ariel. *"You are not who you were, nor who you are meant to be."* He saw how his path led him to this place and time and recognized the way that his experiences forged both deep empathy and quiet disgust with mankind. For though men could be great, they also possessed the ability for evil beyond imagining.

Malak was susceptible to the belief he could somehow change that propensity, could alter what was inherent to humanity. He'd been doing it for two thousand years. He still believed in the essential goodness of most men, in spite of the atrocities he'd witnessed.

"You are the Messiah, returning to the earth in the moment of our greatest need," the President said. "Whether you believe it, doesn't matter. Everyone else does. Those who haven't heard, will. It is a self-fulfilling prophecy. You will unify our monotheistic religions and the nations of the world simply by your existence. Can you imagine the good you will do? How many billions of lives will you save?"

The vision of the future that the devil inflicted upon him danced before Malak's eyes, and he remembered, there in the Vatican, sitting across the table from the President. He saw the tanks in the valley and the blinding flash and the era of plague and darkness that followed. Centuries of tribulation, famine, and death. If he would just agree to become the savior, perhaps mankind could avoid this strife. That was the implicit promise, the veiled threat, and the lie.

Malak still believed that his choices were his own, for better or worse.

He wanted to give humanity more time to live, love, and grow. He wanted to save them from themselves. Yet he knew that ultimately, he could not be that hero. He never was. He saw what he had to do.

"Let me tell you something, President Shaker. I planned on killing you today."

"What? Why?" The Secret Service agents moved fast to restrain him, as they were trained to do. He broke the first man's knee, launching himself from the chair, spinning on the ground, and lashing out with his foot. He jumped to his feet and threw a golden crucifix from the desk at the second attacking officer, striking him in the center of the forehead. The man slumped by the door.

"I was certain that you were the antichrist," Malak said, spinning, looking the President in the eyes. "I thought that by killing you, I might buy humanity some time." Malak snatched the Spear of Destiny from the table.

The door burst open, and men in suits swarmed into the room, too late. The Secret Service officers screamed at him, and they fired, the sound terrible and deafening in that closed room.

He grabbed the tip of the lance, the jagged spear of destiny, and jammed it into his own heart. He'd killed enough men to know how to do it right.

CHAPTER FORTY-NINE
YESHUA

The Rock, now

Waves hushed along the beach, the distant crash of the breakers at the edge of the reef mingling with the easy ebb and flow across the sand flats and tidal waters.

Malak lay on his back, gazing at the night sky. The Milky Way stretched from horizon to horizon, diffuse light emanating from one small galaxy among billions.

A crab skittered by his head, and he smiled. He lay on his back, with the sand pressing into his hair and the back of his legs and in between his toes, cool and honest.

He laughed out loud, hearty and meaning it. He felt peace. He marveled at the quiet beauty of the universe for a time, inhaling the clean salty air into his lungs and tasting the sea. Here on this island, the struggle of man ceased to matter. He could simply *be*, without pressure or self-induced guilt. He would remember, and try to commune with the Creator, and if he was lucky, he'd feel that connection again.

"You are loved," said someone behind him.

Malak stood and turned, shocked. He'd always been alone here. This was his refuge, a place of solitude.

Night became day. One moment, Malak stood in the darkness, and the next, he faced the Son of man in the light. The sun shone bright against a perfect blue sky.

Malak fell back to the sand and lay prostrate before the smiling, bearded man with kind eyes.

"Yeshua, I am yours," Malak said. His heart thumped

in his chest, and his eyes filled with tears. "Forgive me. I am unworthy." His chest was hollow, and his mouth was dry. He found it hard to form words.

"Rise, beloved," Jesus said in a gentle voice that was almost a whisper.

Malak stood again and stared at Yeshua, hundreds of questions assailing him, but speechless, overcome with awe and wonder.

Jesus opened his arms wide. The loose white robe He wore was radiant and shining with inexplicable intensity.

"Come to me," He said, wrapping his arms around Malak in a warm embrace.

Malak wept, the tears flowing down his cheeks, overcome with love and gratitude. It was the feeling of a child lost and starving in the wilderness, found and saved at the final hour by his father.

"You have suffered much, Malak. But you have helped many. You have been a flame in the darkness. Do you understand now?"

"Teacher, no, I do not."

"In this world, there is trouble, yet I have overcome the world. You know this. You see the truth in it."

"Yes. I. But… I have lacked faith many times, made terrible mistakes."

"It does not matter now. Your faith is stronger than you think. Love is more powerful than hate. *Always.*"

"But Lucifer —"

"He is part of creation. He fights to place himself upon a pedestal, though he knows no crown is his. Men must feel darkness to see light."

"Is this the end for mankind? Is this the hour of your return?"

Jesus smiled, a hint of mischief in his eyes.

"Not now," he said. "Soon."

Jesus kissed Malak on the forehead, and infinite universes danced exploded and danced before Malak's eyes, stars and galaxies dying and born again, and in some of those possibilities, humanity soared among the farthest reaches of space and time, flitting from star to star, along with races older than man.

Jesus transformed into pure light and ascended into the heavens like the rays of the sun in reverse, and Malak trembled, wiping the tears from his face. The sense of joy in Malak fled as he watched Jesus leave, and he was utterly alone and desolate with loss.

He sat for a time with his back perched against a piece of driftwood, looking out across the shimmering water with the sun warm on his face. He'd not asked any of the important questions that had been tugging at his brain for two thousand years. Questions like *What am I? Why am I here?* He decided, though, that Jesus had actually answered those questions for him.

When the sun sank into the waters, Malak returned to his campsite, which was exactly as he left it. He made a fire and drank fresh coconut juice. Sometime in the dark of the night, he drifted off to sleep.

He woke with a pressure in his chest, a tingling at the base of his head, and a sense of euphoria.

She was close.

He stepped out of the cave and walked down to the ocean, and Ariel was waiting for him there, sleek and beautiful. They ran to each other, and Malak kissed her, needing her more than ever. They made love on the beach while the waves crashed and the stars shone like diamonds, and he figured that if this was heaven, it was better than he deserved.

The End

Sean T. Smith's journey as a storyteller began in the snow-laden cabins of the Canadian wilderness, where he fell asleep to the rhythmic keystrokes of his father's typewriter. This early exposure to the written word ignited a passion that would shape his life. Transitioning from Ontario's chill to Miami's warmth, Sean pursued Political Science at the University of Florida. His love for storytelling then led him to Nashville, where he dedicated over a decade to songwriting, crafting around a thousand songs under the mentorship of some great tunesmiths.

Returning to Florida to start a family, Sean embraced fiction writing, finding the expansive canvas of novels a liberating medium. His debut, *Objects of Wrath*, marked the beginning of a trilogy published by Permuted Press. This series garnered attention and was in development for television with a Hollywood production company. His subsequent work, *Tears of Abraham*, was published by Post Hill Press and distributed nationwide by Simon & Schuster.

Sean's latest novel, *The Angel's Last War*, is slated for release by World Castle Publishing in 2025. Currently, he is delving into a contemporary military/political thriller. Beyond writing, Sean finds solace kayaking Florida's springs, savoring margaritas by the water, and hiking with his family.

Connect with Sean T. Smith:
Website/Blog: Author Sean T. Smith | Writing, Religion, and the Apocalypse!
Amazon Page: http://www.amazon.com/Objects-Wrath-Volume-Sean-Smith/dp/1618682245
Audible Page: http://www.audible.com/pd/Sci-Fi-Fantasy/Objects-of-Wrath-Audiobook/B00IS985T8
Goodreads: https://www.goodreads.com/author/show/7873199.Sean_T_Smith
Facebook: https://www.facebook.com/wrathiscoming
Twitter: @scribeSeanSmith

www.ingramcontent.com/pod-product-compliance
Lightning Source LLC
Chambersburg PA
CBHW021508240626
47154CB00002B/542